THE CLAW

'Miss Lofts knows how to set the pulse racing'
Sunday Telegraph

'An intriguing, chilling tale'
Manchester Evening News

'A remarkable atmosphere of fear...
a super book'
Eastern Evening News

The Claw

Norah Lofts

CORONET BOOKS
Hodder and Stoughton

Copyright © 1981 by Norah Lofts

First published in Great Britain 1981
by Hodder and Stoughton Ltd

Coronet edition 1982

British Library C.I.P.

Lofts, Norah
   The claw.—(Coronet books)
   I. Title
   823'.912[F]   PR6023.035

   ISBN 0 340 28104 9

Printed and bound in Great Britain for
Hodder and Stoughton Paperbacks, a
division of Hodder and Stoughton Ltd.,
Mill Road, Dunton Green, Sevenoaks,
Kent (Editorial Office: 47 Bedford
Square, London, WC1 3DP) by
Cox & Wyman Ltd, Reading

Contents

Mary Anderson

Every window in the front of the house has been broken and the tubs in which the crocuses were blooming have been overturned. I dare not go out even for the most necessary shopping: I dare not send the children to school. Of all my friends only Lilah Noble has been faithful. She brings pre-packaged meals and books – but always after dark.

There is a great deal of ill-feeling against me everywhere in England: every post brings me abusive letters – not all of them anonymous. A number of people have telephoned to tell me exactly what they think of me. Naturally feeling runs highest here in Hillchester where the terror reigned for six months. People believe that I was an accessory, that I shielded Greg and by so doing allowed the horror to escalate. I cannot blame them. I should myself find it difficult to believe that a man could do the things that Greg has done and then come home and play the part of good husband, good father, good neighbour, and do it so well that his wife suspected nothing.

I could lift the telephone and tell what I now know and nobody would believe that, either. They'd say I was mad and then what would become of my children? Of Jimmy and Anna and Emma? In any case what will happen to them? I'm trained in nothing and what little domestic skill I have was acquired through trial and error and is not of the marketable variety.

We could go home to Mother, but since she was instrumental in bringing this whole tragedy about I feel that I never want to see her again, let alone live with her. And besides, I don't want my children to grow up in a place where their white skins would be a disadvantage.

The house, Number 12, Forest Road, Malwood, Hillchester, would in the ordinary way fetch a good price. But who would wish to buy it now? The place to which the Hillchester Terror came home. The darling little house in which we were all so happy and so ordinary, until . . .

It all began on the first Saturday of June last year, a lovely hot day. The Sullivans who live next door had an old apple tree which had been slowly dying and this year had produced neither leaf nor blossom. Dick Sullivan looked in at lunchtime and asked Greg to help him to cut it down.

Greg went and came home at about five. He was hot and dusty and had a lump the size of an egg on his head. It was nothing, he said, just a knock from a branch which Dick had let fall. I looked and the skin was not even broken. He did admit to feeling a bit tired, and that I could well believe: I know Dick. He'd leave all the heaving and hauling to somebody else. I offered to make tea but Greg said he'd had a beer. "I'll take a shower and have a bit of a snooze. Be seeing you."

Soon after six I took Emma up, bathed her and put her to bed. Afterwards I looked in on Greg and he was asleep, wearing only his summer dressing-gown and lying in the middle of our bed. He looked very peaceful.

Downstairs again I played a cut-throat game of Monopoly with Jimmy and Anna, gave them their supper and sent them to bed, promising to come up and say good night. Having done so, I looked in on Greg again. He lay as before. I thought of my mother and her very tentative plans – tentative because the West Indian island, my birthplace and her home, changes governments as people change hair-dos and what one regime allows the next forbids, and vice versa. In her last letter Mother said that she hoped to be on the train which arrived in

Hillchester at ten fifteen. And of course Greg would meet the train.

But it was now a little after nine and he was still sleeping peacefully. I thought – after all he does have an exacting job and an exacting family, he's always in demand to mend or make or invent. Half of my mind said; Let him sleep! The other half asked; What about that train? I touched his leg which the dressing-gown left exposed. It felt cool. Let him sleep gained the upper hand with me and I went to the airing cupboard for a blanket and spread it gently. Then I went down to the telephone.

Hillchester has two taxi firms, Hillchester Taxis and Call A Cab. The former was fully booked up, the latter had a cab available but sounded rather aggrieved when I mentioned Malwood. Malwood is not actually very far out, under three miles, literally a suburb. But within living memory it was a self-contained village and the voice sounded as though I were asking it to convey a passenger into the Breckland wilds. However, I took comfort in the thought that the cab driver would be well rewarded. Mother, when she has money, is very generous – and she would not come to England unless she had money.

I did a bit of mending and presently it was twenty minutes to ten and I thought that Greg would be terribly annoyed if Mother arrived and found him in his dressing-gown. Theirs had never been an easy relationship. Mother had, absurdly and uselessly, said that she had hoped for a better match for me, and though twelve years had elapsed he had never wholly forgiven her. She had offered to buy the house in which we now lived and give it to us as a wedding present. Greg had turned surly and said he preferred to have a mortgage. On her last visit – two years earlier – she'd wanted to lend Greg the money for a new car to replace his already ageing Ford. He would not even consider it. He was always on the defensive with her though he called her Belle Mère.

Not wishing to disturb the children, I did not shout at the foot of the stairs, but went up, into our room and called his

9

name. No response. I shook him by the shoulder and realised that, despite the blanket and the warmth of the evening, his flesh felt chilly through the thin fabric of the dressing-gown. I was alarmed, but my thought was of death-like comas not of death itself. As a matter of fact I had reached the age of thirty without seeing a dead person.

I ran down and telephoned to Doctor Roper who lives in the road parallel to ours. He sounded rather gruff at first but when I'd gasped out the facts his manner changed and he said he'd come round immediately. And did.

Pulse; heart; even, dear man, the kiss of life about which I had read but never seen applied. After what seemed an age he said apologetically, "Mrs Anderson, I'm very sorry. He is dead." I stood there, too stricken to speak or move. It was inconceivable. It was for me the end of the world. I heard the words "cerebral haemorrhage" and "death certificate". Then he said I should not be alone. What about a neighbour?

I didn't want Peg Sullivan – her husband through clumsiness had killed Greg. I said, my voice sounding a mile away, "I am expecting my mother." Even as I said it there were sounds of her arrival. The paralysis that had gripped me let go. I flung myself downstairs, crying, "Mother, Greg is dead! Greg is dead, Mother!"

She said, "I am here. And I know what you need."

Whenever she was able to come she brought what she called real rum, far more potent than any one could buy in England. The hot drink she made for me tasted strongly of it. And quite possibly there was something else in that drink. Mother rather fancied herself as a herbalist. Whatever it was it worked so quickly that I have no memory of her taking me up and putting me to bed in the little slip of a guest room which I had made ready for her.

I woke to early morning sunshine and birdsong and my first thought was that the window was in the wrong place. Then I remembered everything and began to cry again.

Mother came in very quietly, took me in her arms and said, "Darling, there's nothing to cry about. Greg is all right. It was all a mistake. He's alive. I've just made him a *huge* breakfast.''

I stared. I thought she was out of her mind. She looked ghastly, eyes very wide in a paper-white face and her usually smooth hair disarrayed. Her manner, however was calm and authoritative. ''Be guided by me and say nothing. He thinks he had a long sleep and woke up hungry.''

I said, ''I must see for myself.''

''Do. But remember, act naturally.''

An order that was difficult to obey, all things considered, but I managed it. Greg looked perfectly ordinary; the bump on his head had gone down. A plate showed that he'd eaten bacon and eggs. He'd reached the toast and marmalade stage and was eating with his usual hearty appetite. He was most apologetic to Mother about having failed to meet her train. ''I just went out like a light,'' he said. ''And slept thirteen hours! But I'd been lumber-jacking all afternoon. Dick Sullivan is – if you'll pardon the expression – a damned idle sod.'' He often swore, in a light-hearted way, and I had only objected when the children were small and imitating all they heard. Then Jimmy and, after a year, Anna had gone to the Malwood Primary School – very good of its kind. Soon they were effing and b-ing all over the place and saying, ''Ker-ist!'' if a thrown die turned up the unwanted number. Everybody, including Peg Sullivan whose son, Ricky was very near Jimmy's age, said that it was only a phase. Not to worry. They'd grow out of it.

I kept looking at Greg, restraining myself from touching and kissing. I thought about the story of Lazarus in the Bible. How did Martha and Mary feel when Lazarus was raised from the dead? And I thought of Doctor Roper, soon to be writing out a death certificate. I must let him know.

Then Anna came down, crying because she could not find Ginger. Ginger was a marmalade tom cat, a stray, rescued by Polly Inskip, one of our near neighbours. Ginger had been neutered, Polly assured me and would not go out at night making hideous mating cries, and he never had, but he was

11

still a hunter and had once presented Anna with a dead, mauled young rabbit.

To the south of us a good stretch of the original forest of Malwood still stood and gin traps, though illegal, were still used by some people. I said nothing of that, just, "He'll come back when it suits him." Anna forgot Ginger in the joy of seeing Mother whom she associated with happy outings and lavish presents.

Hard on Anna's heels came Jimmy with *his* pet, another of Polly Inskip's strays, though he was a dog of quality, a black and tan dachshund. We called him Fritz. As he generally did, Greg offered the dog his last toast crust, and Fritz backed away, hackles up, tail down. Jimmy said, "Well, Dad, you can't wonder. Yesterday you did tread on his paw."

Our telephone is in the hall. I dared not use it until Greg had gone up to the bathroom to shave. I was prepared for incredulity. After all I could hardly believe it myself. Doctor Roper obviously thought I'd gone raving mad and asked to speak to Mother. I called her and she came and cooed in her most seductive voice and convinced him. Putting down the receiver, she said, "He believed me. Apparently there are rare cases of people coming round again on the mortuary slab. And now, after all that, don't bother with lunch here. Let us eat at that nice place, the White . . ."

"Horse," I said and sighed inwardly. Mother always suggested some such outing and Greg always went all archaic and insisted on paying. Then he'd grumble to me about the unwarranted expense. Upstairs at the White Horse was quite expensive and they charged full price for the children. Still, perhaps he'd learned his lesson or realised that this was the twentieth century, he said quite gaily.

"And this time she'll damn well *have* to pay. I'm broke." I remembered then that he'd had something done to the car during the week.

It being Sunday we got a good table with a view over Market Square which is not really a square, more of an L-shape. The far side of the wide space within my view was a happy medley of shops and office premises. I could see the façade of the place where Greg worked – Turner and Noble. Accountants. It was flanked on one side by a flower shop, on the other by a wine and spirit merchant's. Beyond the flower shop was a building that housed several enterprises, amongst them Hillchester's most stylish hairdresser's on the first floor. Outside it on this particular morning was one of Mr Sims', the house agent's, boards bearing the words – becoming increasingly rare – To Let. There were other words which, being rather short-sighted, I could not read. I said, "Greg, that place under Antoine's is to let." He didn't even turn his head. He said "All three hundred square feet of it! The bookie has moved to a very sumptuous place in The Arcade."

Mother leaned forward, inspected the board and having learned her lesson, merely said, "It's in a very good position."

"Rated and rented accordingly," Greg said, but without the usual bitterness with which he spoke of rented premises. He did so desperately want to set up on his own, yet twice in the past he had refused Mother's help. He'd stuck to Turner and Noble partly because we liked our house and the neighbourhood – and presently the good school – and partly because he'd hoped for a partnership, not too far-fetched a hope since there was now no Turner and only one Noble, Chris, my friend Lilah's husband, getting middle-aged and lethargic. Greg did much the greater share of the work and was poorly paid.

"Do you know the rent?"

"Twelve hundred a year. Rates vary of course, but they'd come to about as much again."

Mother lifted the handbag which always seemed too big and heavy for her frail elegance and rooted about in its contents. Then, as blithely as though she had not been snubbed on former occasions, she said, "I could stake you for six months."

Expecting Greg to refuse and her to be hurt, I cursed myself for mentioning the board; but Greg said, "By Christmas I should be self-supporting and I'd pay interest at twenty per cent. And be everlastingly grateful."

I felt deliriously happy and in my mind planned small economies in order to help.

Mother said, "Better clinch it now." I should not have been, yet I continually was, surprised when the rock-hard business woman peeped out. After all she was the woman who had turned a sugar-mill – disused since the First World War – and a vast, decaying, plantation house into a tourist attraction, the sugar-mill like something out of *Uncle Tom's Cabin*, the house a most expensive hotel but like something out of *Gone With The Wind*, and Mother the living image of Ellen O'Hara. She had also instituted a souvenir shop, supposed to sell stuff of native origin, but since the old arts and crafts of the islanders were dying out, most of the souvenirs were made in Birmingham. That was why, when Santa Barbara was enjoying a rational regime, Mother was allowed out with some of what was, after all, her own money. (Greg had come to Santa Barbara as a tourist, part of a package deal. He was an orphan but his parents had left enough money for him to be educated and trained to some profession. He'd just passed his final examination and was spending the last of his legacy on a super holiday when we met and both fell in love at first sight.)

Mr Sims did not in the least mind being disturbed on Sunday afternoon. He came along with the keys and we all went to inspect the premises. Just two rooms, one much larger than the other, a minute cubby hole with a sink and a gas-ring, and a lavatory. The larger room was at the back and looked out over a stretch of parking space into Charity Lane. The walls were in need of redecoration, but Greg is handy and even I can slap on distemper.

"Old Chris isn't going to like this at all," Greg said gloatingly. "Bang on his doorstep, too!"

I thought of the former offers from Mother which he had rejected out of hand. In neither case was the place to let so

14

central. Perhaps he had been wise. Perhaps things did work out.

I spared a moment to wonder how this move would affect Lilah and me. Ours had never been an easy friendship, Chris Noble had such inflated ideas about his own importance and did not like his wife being friendly with the wife of an employee. But Lilah and I had been drawn together from the first. We both liked books: we were both newly married and neither of us had ever kept house before. She came from a tumble-down castle in Ireland, where as she said, everything was in short supply except labour. We used to ring each other up and report the latest failure on the culinary front. Then she had had no children and I had had three, and instead of being envious she'd been so nice, acting as a kind of fairy godmother. I had noticed, though, that the days when she had us to her splendid house or took us for outings always coincided with Chris's absences. And to be honest, Greg had been a bit difficult too, calling Lilah "Lady Bountiful".

Still, I didn't let any thought of Lilah perturb me on this happy day. It was slightly marred because Ginger had not come home and Anna cried on and off.

After supper, leisurely and prolonged because we had had so many plans to discuss − even Mother had plans for buying novelties for the shop on credit, as she had done once when currency restrictions were very strict − I looked at the clock and thought: At this time yesterday I believed Greg to be dead!

Now I know that death is far from being the worst thing . . .

Case One: Miss Marcia Lowe

Miss Marcia Lowe put her own key into the lock of her own front door and stepped into her own house. She had performed this action countless times during the past year, but the satisfaction was undimmed.

The taxi-driver, rather more hirsute than she could fully approve of but civil, heaved her suitcase into the tiny hall, took his fare and a tip, wished her good night and departed and Miss Lowe was, except for a late evening cleaner or somebody working overtime, the only person in Charity Lane.

A year earlier when a timely legacy enabled her to retire and buy Charity Cottage, a number of people had asked: But won't you find it lonely there? She had repudiated the idea. Life owed her some solitude. Orphaned young, she had spent her life amongst crowds: boarding school, university, residential jobs in various schools and finally the muted grandeur of the Headmistress's apartments at St Ethelreda's, Hillchester, a school of some renown. During her nineteen years there she had done much to add to its reputation, yet she was glad to retire before anybody could say that she was old-fashioned and − at fifty-two − able to enjoy her freedom and her privacy.

She was a methodical woman; her suitcase which contained things which belonged upstairs she left in the hall: two bulging hold-alls she carried through into what she always called her parlour. One hold-all held gifts − she had tried to remember everybody. The other contained personal things, her purse, her passport, her few uncashed travellers' cheques, her camera and a thick notebook in which she had kept a meticulous day-by-day account of all she had seen and done during her holiday.

She was greatly in demand as a speaker at Women's Institutes, Townswomen's Guilds and Rotary Clubs. And twice she had reached wider audiences with an article published in the *National Geographical Magazine* and another, less erudite, almost chatty, in *Women's View*.

She thought: Now for a cup of real English tea! The Greeks were most interesting, most estimable people, but they simply had not the knack of making tea. As she drank her own brew, Miss Lowe glanced through the mail which had accumulated during three weeks. Several letters from Old Ethelredians. Nice to be remembered so long and so kindly! Really, she thought, allowing herself a moment of complacency, I am a most fortunate woman; so many friends and not an enemy in the world!

Her tea drunk, she unpacked and mentally allotted all the pretty and/or useful things she had bought. After that a simple supper, bread and cheese brought in by her most faithful cleaning woman, Mrs Packer. With it she drank a glass of Greek wine. People could say what they liked about it tasting like turpentine, she enjoyed it.

As, at last, she went up to bed she paused by her landing window, opened it and looked out over the jumble of roofs and back premises. One window still lighted. Perhaps Mr Anderson, working very late. Mrs Packer, always the first with any bit of gossip, had reported that Mr Anderson had left Turner and Noble's and set up on his own and Miss Lowe had said, ''I do indeed wish him well.''

She remembered him vividly though she had seen him only once. A very nice-looking young man who wanted his daughter to be a day pupil at St Ethelreda's kindergarten. She'd been forced to tell him that the kindergarten, an unsuccessful experiment, was being phased out. He lived at

Malwood and she had been able to say with complete confidence, that the primary school there was very good. Its Headmistress was an Old Ethelredian. He said he knew, his boy was a pupil there, but he'd wanted something a little better for his daughter. He'd looked very disappointed and when, six months later, Miss Lowe had stretched a point and accepted a new kindergarten pupil, the orphaned daughter of an Old Girl, she had, for a second felt the hope that Mr Anderson would not hear about it and feel hurt.

Leaving the landing window open for the September night was warm, she unpacked in orderly fashion. Soiled clothes into the basket in the bathroom, those in need of dry-cleaning neatly folded and left on a chair, the lightweight coat, seldom worn, back in the wardrobe.

She gave a moment's thought to clothes. Often on this holiday she had regretted not wearing slacks. They would have been far more suitable for scrambling amongst ruins, getting into and out of boats, riding on muleback. It was not that she was old-fashioned: she had allowed her girls to wear shorts for tennis and slacks in the evening. She told herself that slacks and short hair were not her style. Or – the thought hovered – just a trifle too much so.

It was natural that she should dream of Greece: not of any place she recognised, just a hillside covered with thyme-scented grass, some bits of broken masonry, some tapering, dark yews. And she was blissfully alone, no fellow tourists, no chattering guide. Then something moved and loneliness became not a blessing but a danger. She thought – How foolish of me! It is only Pan and he belongs here!

The thought jerked her into half-wakefulness and automatically she reached out and switched on the bedside lamp. She saw Pan where he had no right to be, advancing towards her with a sneering, leering, *lecherous* look. Then he threw the lamp down and in the darkness ravished her fifty-two-year-old virgin but not wholly resistant body. A slight pain and then indescribable pleasure.

The man vanished into the dark and for a few moments she

lay inert, wondering that she should feel so little sense of outrage. She thought: I have been raped, and surely in a most brutal manner! And still no anger came, only a lassitude from which she could easily have drifted into sleep. It seemed to demand a vast effort to get herself on to her feet, and to go, feeling her way, to the light switch by the door. Instantly she was seized by an overwhelming sense of physical repulsion. What a hideous mess! Her nightdress was torn and soiled, her bed in an indescribable state.

The habit of orderliness came to her aid. Within half an hour everything soiled had been made into the smallest possible bundle and her bed spread with fresh sheets and she had taken a bath and donned a clean nightdress. She had an incinerator in her garden for the burning of garden rubbish and dead leaves. What she had to burn might be less easily combustible, but she had a small container of fuel for her cigarette lighter. Not much, but it must serve. At this time of year it was light by seven and Mrs Packer would be here, at the very earliest, at nine.

Sleep, so rudely repelled, was not to be lured back. And now that she had done what was to be done, she could *think*. In a new way. Utterly new.

Once she had been trying to buy a new pair of shoes, rather difficult because her feet were long and narrow. The girl serving her looked frail and tired and she had apologised for being such a nuisance. The girl had said, "You can't help it. We're as God Almighty made us, Miss." An undeniable statement: and God had so made her that she was over-fond of her own sex.

She prided herself on never giving the smallest betraying sign. She had no favourites and was in fact inclined to deal harshly with those to whom she felt most tenderly. Now the carefully erected and buttressed barrier had been broken down and she could think shamelessly of pleasure shared with a woman. With Dorothea!

Of all the many girls who had passed through her hands Dorothea Gilman was the most attractive and the most

19

dangerous. Dangerous because she had always seemed to be inviting the affectionate word or gesture. She was a brilliantly clever girl and had won a scholarship to Girton. Taking leave of her Headmistress on the last day of her last term, she had burst into tears. "Come, come," Miss Lowe had said bracingly, "you have nothing to cry about. You have a wonderful future ahead of you." For answer Dorothea flung herself upon Miss Lowe and sobbed out.

"But I shall never see you again!"

A bad moment! Disentangling herself, Miss Lowe said, "Nonsense! I go to Cambridge quite often. We'll lunch or dine together."

Over the intervening years they had maintained contact. Dorothea had been very successful academically and had then set about gathering varied experience; a year in America, a year in Germany. When Miss Lowe was thinking about her somewhat premature retirement she could think of no one better able to take her place than Dorothea, and the School Governors had such confidence in Miss Lowe that they practically allowed her to choose her successor.

There'd been another bad moment when Dorothea had said, "I know that I owe all this to you," and kissed her. And once again, holding to her self-imposed rules, Miss Lowe had jerked away and said,

"Nonsense! Of all the applicants you are far and away the best qualified."

Now all was changed. And she began planning an intimate little dinner for two . . .

Case Two: Becky Dalton

Laden as she was – handbag, overnight bag, a plastic carrier and a bottle of wine – Becky Dalton mounted two flights of stairs, one steep, briskly and without becoming breathless. And for the thousandth time she was glad and grateful that she lived in such an ideal place. Her little flat gave her privacy and freedom yet there was absolutely no danger of her being left alone in the house after dark – a thing of which she had an irrational dread. Even now as she gained the dimly lighted landing, she could hear Commander Lucas's T.V. Poor man, she thought. His arthritis had worsened so rapidly that he was now unable to get downstairs at all.

St Luke's Vicarage – now inevitably known as the Old Vic – had been built when many incumbents had private means and labour was cheap. The present vicar lived in a small labour-saving house in the short elm-lined avenue between the churchyard and Castle Street. The Old Vic, after standing empty for four years had been bought by an enterprising builder who had turned it into living units of various sizes. Becky's was the smallest, one room and a cupboard-sized kitchen. She shared a bathroom with the Lucases. Shared also was a space beyond the bathroom door where trunks and bags, Hoovers and brooms and such things as hockey sticks could be housed. Becky turned out, with commendable regularity, for the Old Ethelredians.

By far the greater part of this one-time attic floor was what was known as the penthouse. It occupied the whole of one gable end and was said to be very luxurious. It had two means of access, the door at the end of the passage and the fire escape which the law demanded if any second-floor rooms were rented. Fire escapes were stark and ugly, but the two men, one young, one older, who lived in the penthouse, had transformed this one into a thing of beauty by means of climbing plants, plants in pots and hanging baskets.

Becky's one room was scrupulously tidy; she never accumulated litter and had an almost old-maidish regard for the rule of a place for everything and everything in its place. The man in the wine shop had told her to open the bottle, allowing the wine to breathe, and to let it stand at room temperature for an hour. She placed her overnight bag on the bed and carried the wine and the plastic holder into the tiny kitchen.

She had been home for the weekend and though her parents disapproved of what they called "her way of life", they had been generous. She had brought back with her a brace of partridges, home-grown Brussels sprouts, home-made butter and cheese. Counting upon some such bounty she had asked Alan to dinner at seven and shortly before St Luke's clock struck the hour she was ready. As she set her small gate-leg table – nothing matching but each individual piece pretty – she regretted that she had not gone the whole hog and bought a few flowers, but Mr Noble whose personal secretary she was, had kept her rather late and the wine had seemed more important.

Alan was punctual. He carried a paper cone containing half a dozen pink rosebuds. She said, "Exactly what I needed," and he said,

"Lucky. They match your gown." The word, seldom if ever used nowadays, was somehow typical of him. Her friends called him a dour Scot and wondered what she could see in such a dull, old-fashioned fellow. She could have told them – she was sick of the other sort.

"Oh this," she said, touching the kimono-like sleeve of the

garment. "Shirley Morrison gave it to me. She bought several. She said they were dirt cheap in the ship's shop. And she seems to think I did her a favour by mentioning her to Mr Anderson when he set up on his own. She loves working for him and being left in charge of the office when he goes out."

Shirley's thank-you present was not deliberately seductive; it had a little stand-up mandarin collar and full sleeves. It was toe-length and buttoned the whole way down. On its front, just below the shoulders, it was embroidered with birds, flowers and butterflies.

"And how was the weekend?" Alan asked.

"As usual. Awful. You know."

He knew, for as soon as Becky began to take him seriously he had spent a weekend at Brook Farm. At some point wages had come under discussion and Alan, a wage-earner himself, had said something about the labourer being worth his hire. Becky's father had immediately called him a Marxist and her mother, a faint, faithful echo as a wife should be, had told Becky not to bring Alan Douglas again.

The wine was very good — as it should be at the price. She had not minded seeming ignorant and had asked for something to go well with partridge. Now, raising her second glass of it, Becky said, "Here's to tomorrow."

"If I go. Becky I want to talk about that. I've been wondering . . . You like Hillchester, all your friends are here, you can get home whenever you want . . . Do you think you'd be happy in Dagenham?"

It was the nearest he had ever come to suggesting that they should share a future. She had always been certain that the moment would come but she had expected it later, when he'd landed the better-paid, more prestigious job with Ford's.

She said, "With you, Alan, I should be happy anywhere." She spoke calmly, stating a fact.

"Bless you," he said. "Well then, I . . ." He stopped eating and reached into a pocket and produced a little jeweller's box. He displayed a ring set with a modest-sized sapphire. "It seemed to be you, somehow. But of course if you don't like it, it can be changed.''

"Darling, I love it." She held out her left hand. He slipped on the ring, kissed it, then the inside of her wrist, and finally her mouth. They were controlled kisses: some girls would have found them lacking in warmth, but Becky much preferred them to some that had been forced upon her in the backs of cars. He returned to his place at the table and she flaunted her ring for the rest of the meal. She would have something to show her friends, including Coralie and Rosanna who shared a larger flat on the floor below. They lived what she thought untidy lives, indulging in brief, tumultuous love affairs which did not lead to either engagement or wedding rings. They had dubbed Alan ''dour'' and had teased her about sticking to one dull fellow for nine months. Walking out, they called it, like Victorian housemaids.

As always, Alan helped with the washing up. Two made a crowd in the small kitchen, but despite his size he was compact. All his movements were neat and economical. Becky made a great show of removing the ring before putting her hands in water, and of donning it again afterwards. ''It really is lovely, Alan. If I'd had a thousand to choose from, I'd have picked this.''

"I thought it was just about the colour of your eyes," he said, looking pleased. Actually her eyes were much paler than the sapphire, just as her hair was too pale to be called golden, it was almost straw-coloured. It was naturally curly and she wore it very short, a fashion of which her parents disapproved: there'd been a fine row when she first went home with her hair short. Now, nearing her twenty-third birthday, she was as comely as she ever would be.

Now that they were properly engaged they had a great deal to talk about. Alan had been short-listed and invited for an interview and he was confident of success. He knew just how good a mechanic he was and his opinion of himself had been boosted by his present boss, Big Daddy Bramble, who said that if he would stay with Hillchester Motors until the end of the year he should have a substantial rise in wages and the promotion to justify it.

They drank coffee and talked about the house they would find – preferably in the country, outside the town which, never having seen it, they thought of as new and ugly; they talked of the furniture they would buy and the possibility of Becky finding at least a part-time job. When the coffee was finished they drank the last of the wine.

At last Alan looked at his watch and said he must go, he must catch an early train in the morning.

"I'll come down with you," Becky said.

"It'll mean coming back alone." She'd told him about her phobia – he must know all about her and not be misled in any way.

"I know. But tonight I'm so happy I shan't be in the least nervous." She added characteristically, "Or it may be the wine."

They said goodbye at the front door which, being the common entry, was never locked. The near-midnight air was crisply chill: and Becky gave a little shudder so Alan cut the leave-taking short. "Get back in the warm, darling."

"See you tomorrow. But, Alan . . ."

"Yes, love?"

"If you know anything for certain early in the day, give me a ring. It's not that I'm anxious, just interested."

Mr Rand who owned the Old Vic provided lighting in the hall, on the stairs and landings. Very low-powered bulbs placed high, shed a feeble light. Doctor Brunning who occupied one of the big ground-floor flats had installed an old carriage lamp over his front door, and Mrs Peacock across the wide hall, not to be outdone, had installed two torch-like lamps, one on either side of her front door, so for most of the evening the hall was brightly lit; now only the dim bulb was alight: just enough to show up the shadowy places. Courage drained away as Becky climbed the first stairs.

At such moments she had no specific fear, just a feeling of being watched – and by something hostile. The flesh-crawling sensation increased as she reached the first landing and heard St Luke's clock boom the first stroke of midnight. The most eerie hour: "when churchyards yawn and graves give up their dead". Not that she was actually afraid of ghosts. She was simply afraid. And before she reached the sanctuary of her own bright, cosy room, she must face the truly dark end of the upper corridor. I just can't, she thought weakly and swerved aside to the door of Coralie's flat.

Showing off her ring was a valid excuse, but it would not serve her purpose. No, she must say that she'd brought back more farm produce than she needed and say casually: If one of you likes to come up and fetch it . . . One of them would come willingly: they lived in a state of chronic impecunity.

There was no answer to her knock. And although all the flats on this floor were occupied, with nobody else was she on such terms as to justify a midnight call with bribery in mind. There was no help for it. She drew a deep, unsteady breath and took the stairs at a run. Before she reached the top she was saved. Commander Lucas opened his door and light streamed out. He was wearing only his pyjamas and was about to make his hobbling way across to the communal bathroom. This sharing of what Mr Rand called toilet facilities could be embarrassing. The Lucases, because of their age and Becky, because of her strict upbringing, were all shy about natural bodily functions. The unwritten rule ran that anybody seen going towards or coming out of the bathroom was invisible, and if an actual confrontation was avoidable evasive action was taken. Tonight Commander Lucas having seen her, backed awkwardly into his sitting room and closed the door; but the mere sight of him had reassured her. For the few necessary seconds his figure had stood and the extra light had fallen between her and the dark space which had become the focus of her dread.

The door to her room stood open. She'd meant to close it to keep in the heat, but it had been an exciting evening and she'd obviously forgotten. Now the glowing gas fire and the red shaded lamp were there to welcome her. Safe! she thought and bolted in like a rabbit to its burrow.

Aftermath of Case Two

(i)

Commander Lucas waited for what he considered a decent interval, made his visit to the bathroom and came back. He realised that he was in for a bad night despite the pain-killers and the sleeping pills which Doctor Brunning had said should be taken half an hour before retiring.

Perhaps a little whisky. A *very* little for the stuff was now inordinately expensive, but he'd had a bad evening. He was always distressed when forced to face the situation to which he had reduced poor Lorna. She never complained but she did look so frail and so tired. The flat which had seemed such a Godsend – unfurnished accommodation being so rare – was now, since he could not do the running up and down, a curse. Lorna now had to carry kitchen debris down to the dustbins in the small enclosed backyard. And then, some time later he'd made a mistake and said, "Something smells good!"

Lorna said with her little painful smile "Next door, I'm afraid. We have hot-pot." The two kitchens were adjacent, each served by half a casement dormer-window. Lorna Lucas had opened hers to let out the smell of onions which alone gave flavour to the hot-pot, and Becky Dalton had opened hers to let out the steam of Brussels sprouts boiling.

After that Fred Lucas, while ostensibly watching television or doing the *Telegraph* crossword, had been thinking of all the mistakes he had made since his retirement from

27

the Navy; free-range fowls and Cox's apples in Wiltshire; pigs and blackcurrants in Suffolk. All unprofitable. Then the job with Sims, House Agent and Auctioneer – that was how he had come by this flat! Not a particularly well-paid job but steady. Then this blasted arthritis and – Here a sheer hulk lies poor Tom Bowling! Poor Fred Lucas!

He meditated – not for the first time – the obvious way out. Lorna would be far better off without him. She could take what remained of what had once seemed a sizable dowry, and go to live with her cousin, Veronica.

He eyed the instruments of self-destruction; twenty barbiturate capsules, half a bottle of whisky. Enough?

Then the screaming began. In his life which had not been uneventful, he had heard many screams. Nothing quite like this. It sounded as though a mechanical screaming machine were at work. Three screams, a pause, three more. Some sort of game? There was no knowing what the young these days thought amusing. The sound came from next door, from the flat of Miss Dalton, hitherto such a quiet and desirable neighbour. But if it went on, it'd wake Lorna, poor dear!

He hoisted himself up on to his two sticks and went out, braced for protest and perhaps, even, argument.

Miss Dalton's door stood wide open and the almost automatic screaming went on.

In his day he had seen many horrible sights; victims of bombs, torpedoes, massacres, but nothing quite like this. The poor girl lay on her back in a widening pool of blood. Except from some tatters she was naked and from her throat to what were – there was no other name for it – her private parts, there were long bleeding furrows. Clawed, he thought, well aware of how ridiculous the thought was, but at the same time, skilfully handling his sticks, he struggled out of his pyjama jacket and laid it over the worst . . . The girl went on screaming; one, two, three; a pause and three more.

He said, "Miss Dalton! Miss Dalton! It's all right. I'm here."

Behind him, Lorna said, "Oh, Fred! What is it?"

He tried to swivel on his rigid hips, interposing his body. "Dear, get Doctor Brunning. Telephone would be quickest."

When Lorna had gone to their telephone he tried again to stop the terrible noise. "Miss Dalton! Everything is all right now. It's over. I'm here. The doctor is on his way." She went on screaming and the senselessness of the noise began to irritate him so that, for all his shock and pity, he wanted to say; Shut up! Not that that would have served; behind the automatic screaming was the empty, idiot stare.

Lorna slipped back. "He's on his way up." She had put on her own dressing-gown and brought his.

"Stay clear," he said. "No sight for you." She was sixty-two and had nursed throughout the war but this was no sight for her. For once she ignored him. "Perhaps a *female* voice . . . Miss Dalton. It's all right. You are with friends." That was stretching the truth a bit since she and Fred had always held aloof, not only from their nearest neighbour but from all their fellow tenants – except, of course, Doctor Brunning.

Considering his bulk and the fact that he had been asleep when his bedside telephone rang, Doctor Brunning had made good speed. He wore a dressing-gown of rich brocade and carried a bag of a quality seldom seen nowadays. Coming up the first flight of stairs he had imagined that poor Fred Lucas had had the almost inevitable fall: on the second flight he had heard the screaming and visualised a case of hysteria.

He, too, was accustomed to horrible sights, but he said, "Sweet Christ!" when he saw what he had to deal with. The professional calm took over. Sedation: Hospital: Police. In that order. Setting his bag on the table where two glasses and a bottle stood, he loaded a syringe He used it dexterously and began silently to count. At seven the screaming stopped, but instead of falling instantly unconscious the poor girl lifted her head and staring past them said in a terrible voice, "The Devil – The Devil behind the door!" Then she fell back.

Into the silence Doctor Brunning said, "I can do a temporary job, but she needs more. Mrs Lucas, will you go and dial 999 – that is emergency. They'll ask you what service you need. Say Ambulance and Police. Then call the hospital. Ask for Accident and Emergency. Mention my name – be sure of that! Say that I am sending in an accident case and that a blood transfusion will be needed.'' He chose Lorna as his messenger because she was quicker on her feet and also he had been impressed by her manner when she called him. Surprisingly calm.

Doctor Brunning worked for a minute or two in silence.

''That should hold it for a bit. All but this,'' he pointed to a claw-mark on Becky's breast – it had just missed the nipple – ''which needs a couple of stitches, are fairly superficial. But what a bad business!''

''I never saw anything like it.''

''I did. Once. I spent some of the war years in India and some natives brought me a woman who had been clawed by a leopard. Deeper wounds, less symmetrical. It was a backward place and they'd tried plastering her with cow dung. She died, poor thing. What puzzles me about this – well, even the most savage rapist has only what you might call human equipment. This poor girl might have been raped with a barge pole.''

''Most extraordinary! And why didn't she yell sooner? I know I'm a bloody cripple, but I'd have come. And used my stick!''

''When she comes round, with the shock worn off, she should be ready to explain . . .'' A solid uniformed figure appeared in the doorway. ''Ha! Good evening, Sergeant.''

The police had arrived.

Not only to Doctor Brunning but to most of Hillchester, Tom Saunders represented the police. Other police officers came and went; Sergeant Saunders was always there.

He was, by several years, too old, and by every other standard too good for his rank. But in the police force promotion always postulated a move and to Tom, and to Amy, his wife, any move was inconceivable. They were so well dug in, with wide-stretching roots. One of Tom's brothers was the one remaining independent butcher, the other was a fishmonger. Amy was similarly usefully connected; one of her brothers had a very prosperous market garden out at Salford and the other owned the increasingly less remunerative Comet Cinema. And there were minor connections; aunts who would baby-sit, and cousins. It had been one of Amy's cousins, temporarily serving an apprenticeship, so to speak, at Sims, who had been able to direct Tom and Amy to their most desirable house.

Any man in Tom's position would have been a fool to move. And there were the girls to consider. Kate and Alice who were deemed clever because they had inherited their father's computer-like memory, and were now day girls at St Ethelreda's.

There was also something called job satisfaction, and Sergeant Saunders enjoyed it. He knew Hillchester like the back of his hand. New, high-ranking officers would call him in and say, "Sergeant, where the hell is a place called the Puckles? I can't find it on any map." He knew all the answers and over the years had grown not exactly conceited but comfortably sure of himself.

He was first on the spot because he had been nearby making his round of constables on duty. These, since the new rules about sex equality, included women and Sergeant Saunders was not the only one to feel uncomfortable about it. As far as was humanly possible the women were spared allocation to known trouble spots. Monday nights were usually quiet everywhere, rowdies had expended their money and their energy over the weekend, so it had seemed safe enough to assign the Market Square area to WPC Collins who had just reported that all was well, when the call came for police at the Old Vic. Tom had driven the short distance quickly, not expecting anything very serious; a burglary, maybe. The three ground-floor flats and the penthouse could have attracted some thief.

Tom stopped his car near the front door, entered the hall, now brightly lit by Dr Brunning's private lamp. The door below it was half open and Tom stepped in and called.

Nobody answered, though the flat was not unoccupied. In a room to the rear of it, the doctor's housekeeper lay, resolutely pursuing her policy of hearing nothing after nine o'clock when she retired. She'd made that clear from the first; if she shopped, cooked and served meals, kept his clothes in order and did such cleaning as Mrs Packer could not manage in her daily two hours, then she needed her rest at night.

The rest of the ground floor was quiet enough. And the next. Tom climbed steadily, saw a wide-open door, heard voices. Was greeted and stood staring and for all his long and varied experience, horrified. He had two teenage daughters and he recognised the poor girl. Now and again, when hours of duty permitted, he had gone, feeling rather conspicuous, with Kate and Alice to hockey matches.

"Rape, Sergeant. Aggravated rape. I have rendered first aid and the ambulance should be on its way." Doctor Brunning spoke crisply, wanting this over and done with; needing a drink. Commander Lucas was also anxious to get away. He also needed a drink but his more urgent need was to sit down. The one easy-chair in the room was far too low, once in it he could never get out, and the others looked suspiciously frail. And where was Lorna? He said,

"Well, if there's nothing more . . ."

Tom Saunders said, "If you don't mind – just stay where you are. I'll be back in two minutes." He spoke almost placatingly, but he spoke with the voice of the law.

He literally threw himself down the stairs, three, four steps at a time. Well over forty, an old has-been, but lean and lithe as a boy. Using his car radio to transmit the truth as far as he knew it, Tom thought: Poor old G.H. he'll hate this! Tom liked and respected Detective Chief Inspector Hardy but considered him over squeamish and fastidious for his job. Chief Inspector O'Brien, head of the uniformed branch, though superficially more jovial was far tougher.

He did not waste time asking for a policewoman. Rape told its own tale and whenever a woman or a child was concerned a WPC was always sent. He loped back upstairs and considered

32

that he could usefully employ the time of waiting by taking a few preliminary statements.

"Who found her?"

"I did and my wife immediately called Doctor Brunning." Commander Lucas told, for the first time, the story which was not to vary one iota and was, as might be expected, very precise about time.

"Miss Dalton entertained her boy friend this evening as she often does. The partition between the apartments is rather flimsy. Certain sounds carry. I could hear his voice, but no words. He left at three minutes to twelve. I heard her door close. I imagined that the coast was then clear for me to go to the bathroom. Nowadays it takes a little time for me to get underway and the church clock had just struck twelve when I opened my door and saw her on the stairs. She must, contrary to habit, have gone down with him. I backed away and allowed her sufficient time to make use of our shared – facilities. I then went across, came back, drank a small nightcap – whisky. Then the screaming began. I admit that I hesitated before interfering, thinking it some game. But I feared that my wife would be disturbed and came along to protest. It was then precisely twelve minutes past twelve – I looked at my watch . . ."

"And a quarter past twelve when Mrs Lucas called me," Doctor Brunning said anxious to co-operate and equally anxious to assert himself. After all, if the poor girl survived it would be thanks to his ministrations. "And where the hell is that bloody ambulance?"

"On its way, sir. I think I hear . . ." But it was WPC Collins who had run all the way from her beat. She looked at Becky and turned green but she forced back the nausea and said, "The ambulance was just drawing in, Sergeant."

"You go with her and stay until relieved." There was another sound of feet on the stairs. The ambulance men.

Doctor Brunning looked at Becky and was moved by an outdated sense of chivalry. He slid out of his dressing-gown, and said to WPC Collins, "Lend me a hand. Put it on her –

back to front.'' They slid her flaccid arms into the sleeves. Then he detached the wide sash and with it tied the spreading folds of brocade round her knees. Decency preserved!

In the truly luxurious penthouse it had been a good party; Georgie Turner – sometimes called Georgina – was rich and generous and Matthew Waterson catered well. But when St Luke's clock began to chime, the young man from the Customs and Excise – new to all this – said, ''I must go. I have to work for my living!'' So did most of the other guests, but they were more hardened. Georgie said, ''One for the road, dear boy,'' and with a lavish, wasteful hand poured more champagne which the young man, anxious not to offend, obediently drank. It was his first visit and he had come to the penthouse by way of the front door and stairs. He'd observed later guests using the fire-escape door, but curtains had now been drawn across it and the way to it blocked by a sofa: so he went out by the way he had come and just caught sight of Sergeant Saunders entering Becky's room. He returned to the party and said, ''Police on the premises!''

There followed a general stampede. One young man had a head-lamp out of order. The rest ran because they had no wish to be involved in anything, or to be caught *here*. Everybody knew what Georgie and Matthew were: they made no secret of it and people like them were supposed to be tolerated, even by the law. But Hillchester was a hopelessly old-fashioned place, where men laughed at what they did not understand, used coarse terms and made jokes in bad taste. Few, if any, would believe that some young men regarded the penthouse as a centre of culture: a place where books and serious music could be discussed and any small show of talent fostered, indeed over-praised.

Graham Harper, a young journalist employed by the *Hillchester and District Daily Times*, ran with the others, but did not go far, merely from the side to the front of the house and into the hall. In his job so much depended on being in the right place at the right time. He noticed Doctor Brunning's lamp

34

and open door – that might mean anything. He went up the stairs and presently saw Becky's room, almost like a stage-set, rather crowded. Sergeant Saunders, Commander Lucas and Doctor Brunning. He slithered past and took his place amongst the odds and ends in the dark end of the passage. He saw the arrival of WPC Collins, closely followed by the ambulance men. He remembered the ribald remarks of Georgie Turner and Matthew Waterson. Matthew who did the shopping and had watched Mrs Lucas's parsimonious purchases had suggested that she had been caught shoplifting. Georgie said that the prim little typist – they were always the worst – had been cooking the books. The presence of Doctor Brunning, and now of the ambulance men, hinted at other things. Murder, he admitted to himself, was a bit much to hope for. Perhaps a suicide attempt.

The stretcher came out. The brown blankets of former days had been replaced by white nylon. It was hardly whiter than the poor girl's face. She looked very dead indeed. And Detective Chief Inspector Hardy and the Scene-of-the-Crime officer, both known to Graham by sight, must have passed the stretcher on the lower landing. It must be something pretty serious to have brought them both out at this time of night. Rape at the very least! Graham was suddenly aware of his own vulnerability, lurking here in the darkness.

Presently the wished-for thing happened. The two civilians came out. Commander Lucas said, "I don't know about you, but I need a drink! Care to join me?"

"Thanks all the same, but no. I left my door open."

"You did a marvellous job."

"So did you. I just hope we were in time."

Doctor Brunning, moving now at an old man's gait, in sharp contrast with the gaudy colours of his pyjamas, went downstairs. Graham slithered after him and just as he was about to enter his own flat, said, "Doctor Brunning," in a tentative voice.

"What now?" the old man asked, his voice sharp with irritation. "Oh, you! Come in, my dear boy. Brandy on the

sideboard. Help yourself and pour me a double while I just
. . .'' He went into his bedroom and by the time Graham had
poured two drinks – his own carefully measured, the other
rather more than the requested double – was back wearing a
dressing-gown. He dropped, rather wearily, into one
armchair, accepted the over-large drink, took two avid gulps
and felt better.

"Ha!" he said. "Man's best friend. Used with discretion,
of course . . . Do sit down. You make me feel uneasy." He
took another gulp and said, faintly aggressive, "And what
can I tell you that you don't already know? Not that you could
print it. Too horrible. Nobody would believe it. I've seen
some horrible things in my day but . . .''

He proceeded to give details. The relief of talking or the
brandy brought the colour back into his face, patchily at first,
then smoothly rosy.

Graham listened, slightly sickened, but fascinated. He
could imagine what Sergeant Parsons, the Public Relations
officer would make of this – if indeed he mentioned it at all.
Everything possible was done to conceal the identity of rape
victims; even the locality of the crime was withheld. Graham's
mind toyed with innocuous phrases: Not far from the town
centre . . . He wondered if, by morning, suspicion would have
centred upon somebody so that he could use the hoary old
phrase about a man helping the police.

"A spot more?" Doctor Brunning asked, coming to the
end of his tale and lifting the decanter.

"No thank-you, sir. I know my limitations. This sounds
like the work of a maniac. Don't you think women should be
warned?"

"They should all be warned! About going round half-
naked; rousing men's lowest instincts. Last month when my
car was in dock, I went on a bus. There was a girl. When she
uncrossed her legs I could see more than was decent. *I* found
the display more disgusting than enticing but then I'm getting
on.''

"I don't know Miss Dalton but I have heard her described

36

as rather prim and proper.'' The old man took a gulp of his second drink and said. ''That in itself can be a danger. By all accounts she'd been entertaining a man all evening and from what remained of her clothes I judged her to be most improperly dressed. *And* they'd been drinking – the bottle stood there. The wretched man tries to take the next logical step, is resisted and goes berserk. That would account . . . But not in this case.'' He gave Graham a curious glance, wary, cunning, defiant. ''I know you'll say I'm prejudiced. I noticed that when you did that article about me you cut out all reference to Quarry Lane.''

''Not I. My editor.''

''Same thing! I've just told you that the poor girl reminded me of an Indian woman I'd seen after a leopard clawed her. But I did not do all my service in India; I was in West Africa for several months and there I heard about the Leopard men – a very sinister, very secret society. The members go about disguised as leopards. Now mark this! In the few seconds it took for the injection to work, Miss Dalton said a very cogent thing. She said; The Devil! The Devil behind the door! Now to me that was highly sig – significant. So was another thing . . .'' The brandy was beginning to take over. ''While I was in India I witnessed a most indecent phallic festival, the men wearing – shall we say appurtenances? Miss Dalton's injuries, apart from the claw marks, were worse, far worse than could have been inflicted by natural means. You understand me? If I were Detective Chief Inspector Hardy I should concentrate on Quarry Lane and look for a Hindu who was on friendly terms with a West African – or vice versa. This whole thing smacks to me of a combination of two very pernicious cults. But of course, to say so to anybody but you, so discreet, is to dub oneself racialist or a can – candidate for the psychiatric ward. However we shall see.''

Graham went to his grim bed-sitting room in a house which contained six identical ones. It stood in a cul-de-sac called Smith Square, to the rear of the Smiths' Arms in Guildhall

Street. A poor relation of the Old Vic, it was an enviable place to live, and very central. Residents were allowed to do what cooking was possible on a small gas-ring. He used his to heat up a judicious mixture of milk and water, added instant coffee and settled down to tap out his article, presenting facts in the form of questions. Was Hillchester about to suffer a similar reign of terror as had recently afflicted Cambridge? Would women living on their own be wise to take precautions? It would probably never be printed, but he'd done his best.

In the morning the official police release concerned a stolen car, recovered without hurt except for an empty petrol tank.

"Nothing about the rape?"

"What rape?"

"Come off it, Pete. I know about it. I was there."

"With the gay boys?"

In his mind Graham heard the cock crow thrice as he said, "No. I was having a drink with Doctor Brunning."

"And he talked. Garrulous old fool! But forget it. G.H. wants this given the least possible publicity. He has the idea that most crimes are imitative, so the less said the better."

"He could be right."

Hardy, being right, was also immensely handicapped. Not a sensible word from the victim. Becky had been taken to the New Hospital and placed in a room, the recovery room, wedged between Casualty and Geriatrics. WPC Collins sat beside the bed, waiting and watching. Just before four o'clock in the morning Becky came round and began to scream. Then all the old people not under the influence of some kind of dope, woke and began to scream, too. The resultant pandemonium was quite intolerable and Sister Watson rang the young house surgeon who was serving his comprehensive but gruelling apprenticeship. He prescribed, for the inmates of the ward, hot cocoa and a harmless digestive tablet which they accepted as a sedative – Swallow this, dear, with your nice hot drink. There, there, you'll be asleep in no time. It worked and in no time the old, more or less demented people were asleep again. But Becky went on; three screams, a pause for breath, three more. "This is quite impossible," Sister Watson said. "It's all very sad, but she's a case for Pykenham, not here. For God's sake give her something: anything to stop the noise." Seeing him hesitate she said, "I will take full responsibility. And if you don't, I will!"

Becky could give no helpful lead and her room was singularly uninformative. She had entertained a man that evening and she wore a ring on what was usually regarded as the engagement finger, but there were no letters, no photographs. Her handbag held a cheque-book, about three pounds in cash, powder compact and lipstick, a crushed packet of cigarettes and a lighter.

Two sleepy, sullen girls on the floor below admitted to having been friendly with Becky. They knew she had a steady boyfriend called Alan. They did not know his surname or what he did for a living except that it was something to do with cars. They knew where Becky worked – at Turner and Noble's. They also proffered the information that her parents had a farm, where exactly they did not know.

The immediate post-rape drill was complicated by the fact that that an all-male party had been held in the penthouse. Evidence of that lay all around. Quite a few glasses, Sergeant Saunders quietly observed, left unemptied. And at what time did this party break up? The younger of the two occupants said, "Just on twelve." The older one gaily,

"Matt, you're drunker than I thought! It was well after that . . . Twenty to one when young Adams made the move that broke up the party." Georgie was older, more quick-witted, and reared in a harsher school. He was even prepared for the next question. Had any member of the party left it at any time?

"Quite possibly. But that is one of the many reasons for champagne's popularity. It nullifies, rather than stimulates bladder activity. And anyone in need would have gone through there." He indicated a door. "Quite possibly," he said with an air of delicate self-abasement, "I am comitting a technical offence when I lock my outer door, since that fire escape is supposed to serve all this floor. But last year there was an unfortunate incident. The landing is so badly lighted. One of our guests went that way and sprained an ankle. So now, when entertaining I take the precaution of keeping the landing door locked."

Tom Saunders whose mental vocabulary far exceeded that which he used every day, thought; Specious! But he asked, "Just as a formality", the names and addresses of the twelve guests. These were willingly supplied. None of the twelve was under suspicion, but they might have seen or heard something of significance. Only one, so far as Tom Saunders could remember, had any kind of a record. Maxie Fisher, caught shoplifting two years ago. His age, just seventeen, and his bad family background had ensured him of leniency. He had lately taken to playing the guitar.

As soon as they were alone, Matthew said, "That was damned smart of you Georgie." Georgie acknowledged the compliment with a slight smile as he moved towards the telephone. "Everybody must tell the same tale. They're all on the phone except Maxie. I'd ask you to walk round and tell him, but you might be stopped and it would look funny and actually nobody would take his word against all of us."

The post-rape drill got under way. Police, wearing plain clothes out of consideration for householders' feelings, made door to door visits asking questions that nobody was obliged to answer. How many males were resident in this house? Could they account for their whereabouts between the hours of eleven and midnight? Had anybody seen or heard anything suspicious? Residents within the area to which a man could have run before the alarm was raised were few. In the short avenue between St Luke's church and Castle Street there were, apart from the Old Vic only four houses; the new vicarage, the slightly smaller house where the church-warden lived and two prettier dwellings, both occupied by elderly maiden ladies. Castle Street where it passed between St Luke's Avenue on one side and St Luke's Lane on the other had become frankly commercial; a large garage, a launderette, several small lock-up shops. St Luke's Lane was similarly depopulated at night. One side of it was entirely devoted to offices, the other to the back premises of the White Horse, including a separate bar, known as The Shades which catered entirely for customers who would have felt ill at ease in the main part of the hostelry. Then, veering round the White Horse which stood on the corner, one came to Market Square where only two men actually lived. One was the proprietor of a café called Tony's and a less likely rapist could hardly be imagined, an ugly man, an ex-boxer, with a crooked nose and cauliflower ears, he had somehow acquired a most beautiful, voluptuous-looking and masterful wife, Italian by birth.

The other man resident in Market Square was the husband of Mrs Fullerton who owned and ran the Music Centre. And he, if suspected, had a cast-iron alibi. He'd had one of his attacks – severe and frightening palpitations. Mrs Fullerton had propped him up, administered the prescribed pills and then rung up Doctor Brunning. Getting no answer she had tried Doctor Carter who had come as doctors so often did, when the worst was over. (And underestimated the whole thing, thought her neurotic and Eric *malade imaginaire*.)

The sole even remotely interesting piece of information that the questioning produced, came from the Reverend Mr Lummis, and that concerned timing.

"I knew I was in for an unquiet night," he said, still peevish. "Cars and – worse – motor-bikes, roaring into the Old Vic at about nine o'clock. Hopeless to go to bed and be again disturbed, so I stayed up and read. I heard the clock strike midnight and decided not to wait. So I let out my cat, usually a most docile creature but for once recalitrant. On a warm evening I should have left her, and gone to bed. But there was a chill so I waited, glancing at the clock with some impatience. At twenty-five minutes past the hour the uproar I had anticipated began. Cars and motor-cycles most incon-

41

siderately driven. And after them, one solitary walker, with a dark bundle under his arm. By the light of my porch I recognised him, Maxie Fisher. Underprivileged and I fear, dishonest, but with such a good voice – quite the best choir-boy I ever knew. But I was suspicious of the bundle. I imagined – quite unworthily – that under cover of the party he had purloined . . . So I accosted him. I said, 'Hullo Maxie, what have you got there?' He showed me, a guitar which he said he had bought and paid for at the Music Centre and if I didn't believe him, ask Mrs Fullerton. I felt – rather ashamed and easily forgave his rude manner.''

This long speech offered nothing very useful; just a slight discrepancy about time, but then both the occupants of the penthouse had been drinking.

''Naturally,'' Mr Noble said in his most pompous manner, ''I am anxious to help, Chief Inspector. But I know almost nothing about Miss Dalton's personal life. However, I know who might. A girl named Morrison. They were on cordial terms. In fact Miss Dalton once suggested that she should join the staff here. She now works for Mr Anderson. Just two doors along.''

The news, though it had begun to leak had not yet reached Greg Anderson's office. Hardy began with a half-truth, saying that Miss Dalton had met with an accident. Behind the glasses which, far from disfiguring, magnified the beauty of her eyes, Shirley stared. ''Oh dear, in that horrible old car! I've warned her a dozen times.''

''What old car?''

''Her boyfriend's. He's a typical Scot, mean as they come. He has a well-paid job; he could well afford a decent car. And in all the time he's been hanging round Becky he's never once given her a decent present.''

''You know his name?''

''Of course. Alan Douglas. Is Becky badly hurt?''

''Seriously. We hope not fatally.''

"Where is she?"

"In hospital. And it was not a car accident. We, I, did not want the truth advertised until a few enquiries were made . . . The truth is . . . Miss Dalton was attacked and raped."

"Christ!" Shirley Morrison was truly shaken and felt faint; but just in time she remembered Miss Lowe's advice to would-be fainters. Draw deep breaths and concentrate.

"You mustn't suspect Alan," Shirley said, having breathed and concentrated. "I know I just said he was mean — and so he is. But not lecherous. Monkish! In fact Becky once said she liked him because he was the one man she knew who could keep his paws off."

"She had many boyfriends?" It had occurred to Hardy that the viciousness of the attack stemmed from some grudge such as a discarded lover might cherish.

Shirley meditated. "Fewer than you'd expect; she being so pretty. Only two the least bit serious. One was an airman. He got posted to Germany: but they'd broken up before then. There was Simon Hooper, but he went a bit too far. In many ways Becky was — well, old-fashioned. So they parted. All quite friendly. He found somebody else and she found Alan. Can I see her?"

"Not yet. She's under sedation."

"As bad as that?" Hardy slipped in two more questions. Alan Douglas's place of work and was Simon Hooper anything to do with Hooper and Ransome, the solicitors in St Luke's Lane. Shirley knew the answers; Hillchester Motors and yes, old Mr Hooper's nephew.

Unlike Mr Noble, Mr Bramble did take a keen personal interest in the affairs of those he employed. This was resented rather than appreciated, it smacked of sheer nosiness and when they called him Big Daddy his men were being sardonic.

"Is it about that old heap of his? Frankly I can't see how, clever as he is, he's kept it going so long."

"Nothing to do with cars. I'd just like a private word with him."

"He's not here. Like everybody else I've taken pains with

43

and trained, he got too big for his boots. He's on his way to Dagenham now. An interview with Ford's."

It did not actually surprise Alan to be met at the station but he was slightly puzzled by the ease with which the stout, amiable-looking man had singled him out.

"Mr Douglas?"

"Yes. That's me."

"If you'd come this way . . ." the stout man said and led the way, not to a waiting car but to a small room where another man waited. The stout one then revealed himself, starting with words so often used that they had become automatic. "I am a police officer . . ."

Alan's world exploded. Becky, his dear one, his wife to be, assaulted and raped. It was incredible. And even more incredible the idea that he was under some sort of suspicion. For a moment he looked like a man who, in frenzy, might do anything. Then he partially mastered himself and said, "All right. Take this down, blast you! I left Becky just before midnight and there in Castle Street was Mr Sims – he's an auctioneer – with his car stalled. Merely a jumped lead, but he's ignorant. And the clock struck. I might not have noticed it, but he did and said his missus would have something to say. Then he offered me a lift. Not out of his way. And while I . . . God! Some bastard did that to Becky! I'll find him if it's the last thing I do – and rip him apart."

He was not even an official suspect; just somebody to be questioned, the maker of a voluntary statement. He could not be detained or in any way prevented from going about his lawful business. The stout man said, "Thank you, Mr Douglas. And now, I understand, you have an interview."

"Bugger it!" Alan said and turned and ran. The two policemen followed, but another train had arrived, spilling passengers who, having been jostled by one big, wild-looking man were indisposed to accept another jostling by two men merely in a hurry. The fact that one of them wore police uniform did nothing to help. Who're you shoving, Pig?

44

The police car stood there, its driver leaning against it and enjoying a cigarette. Alan took him by the arm and flung him aside and within half a minute had committed an indictable, if rare, offence. He'd made off with a police car.

Hardy had had that worst of all things, a useless day. Getting nowhere. He found himself – as a rational man – obliged to accept the idea that Becky Dalton's superficial wounds had been inflicted by a knife. And a knife, very sharp and so newly washed as to be a little damp, had been found in her minute kitchen. As to the other, worse damage, opinion was divided. Old Doctor Brunning held firm to his view –. unnatural means. But one of the doctors at the hospital thought otherwise, recalling a case, rare enough to be memorable, when a young bride, honeymooning at Brighton, and, obviously a virgin, had suffered such a terrible haemorrhage that she could well, without help, have died.

And certainly no suspicion could be attached to this wild-eyed young man who now said, "I want to see her. I must. We got engaged last night – and she'd – she'd tell me anything. Like being scared of being alone in the dark . . . She never could say why but it could be. Maybe all the time, and me trying to laugh her out of it . . . God! She may have had some reason."

Hardy thought: A known, a loved, trusted face might be the catalyst. "Certainly you may see her."

"I must tell her," Alan said, speaking with some difficulty, "that what happened to her hasn't made any difference to the way I feel about her."

"Of course not." Hardy's tone was understanding and soothing. "Now look, you've had a rough day. I think a cup of coffee and a sandwich . . ."

"I couldn't swallow."

"You must. What happened is bad, very bad. But you're both young. She stands a good chance." But even as he spoke, Hardy remembered a woman, far less savagely assaulted who had been permanently deranged: and the latest

45

report from the hospital had not been encouraging. Physically Miss Dalton had responded well to the blood transfusion and the small operation needed had been successfully performed. But whenever she was conscious, she screamed. The hospital was not really the place for her. Pykenham would be better.

WPC Collins was relieved by WPC Drabble who came armed for her vigil with a bag of doughnuts, a paperback thriller and some knitting. During her watch, Betty Collins had done some serious thinking and come to the conclusion that she was in the wrong job. All her thinking was over-shadowed by shame. She'd fought the nausea successfully until she was outside the Old Vic. Then the fresh air had had upon her the effect it often had on drunks. Leaning against the side of the ambulance, she'd been violently sick.

She came of a police family. Her grandfather, still alive and with all his wits about him, had been a village policeman; her father had reached the rank of Inspector. She'd been no more than seven when she overheard them regretting her sex, saying if only she'd been a boy . . . She had made up her mind to show them. And they'd both been delighted when she qualified to enter the Force. "Things are different now," her grandfather had said. "Giver her time and she'll make Chief Inspector."

At first she had seemed to be ready-made for the job. She was not timid, she was cool in an emergency, conscientious about details. But she had suspected, over a battered baby case, that she lacked some vital asset – call it detachment. She had then hoped that she might harden up. Now she realised that she never would and that she should quit. There were limits beyond which one could not force oneself. She reviewed her assets; she typed well, could write and read shorthand, could drive anything on four wheels. She'd resign and the already under-manned Hillchester Force would be further depleted! But that she could not help. Headquarters down in the county town of Thorington would have to send somebody.

The place known as Peg's Pantry catered for a very select clientele, youngish women, none with money to throw about and some with weight problems; all by lunchtime rather hungry, ready for stew or shepherd's pie or rissoles – very rarely a joint, or, if dieting, a great heaped plate of grated raw cabbage and carrot. And here, as everywhere else, there was a hierarchy. The big oval table in the bay window was tacitly reserved for Old Ethelredians, and the place at it, looking out over Market Square, had always been Becky's. Her place was unoccupied now. Why? Enlightenment came with the arrival of Student Nurse Barker who, settling in to her lowly place said, "Isn't it terrible about Becky?"

In lowered tones she told them all she knew, and it was a good deal. She used the word ripped rather than clawed. Everybody stopped eating while she told her tale and several did not resume when she had finished. Somebody said, "Becky of all people! The very *last* person!" Somebody said, "We must send some flowers." There were eight of them so fifty pence each seemed a reasonable contribution. For those on a narrow budget this meant coffee and a bun at Tony's instead of lunch at Peg's one day this week. Tony's was perfectly respectable at lunch time. No Ethelredian, in fact no decent young woman, would have set foot inside the café after five o'clock.

Somebody said, "This will upset Shirley. They were great friends."

As though answering to her name, Shirley appeared. She looked pale and had been crying. She had felt like eschewing lunch altogether, but had then thought that the girls should be told. She had been forestalled, but she was first with the flowers; on her way to Peg's she had stopped at Flora's and ordered the delivery of twenty pink – not red so reminiscent of blood – carnations with a Get Well card. Nevertheless she willingly added her fifty pence to the common pool. She was better off than most of her contemporaries, for she lived at home and had bed and board and various other amenities absolutely free.

47

From Peg's Pantry the news spread outwards; a shock wave. But there were other leaks . . .

(ii)

Eying his breakfast, three rashers, two eggs and a slice of fried bread, Doctor Brunning said, mildly, ''Rather too much again, Mrs Garland.'' She herself was lean to the point of being scraggy, she ate voraciously and had no patience with diets and talk about calories. There had been a time when she had expressed her opinion in words; now she had no need to speak. She swivelled round and stared at the brandy decanter. God! he thought: in the agitation last night I forgot to top up! Mrs Garland had been so outspoken about the connection between unwanted weight and alcohol that he had resorted to a little harmless smuggling. He brought home, in his black bag and kept in a locked cupboard, a private supply and whenever he took a drink above the amount Mrs Garland would tolerate he replenished the relevant decanter. He must not offend Mrs Garland who was, to the best of his knowledge, the only resident cook-housekeeper within a radius of twenty miles.

''I know. But last night – or rather this morning – I had a visitor. And I was very upset. I really *needed* a drink.''

Her look, a nice blend of disbelief and scorn, provoked him. He told her exactly what had upset him. Ten minutes later she told the milkman.

His name was William Selsey and he was sixty years old. Happily married; two sons, both grown-up and flown the nest now; one daughter, late-born, whom he loved, adored, worshipped. He did not realise it but Lorraine represented all that his humdrum life had experienced of romance. He'd started work with Farmhouse Dairies when he was sixteen. At twenty he had gone to the war and in North Africa, doing what he always said, in his stolid East Anglian way, had been the only thing *to* do, had won a Military Medal and a wound in the knee. He still limped and whenever the weather

48

changed, suffered some pain. Hillchester, for its size rather short of heroes, had given him a tumultuous welcome. Then he'd married Liz because he liked her as well as he'd ever liked any woman, and she plainly wanted to marry him. Also the Council gave priority to ex-Service men when it came to the allotment of Council houses.

A dull life. Everyman's life – except for Lorraine.

Now Mrs Garland said, "rape", mouthing the word with delicate distaste. William Selsey turned as nearly pale as his out-in-all-weathers complexion allowed. He said, "Poor girl!" He said, "I hope they catch the brute!" Then he drove to the nearest call-box and rang up the Music Centre where Lorraine had taken a job. Much against his wishes. Some of the customers there were what he called in his mind bad types, but Lorraine had said that of all the many jobs offered her, this was the only one with the slightest appeal.

The voice answering was Mrs Fullerton's. Upper-class. Odd how you knew.

"I'm Lorraine's Dad. Mrs Fullerton, I want she should catch the four o'clock bus. I just heard there's a rapist on the rampage."

"Oh dear!"

Mrs Fullerton did not fear rape herself: it was burglars she dreaded; but every sign of the breakdown of law and order dismayed her.

"You will see that she's on the four o'clock."

"I will see that she leaves here in ample time, Mr Selsey. I cannot escort her to the bus station."

Lorraine's early departure would not be very inconvenient this afternoon: trade was never brisk on Mondays or Tuesdays, Wednesday was market day and the Music Centre fairly busy. Thursday was early closing. The bulk of the trade was done on Friday and Saturday when the shop stayed open until seven. To compensate for these unsocial hours Mrs Fullerton allowed her assistant to take the whole of Thursday instead of the half day and never expected her to come to business earlier than eleven in the morning. Despite these concessions she did not find it easy to get the right kind of girl. Had there been any alternative to Lorraine Selsey she would never have employed her. Vain, surly, lethargic, untidy, unhelpful: the only thing in her favour was that she understood pop music which Mrs Fullerton did not.

William Selsey continued on his round, spreading the news as he went. He liked to have a chat with his customers especially old people whom he thought lonely. For those unable to get out and about much he did little kindnesses, posting letters, conveying messages, buying things. He had twice been instrumental in saving life because people usually waiting and on the look-out for him had failed to appear or respond to his knock. One old man had turned on a gas burner and then failed to light it. He was far gone when William looked in at the window and then broke down the door. The other near fatality was an old woman suffering from hypothermia.

Mrs Garland told everybody with whom she came in contact and that included Mrs Packer who worked for Doctor Brunning for two hours every weekday. Miss Lowe could afford help only twice a week and Tuesday was not one of her days for Charity Lane; nonetheless, on her way home she just looked in to impart this red-hot piece of information. Miss Lowe reacted as thoroughly as the most ardent gossiper could wish. At the words raped and ripped she turned very pale and then, at the mention of the victim's name, seemed on the verge of tears. "Becky Dalton! Oh no! One of my very best girls. Is she much injured?"

"Bad enough to be in hospital. But Doctor Brunning told Mrs Garland he had fears for her mind. Apparently she said something about seeing the Devil. Behind the door. She might have to go to Pykenham."

Miss Lowe again said, "Oh no!" and pressed her hand to her mouth.

"Thought I'd just let you know. See you tomorrow."

Left alone, Miss Lowe did some swift, painful thinking. She was largely to blame. She should have reported her own

50

experience. The link between Pan and the Devil was only too plain. Obviously the same man. And although she had seen him but briefly she could give a fair description of him, which poor Becky was unable to do.

She must now write to the police, taking pains to remain anonymous. How could that be done? One's handwriting could never be wholly disguised. She owned a typewriter, but had read somewhere that every machine had individuality and that type could be traced as easily as writing. She'd always rather enjoyed crime stories and one came to her aid now.

In Woolworth's she bought the smallest possible quantity of writing paper with matching envelopes. Then she moved on to the racks of paperbacks and chose one with a lurid cover. Paste she already had in the house; she used it for mounting photographs. She visualised an afternoon of work demanding intense concentration; and that would be a relief. It might take her mind off Dorothea and the miserable thought of how things had gone wrong.

Her first invitation had been refused: "Dear Marcia, I have no need to tell you how hectic the beginning of term always is. And I'm still without a secretary. I shall have to advertise." The word was repellent to them both for it signified the failure of the Old Girl network. The second invitation was cordially accepted and Miss Lowe happily planned a dinner as different as possible from school food. She already had the Greek wine: she bought sherry, small pink chrysanthemums for the table, great mop-headed ones for the stand in the sitting room. She was arranging these when the telephone rang. It was Dorothea asking dear Marcia would she mind too terribly if she brought someone with her. "It's the new gym mistress. Very shy and rather gauche. She's heard so much about you and would love to meet."

What could one say?

The girl would still be gauche when she had ceased to be shy: she had large feet and coarse hands. She was a trifle uncertain about the cutlery and her accent was insecure. She looked at Dorothea with dog-like devotion, just as Dorothea had once looked at Miss Lowe. And she was being encouraged! Really, how dreadfully obvious and what bad taste on Dorothea's part! Scorn salved the wound – but only temporarily.

As she had hoped, Miss Lowe found the paste and scissors job wholly absorbing. Punctuation was the real problem, one could not cut out and paste on the full stops and commas one needed. She compromised by leaving long spaces between statements. When she came to addressing the envelope she was obliged to cut the word Hillchester from the daily paper. She made and drank a cup of tea while the paste dried, and then, hoping that she did not look as furtive as she felt, went out to the main Post Office.

"Over to you George, and a real beaut," Terry O'Brien said with his mischievous, not-quite-unmalicious grin. He handed Hardy the letter which was addressed to "The Chief Inspector". Very few people could differentiate. Hardy unfolded the stiff sheet and read:

Sir
I blame myself most severely for this latest atrocity
I was myself raped three weeks ago and I can describe the man
He is rather above average height and well-built
His movements were those of a young man
He wore a disguise which made me think of pan
The latest victim speaks of the devil
There is a connection
he did not hurt me otherwise
He had a distinct animal odour and a nasty jeering laugh
I most deeply regret not giving you this information at the time
rape at my age seemed so ridiculous
he entered my house by a window overlooking adjoining roofs

I greatly fear that his condition is progressive and if left at large he may do worse

The last statement echoed the fear that Hardy had felt since he first saw Becky Dalton's injuries. For plain rape there was a reason, occasionally even an excuse: the senseless savagery of this attack hinted at mania. And allied to it was the element of low cunning which enabled mass rapists and murderers to elude the law for considerable periods.

The letter's comment on the connection between Pan and the Devil was also worth noting. There were still people about who thought of the Devil as horned and cloven-hooved. And the poor girl's parents were of that number; complete Fundamentalists. Their reaction when told of what had happened to their daughter was most extraordinary. Most inhumane. It was a judgment on her for her way of life. When she first went to work in Hillchester they'd found her good safe lodgings with a woman of their faith; and she'd left to occupy a flat of her own where she could smoke; drink perhaps, who knew? since one vice led to another. She'd had her hair cut, wore trousers and went around with young Communists. They evinced no desire to see her and seemed unconcerned by the possibility that she might be moved to Pykenham.

Alan Douglas, as near tears as a man could be without betraying his manhood, had happened to say that Becky was a very nervous girl, always afraid of being alone after dark, and she had spoken of the Devil. It was possible to suppose that Becky's assailant had known her rather well. And fright would account for the lapse of time – by Commander Lucas's meticulous timing – before she screamed. Dumb, probably fainting from terror. One could only hope that she was unconscious when the outrage was committed.

"Well, what do you make of it?" O'Brien asked.

"What do *you*?"

"A nut case. Or wishful thinking. Like the bogus murder confessions. Walter Mitty stuff."

"This mention of age," Hardy said. "Down at

Thorington when a fellow was nabbed, two quite reliable women said they had been raped, but had kept quiet, fearing the publicity and the ridicule. Both over sixty.''

''Well if you're going to take this seriously you'll be interested in this. The Scene of the Crime officer said that he expected to find cat hairs amongst his cleanings. He said he thought he could *smell* a cat but nary a hair turned up.'' He spoke lightly. Anyone not knowing him would have misjudged him, thinking that he was finding the whole affair amusing, but Hardy knew better: the flippant manner concealed a very conscientious, on-the-verge-of-ruthless police officer. And a good colleague.

It was now Wednesday morning and they had got exactly nowhere. The house-to-house questioning had yielded nothing and every known sex offender in the area had been accounted for. It had hardly been necessary to consult the files; Tom Saunders could name them all and knew what had happened to each.

It was unlikely, but not impossible, that one of the pent-house guests had turned rapist. The swift contradiction about the time, the glib story of the locked door to the landing had not passed unnoticed. But not one of the twelve young men, traced to their homes or places of work, had shown the slightest hesitation about taking a saliva test. Such a test was entirely voluntary but a refusal would have quickened suspicion. A man's saliva and seminal fluid were indications of his blood group.

On Hardy's desk, beside the already-mounting, negative reports, was the morning edition of the *Hillchester and District*, with Graham Harper's article on the front page. Not in the most prominent position, but still, the front page. Hardy, a quick reader, took it in at a glance. Very clever, the way facts were presented as questions. And again, as when reading Miss Lowe's letter, Hardy heard the echo of his own fear. Was Hillchester indeed to suffer a reign of terror?

Tom Saunders came in and Hardy handed him the anonymous letter saying, ''If we take this as fact, it might help if we could find something in common between the two victims. One a woman conscious of her age and a girl of twenty-three. Any idea, Tom?''

Tom went into one of those sessions of self-communications which often prefaced some cogent words. At the end of it he surfaced and said, "I can only think of Miss Lowe, sir. Pan. Greek if I remember rightly. Horns, feet like a goat's. And that poor girl talked of the Devil. Miss Lowe gave a lecture, illustrated by colour slides. My girls insisted on my going. It was in aid of Oxfam. And now I come to think of it, one of her windows is easily accessible. The neighbouring roofs go up like steps. But let's say Miss Lowe composed this . . . Then the only common denominator that I can think of is the school. St Ethelreda's. Miss Lowe, until last year, Headmistress, and Becky Dalton, years ago, head girl and hockey captain . . . No real link . . .''

On the first part of his round William Selsey preceded the paper boy; later on the papers had preceded him and a number of people called his attention to the article, saying: Look at this! Saying: What are we coming to? Four elderly women asked him to buy door chains for them, and then, in their varying ways, asked his help in the fixing of them: would it be too much to ask? Did he know a handyman? He made reckless promises.

Smith Square was on his round and he was placing the requested amounts in the communal hallway when Graham Harper ran downstairs.

"Morning, Bill.''

"Morning Mr Harper. Mr Harper, half a minute if you don't mind . . . That article you wrote. I'm grateful to you. Lorraine – that's my daughter – reckons I'm too fussy and careful. Now it's down in black and white, women should be careful. Lends strength to the argument, if you see what I mean.''

Graham's mind, not quite the equal of Tom Saunders' yet, but framing up, went click! Click! Click!

"Look," he said. "She goes to that Disco? Right? I remember your telling me. Well, tell her to lay off for a bit. Quite apart from this raving maniac being at large, I happen to know that the Disco is being watched by the police."

"Why?"

"That I can't tell you. Just a tip. I must rush. Late already."

William limped away, pleased rather than concerned with the crumb of information. *Now* in his arguments with Lorraine he had a real reason to bring forward. She'd always accused him of being blindly prejudiced against the place which she adored; the one place where she was really happy. Actually he was not prejudiced, he wanted her to be happy. What he hated and worried about was after the Disco closed down Lorraine was always left to come home alone. He just could not understand it. In his youth girls were always seen home. There were more girls than boys then and often enough, after some sort of do, he'd walked Liz and two or three other girls who had no escort of their own, safely home. Now there were more boys than girls, yet Lorraine never found an escort. He simply could not understand it: she was so pretty! She was very slim; her skin was white. She had blue eyes and a mass of curly, nut-brown hair, shoulder length. He was oblivious to the fact that her usual expression was peevish and the blue eyes, except when she was in a temper, quite blank.

When she had first begun to frequent the Disco and come home alone, he'd gone to meet her, skimming down from Copplestone Close on his old-fashioned bike and waiting patiently outside the Disco called, for some reason, The Roaring Twenties. He had then seen for himself that no one came out of the place reeling drunk or in any way disorderly. Lorraine had said that the only drinks served were coffee and Coke. And she had objected to being met. She said it made her look silly, made her look like a child being fetched from school. All the way home she'd walked just that little away from him, setting a pace which he with his stiff knee and pushing the heavy, old-fashioned bike had found difficult to match. And, once safely home, Lorraine had turned on him and said that if ever he shamed her that way again she'd simply leave home and ask Mrs Fullerton to let her one of the spare rooms over the Music Centre.

Then there'd been the rape and Lorraine had said, with some truth, that that had not happened to a girl walking home alone across the Common. Had it? Had it?

Now he was armed. He could say: honey, I'd stay away from that Disco for a bit: I hear the police have their eye on it.

That would carry weight with Lorraine who was at heart rather prim and proper. He and Liz had never had reason to worry about her *behaviour*. She might run around with a rather fast lot – like that Queenie who had first taken her to the Disco, but she often spoke disparagingly of the way Queenie carried on with boys. Queenie, a near neighbour, would call for Lorraine on Disco nights, and they'd go off together on the bus; but when he asked why they didn't come home together, Lorraine said with scorn, "Oh, she's off with some lout." William would certainly have disapproved and felt jealous of any boy in whom Lorraine took an interest, but he did wish she could find a nice, steady, well-behaved escort. Not that she'd find one in that place!

Case Three: Lilah Noble

It was really rather awful, Lilah Noble admitted to herself, to be glad of a weekend alone, but as she entered the house after having driven Chris to the station she relished the thought of freedom to do what she liked, when she liked.

Chris was a devoted husband, generous, courteous, kind, but as he advanced into middle age he had become pompous, pernickety about trifles, slightly dictatorial, and so predictable in attitude and speech as to be a bore.

The kitchen door was unlocked. No need to bother with locking up if you kept a dog like Boru, an Irish wolfhound the size of a small donkey and with a reputation for ferocity. So far cats had been his only victims, but the owner of one – a brown Abyssinian of immense value, had refused to be pacified with mere money. She was vindictive enough to demand the death sentence on Boru. That had not happened, but the thing had caused quite a stir and Lilah had been warned to keep her dog under control.

This evening she let Boru out into the lighted courtyard and while he ran about, went to say goodnight to her horse, Fergus. Tonight she could take her time about it. One could not actually say that Chris was jealous of the animal, but he did make heavily facetious remarks: "I suppose one night, you'll sleep in the stable."

(But never let it be forgotten, Chris had given her both Boru and Fergus.)

Boru's supper stood on one of the working surfaces of the

model kitchen. It was safe to leave it there, well within his reach, he had been trained not to steal. She set the dish down and moved about the kitchen making sure that everything was ready for tomorrow when Mary Anderson and the children were coming to spend the day. Yesterday, the moment that she knew that she would be unable to go with Chris to London for the weekend, she'd telephoned Mary and issued the invitation. Greg had answered the phone and sounded very amiable. So much so that she had said, "If you'd like to come, too . . ." No, thanks all the same, he was terribly busy. And that she could easily believe. Chris had often said that Greg Anderson had defected. It was somehow typical of him to use that word. And taken several clients with him, people of little importance.

She had provided everything that children liked these days; potato crisps, chipolata sausages, fish fingers, beef burgers, chocolate biscuits and masses of ice-cream. She and Mary would lunch on smoked salmon, a thing of which Mary was fond and which she could not afford. Dry Martinis to start with, and a bottle of hock.

She found herself hoping that tomorrow would be fine, then Jimmy and Anna could have little rides on Fergus whose reputation as a steeplechaser was so assured that he could afford to behave like an ambling, amiable pony when occasion demanded. Boru would have to be shut away in his outdoor pen, not because he was unfriendly to children but because they were terrified of him and called him a wolf. Thinking about him, she turned and looked at his dish. He'd eaten rather less than half of the mixed meat and biscuit. "That, my darling," she said aloud, "comes of eating cake at teatime!"

It was nice not to have to bother about making a meal for humans and complying with two of Chris's traits – his love of food and his absolute hatred of seeing his wife in the kitchen. At the time of his marriage, when the renovation of The Grange was taking place, the plans included a very nice flat, suitable for a married couple; but that was an extinct breed.

The most that could be obtained in the way of help was a daily woman five days a week to clean, not to cook. So Chris had fallen into the habit of taking what he called a very *adequate* lunch at the White Horse and saying that he needed only a snack in the evening. But then he would contradict himself, coming into the kitchen where she was preparing the snack and saying, "Darling, leave all that. Let's go out. I hear there's a new place . . ." New eating places were cropping up like mushrooms and Chris would think nothing of driving thirty miles for a good meal.

Lilah, taking a piece of cheese and a crust of bread, reflected, happily, that Chris would eat well all this weekend and he would especially enjoy the Old Boys' Reunion Dinner on Saturday.

In the comparatively snug little room where they usually spent their evenings, she poured herself a drink. And it was whisky! Chris, for no very clear reason, regarded whisky as a drink fit only for men. He'd said, early on, that it never looked right to him, a woman, a lady drinking whisky. But in the ruinous castle in Connemara which was her home place there had been no alcoholic drink but whiskey; Irish whiskey, with its distinctive smoky taste. She'd practically been weaned on it. But in that, as in so many other things, she had given way.

She read as she ate and drank. Rather a good book and one which Mary Anderson would enjoy. Get it finished so that it could be handed over to Mary tomorrow. Switch on the nine o'clock news . . . Everything too awful to contemplate. Wait for the weather. Dry with sunny spells in the Midlands and East Anglia. Good enough. Switch off. And why not go to bed and finish her reading there? no reason whatsoever. Tonight she was her own woman.

She let Boru out again and noticed that he was slow. Well, he was past his prime and earlier in the day, had been well-exercised.

The dog slept in her room in the biggest basket that even Harrod's could provide. Left alone downstairs, he'd howled, like a pack of wolves and since she and Chris no longer shared a room, though they did, with increasing infrequency, share a bed – he visiting her, she had been able to bring the howling puppy to her bedroom.

The sleeping arrangements were mutually accepted. Chris went to sleep as soon as his head touched the pillow and he snored. She slept less easily, liked to read and smoke.

And that they occupied separate, but communicating rooms, had nothing to do with the fact that their marriage was childless. Chris had wanted – still wanted – a son to inherit the small empire of which the accountancy business was only a part, and Lilah would dearly have loved a child, boy or girl. They'd been eminently sensible about the problem of their childlessness, taking the best advice, submitting to tests which proved – or seemed to prove – that they were both absolutely normal and that there was no reason why theirs should be a sterile marriage. But so it was, and so it continued to be.

Boru, unusually lethargic, got into his basket, gave a grunting sigh and slept. And at ten o'clock precisely Chris rang. He never failed in the observance of such courtesies. He told her that he had had a good dinner on the train, was comfortably installed at Claridge's, and had already met two other Old Boys. He was about to go down and have a nightcap with them. "And you, darling . . . Everything all right?"

"Absolutely all right. In fact I'm safely in bed. Having an early night." "Good" he said, "good. Sleep well, darling." "You, too," she said. "Happy day tomorrow."

"You, too," he said. "Don't let the brats get you down."

He knew, of course, what she planned for Saturday. She'd never been secretive.

They exchanged good nights, and she read on, finishing the book at twenty minutes to eleven. She was on, or just over, the borderline of sleep when the main lights in the room snapped on and she saw, between the door and the foot of her bed a nightmare figure, a man, stark naked and with no face and one over-large misshapen hand.

She was not a woman to be easily frightened. She

remembered that burglars liked ready money, instantly usable and usually untraceable. She reared up on her elbows and said in her clear, unmistakably upper-class voice, "My handbag is on the chest. There! It contains about fifty pounds. It is the only money in the . . ."

He cut her short with a jeering laugh and stood for another second or two, fully and grossly exposed, then turned and switched off the lights. She reached down to the side of her bed and grabbed the heavy torch which always stood there under her bedside table. Earlier in the year there had been two power failures, both at night. It was a formidable weapon. She sensed, heard, actually smelt his nearness and hit out with all her might. The blow made contact; she felt its impact and he grunted. But he was not deterred. He, too, struck out in the darkness and dealt a far more effectual blow to the side of her head. Stars danced and bells rang inside her head and she had that feeling of drifting away as though an anaesthetic had been administered. She fought against it, she fought against being raped but she was easily overpowered.

There was no actual pain until afterwards when something sharp dug into her collarbone – twice broken in riding mishaps. She screamed then, knowing even as she did it, how senseless it was to yell when there was no one to hear. Then there was scuffle. A curse from the man. A yelp of pain from Boru.

From earliest childhood she had been trained not to fuss; if you took a toss, well, you took a toss, and the only thing to do was to pick yourself up and start all over again. She switched on the bedside lamp and saw Boru with a deep, slanting gash across his muzzle from just under one eye – Thank God his eyes had been missed – to the edge of one nostril. He looked dazed and puzzled, but the self-healing process had begun; his long pink tongue was already at work, licking off the blood and applying the healing saliva.

She wasted no time in investigating her own wounds. She knew with certainty that she had been assaulted by the same man as had attacked Becky Dalton. And he must be reported immediately. But she must not disclose the fact that she had herself been raped. For one thing Chris would never get over it.

Like all ill-informed people she imagined that a call from a phone-box would be less easily traced than one from a private number. And there was a phone-box within a hundred yards of the opening to the drive. She pulled on a pair of slacks and a high-necked sweater, and bundling up her long black hair as she went, ran out into the night.

Just inside the mouth of the drive was a car finding it difficult to start. It gave three protesting roars. Then it started and turned towards Hillchester. Another car, going in the other direction gave light enough for her to see the slow-starting one in profile. Her mind registered the facts that it was an old car and dark in colour.

The phone-booth was brightly lit; so was the golf clubhouse on the opposite side of the road. By Salford standards – and for Friday night – it was not yet very late. She feared recognition and kept her head down as she dialled 999. A cool, unhurried voice asked, "Which service do you require?"

What the hell did that mean? "Police," she said. There was a maddening long pause before a different, but equally calm voice said, "Hillchester Police Station."

"I wish to report a rape."

"What is your number, please?"

Automatically she began to give her own. "Salford 28 . . ." she began. Checked herself and looked at this number. It was all right, like her own the number began with 28, but there were more digits and ended with X. The calm voice said, "Yes?"

"I have to report a rape. The man responsible is driving an old, dark car and heading towards Hillchester." She dropped back the receiver and scurried home, holding one hand to her face, partly to avoid recognition, partly to console the pain which had begun in her cheek, just below her eye.

Her mind was clearer now and she realised that she had not done enough. She wanted that bloody brute of a man caught and punished. She could describe him – all but his face – in a fair amount of detail. And it was her duty to do so. How? Inspiration came as she re-entered the house. She went into the dining room where, in an unlocked cabinet, Chris kept his collection of antique silver. She ran through the door that led to the kitchen and from a cupboard took a stout plastic bag, plainly labelled Best's The Best Cleaners. Back in the dining room and working with the haste a *bona fide* burglar would have used she shovelled into the bag a pair of candlesticks, a seventeenth-century christening cup and a lidded sweetmeat dish. Enough! A burglar caught in the act and frightened would have dropped the bag down, but she set it down gently – no need to dent the precious things.

Finger prints? Hers only. Well, she often cleaned the silver and she must remember to say that the man wore gloves. She used the kitchen phone and having given her own number, identified herself. "I am Mrs Noble of The Grange, Salford. I have just disturbed a burglar in my house. I saw the man quite clearly. And his car. An old model. Dark in colour."

To the Hillchester police the word *rape* was an exposed nerve, immensely sensitive and Hardy had given strict instructions that he was to be alerted even if a hoax was suspected. There had been some lately – all from call-boxes. He had not gone to bed, but was playing poker when the first call from Salford came, and was at the Station just as PC Stebbings had taken the second. Stebbings vastly admired Sergeant Saunders and Saunders had once told him, "The trick is to notice *everything*, Charlie; it gets to be second nature."

"Peculiar thing, sir," he now said, giving evidence of noticing everything. "It sounded to me like the same voice. Both times I mean. A lady."

Hardy noted the remark, with the reserve thought that perhaps too much attention should not be paid to that. All Scotsmen, for instance, sounded alike to an Englishman. What did strike him as worthy of notice was the similarity in content between the two calls; both mentioning an old car, dark in colour. The two calls were separated by a space of exactly fourteen minutes.

"I'll go and see what I can get out of Mrs Noble," Hardy said. And damn all to Hell, these days even officers of his rank had to hunt in couples! There'd been so much scurrilous talk about bent policemen, accused of everything from the taking of bribes to resorting to violence, nobody was safe. A glance about showed him WPC Drabble, waiting to take over from Stebbings at midnight. As usual, she was chewing something. A ruminant animal. Cow! "You come with me," he said.

South of the town, on the way to Salford, was a road junction called the Triangle. Originally three roads had met there and there had been a triangle of grass. Now there were five roads converging and no grass at all, but it was still called the Triangle. Somehow typical of Hillchester.

Hardy was pleased to see how quickly and efficiently the post-rape drill could move into action. There was a road block on the Salford side of the Triangle and several cars, not all of them old models and dark in colour, were awaiting clearance.

Then he realised that he had come ill-prepared. Where exactly was The Grange? He asked, rather irritably, "D'you know where this place is?"

WPC shifting whatever cud she was chewing, said, "Yes. I had to come one time about a dog that had killed a cat." She was placidly willing to instruct. "On the left," she said. "Third on the left. There's the turn off to Malwood; then the drive to Mason Croft and after that, a fair way on, is The Grange." She shifted her quid and resumed chewing. Well, after all, cows had their uses! And she had directed him accurately.

He had seen Mrs Noble several times, but always from a distance. He'd watched her win a race at the Hickford point-to-point, seen her, last year, acting the gracious Mayoress, but he had never before been struck by her likeness to Julia.

Julia! His wife for four years that swung dizzily between ecstasy and Hell and ended in divorce. Thank God it was easier now! He never spoke of her and few people with whom he now had daily dealings, knew that he had ever been married. He'd let her go, with her satiny black hair, her crystal blue eyes and the impression she gave of looking down on everybody – even, curiously enough, at times herself. Julia had been an expert liar, so expert that he'd never even suspected her of infidelity. But he must not let that fact lessen his belief in this woman's story. It was simple, concise, and well-related. She'd been in bed, but not asleep when she thought she heard a noise. "Possibly my husband's being away made me more alert than usual. I ran straight down and he stood there, in front of the cabinet. He was absolutely naked except for a stocking mask and gloves. When he saw me he dropped the bag, struck out at me and ran away. Through the kitchen." Hardy had no difficulty in believing in a naked burglar. A man quite recently arrested had confessed that he worked clad only in overalls; this character had merely gone one better. But any man would know that to drive a car naked would be to attract attention even if no crime had been committed: so when had the man dressed himself?

"You followed him?"

"Not instantly. I was rather dazed. The shock, and quite a heavy blow." She raised one strong but delicate-looking hand to her puffy cheek and swelling eye. Then she went smoothly on. "Through the daze I heard him trying to start the car and I thought how easily cars can be identified, so I went to the kitchen window and looked out. It was an oldish car – possibly a Ford Pilot: and either black or very dark grey. I think I have said that before."

"You did. Most helpful. And you said the car headed towards Hillchester." From the kitchen window, at the back of the house, she could not have seen what direction the car took when it emerged from the drive on to the main road.

She was in no way disconcerted. "That is true. You see, by that time I was pretty mad. Some horrible little man trying to steal and then hitting me! I thought if only I could get the car's number. From the window I could only see it in profile, so to speak. So I ran after it. I failed to take the number but I did see which way it turned.''

Hardy's vague feeling – too vague to be a suspicion, and certainly not a hunch, since he disbelieved in them – was that this could be another case of an eminently respectable woman having suffered rape and being unwilling to admit it. Yet wanting the offender caught, probably punished, for the lesser crime.

With another feeling – that he was parodying Sherlock Holmes one of whose cases hinged upon what a dog did *not* do, he said, ''Do you still own your wolfhound, Mrs Noble?''

She took that in her stride. ''Boru? Oh yes. But yesterday afternoon I took him a long walk and there is some barbed wire on one side of the Low Meadows. I think he saw a rabbit and mistook it for a cat. He ripped his muzzle a bit and seemed unhappy, so I gave him a Soneryl and he went flat out.''

''You applied Dettol?'' Her hand went up to the front of the high-necked sweater.

''Good gracious, no! It would have deterred him from licking it. The Dettol – I probably reek of it – I dabbed on my face. Merely a precaution.''

''Just now you spoke of the intruder as a horrible *little* man. Is he actually small?''

''No. I used it as a term of contempt. In fact he is rather taller than average, and of muscular build. I cannot describe his face or hair. As I said, he wore a stocking mask. From the swiftness with which he dropped the bag, hit me and made off, I'd say he was young. Oh, and suffers from what is politely called B.O.; in fact he stank like a ferret.''

Believe that carefully composed, anonymous letter, and believe this, and the descriptions tallied. Hardy shifted ground.

''Now who would know, Mrs Noble, that your husband would be away from home tonight?'' A look of indulgence, half-mockery, half-tolerance, crossed her face.

''Everybody with whom my husband has been in contact

for the last fortnight. He is the most devoted Old Lansfordian and the annual Old Boys' Dinner is one of the year's highlights for him.''

"So a number of people would know that you would be here alone?''

"No. Usually I go with him – and should have done this weekend, but the dear old man who does a bit of gardening for us, and looks after my animals when I am away, was smitten down with lumbago yesterday morning.''

"And his name?''

"Archer Fletcher . . . But surely I said that the man seemed *young*. Archie's age is a bit uncertain, but from what he remembers, we think he must be nearly eighty.''

"He has cronies?''

"Not now. He has outlived them all. And, I suspect, was always a bit of a loner.''

Another cul-de-sac. Yet the similarity between the two descriptions was remarkable and it was unthinkable that a man who had just committed rape somewhere in Salford would, in less than half an hour, be caught burgling here.

He had not yet tested her on time; it was an element which often exposed a weakness in an otherwise good story.

"It would be helpful, Mrs Noble if you could pin-point the time of the break-in exactly.''

"Then I am afraid I must be unhelpful.'' There was an edge of impatience in her voice. "The circumstances were hardly conducive . . . All I can say with any surety is that when I last looked at my bedside clock it was twenty minutes to eleven. After I had phoned the police I did glance at my watch and it was then twenty-five minutes to twelve.'' Neatly side-stepped!

She had smoked throughout the interview, and her very way of smoking was another reminder. It was not chain-smoking exactly, she never lit one cigarette from the stub of another; nor did she ever leave the cigarette in her mouth. So far as the act of smoking could be said to be graceful, she, like Juliet, had the knack.

On the low table beside the chair in which she sat there were two cigarette boxes; one silver, one onyx. She had been using the silver one, now opened it, found it empty, and without changing her position in the chair, reached backwards for the onyx box. Before her fingers could close on it, she winced, quickly withdrew her arm and clapped her hand to her shoulder, or some spot just below it. Hardy, without speaking, rose and moved the box to within easy reach, sat down again and asked, "Apart from the blow to your face, did this man hurt you at all?"

"Oh no! The fact is I have twice broken that collar bone. And I always forget that certain positions . . ."

If only he had the authority to say; Take off that sweater! Nothing in this world was ever certain, but he was reasonably sure that she had been clawed. Not badly but enough to hurt now that the incisions were stiffening. But the power to order a woman to strip simply because her house had been broken into – for that was how it would look – postulated a Police State. And who wanted that?

The road-block had been quite abortive, quickly as it had been set up and thorough as it had been. Not only old, dark-coloured cars had been stopped, but, as post-rape procedure demanded, any car containing a single man. Nothing even mildly suspicious. Of the four old, dark cars stopped, two were driven by women, one occupied by a family party, three generations: it was badly overcrowded – but that was not yet a technical offence. The fourth old dark car was driven by Colonel Soames who lived at the White Horse in Hillchester, but played golf and cards at the Salford Golf Club; and he was in a foul temper because he had lost one pound fifty and because, knowing he had to drive home he a true alcoholic, had got through the long evening with only one small whisky.

The old, dark car, driven by a lone man did not come that way. Because the story which Greg Anderson told his wife in the morning was roughly true.

Aftermath of Case Three

(i)

Greg Anderson had attended a Chartered Accountants' Dinner in Thorington and had been careful to see that he was observed by as many people as possible. Inside himself he was certain of immunity whatever he did – he could, he felt, get away with murder, but one must play according to the rules and one rule said; Take all reasonable precautions.

He had slipped away during the first of the dull after-dinner speeches and had had ample time to deal with Lilah Noble as the high-nosed, interfering, patronising bitch deserved.

Afterwards it was only the matter of moments to get back into his clothes. The old car did not start easily. He'd get a new one in the New Year. Business was prospering to an extent he had hardly expected, even in his most optimistic moods. A few quite important people had defected with him but his main clientele consisted of little men, too bashful to face all the mahogany and glass, the glacial receptionist at Turner and Noble. A lot of them had been struggling along, or letting their wives struggle along, with Income Tax and VAT. Most of them were in a terrible muddle and glad to consult him in his anything-but-intimidating office. Others were most touchingly grateful if he'd go to see them – farms mostly, the occasional village store; people who were literally too busy to fill in forms, or to waste a daylight hour in visiting him. Their gratitude took the form of giving him presents, as well as his fees.

70

He thought quite happily about his business, and then less happily, about his domestic situation, and wished with all his heart that he could get Mary to agree to separate bedrooms. He'd made the suggestion several times, saying that now he was so often late he felt guilty about disturbing her. She'd always looked hurt and said either that he did not disturb her, or that she liked being disturbed.

They no longer lived as husband and wife. The failure was in him and had they ever spoken about it, he would have admitted it. Ever since Belle Mère's visit in the summer, he had been impotent with Mary. She seemed to accept that, and yet she looked hurt when he mentioned making a move into the tiny spare room.

Take tonight for example. He was pretty sure that there'd be a bruise in the angle between neck and shoulder – that bitch Lilah had hit him hard. And her bloody dog had left his mark, too, drawn blood just above the elbow – he'd staunched it with the nylon mask as he ran towards the car. Mary would most certainly see the injuries either tonight or tomorrow. He must think of some plausible story.

As he thought that, he saw the big Mercedes ahead of him, parked almost, but not quite on the wide grass verge. Its headlights were on and within their radiance stood a woman, frantically waving one arm. The chivalry of the road was a thing of the past and cars sped by. Greg stopped, not from kindness but because he saw a way of serving his own purpose. He could imagine himself saying to Mary; I was a fool. I thought I could give it a shove.

"What's the trouble?"

"No petrol. *Entirely* my own fault! And now I'm in the most terrible muddle. I'm expecting a call from New York. *Most* important." A diamond-encircled watch flashed as she pushed back her mink sleeve. "It's less than a mile, but I couldn't walk it in the time. Even if I kicked off my shoes." Plump yet shapely legs sloped steeply down to frail sandals with immensely high heels. They resembled pigs' trotters.

"I'll drive you."

"I should be everlastingly grateful. It really isn't far. Mason Croft. The next turn off on that side."

Abandoning the Mercedes as lightly as most people would discard an empty cigarette packet, she climbed into the old Ford.

He'd left his engine running so no bother with starting: and since traffic was thinning out now, no delay in getting across the road and into the drive of Mason Croft. The name rang a faint bell.

"Mrs Hudson-Smith?"

"Yes. How remiss of me! I had this call on my mind."

He could feel her tenseness, her desire to go faster.

"I'm Greg Anderson. I'm going as fast as I can. My car has seen its best days, I'm afraid."

"We may just make it. Look, as soon as we get there I shall dash straight in. Please come, too. We could have a drink and I could thank you properly."

"When you've taken your call, perhaps I could telephone my wife and explain my delay."

"Oh, of course you must do that. Ah, here we are!"

Mason Croft, a white elephant of a house, long disused and falling into decay, but saved from it by a sale which Sims, the house agent, still regarded as a piece of good luck, was ablaze with lights. Mrs Hudson-Smith scrambled out of the car and went in by the front door. Greg could then hear the telephone. And following her in, as he had been told to do, he overheard something quite inconsistent with the image of a silly little woman, wearing silly little shoes, and running out of petrol. Holding the receiver in her right hand, Mrs Hudson-Smith gestured with her left.

To somebody in New York she said crisply, "What? No! Absolutely ridiculous! I am *not* – repeat *not* – a charity organisation! What? Speak up! This is a bad line."

Greg opened the door which the woman had indicated. Almost before he realised that it was a very beautiful room, and yet designed for living in, the old Labrador bitch heaved herself from the hearthrug before the banked-up fire and took

72

hold of his elbow. Teeth blunt with age and the intention to arrest rather than harm.

Mrs Hudson-Smith came padding in. While talking in the most masterful manner to New York, she had kicked off her sandals. She said, "Oh dear! God help me! I had totally forgotten Sarah! Sarah, leave go. It's a friend!"

As suddenly as the dog had attacked, it withdrew and relapsed into torpor on the hearthrug.

"I really *cannot* apologise sufficiently. Let me look. If the skin is broken you should have an anti-tetanus injection."

He assured her that that would not be necessary. The poor old dog had only mouthed his sleeve.

"Oh, good! Now you do your telephoning," she pointed to an instrument on a side table. "I'll let Sarah out. Then we can have a little drink."

Mary sounded agitated. "Oh Greg, is anything wrong?"

"No. Just doing my Sir Galahad act and it's taken me a bit out of my way. I shall be rather late."

"Where are you?"

"At a place called Mason Croft."

"Hudson – Smith? Lilah has mentioned them. Is it *very* plush?"

"What I've seen so far, very."

"Look at everything and tell me in the morning."

He looked at everything until Mrs Hudson-Smith returned without the fur coat and wearing velvet slippers. She went to a drinks trolley and said, "Brandy? Or would you prefer something else?"

"Brandy please. A small one. I still have to drive home."

"Where do you live?"

"Malwood."

"I can tell you how to get there by a way where no breathalyzer will accost you." She poured brandy generously. She handed him a glass and taking her own, curled up on a sofa near the fire; a kittenish pose.

She said, "I'm already so deeply obliged to you, I hate asking another favour."

He gave her his most charming smile and said, "Try me."

"Vic will be in any minute. He'll have passed the Mercedes and he will be furious with me. But his temper never lasts long and he wouldn't scold me in front of you."

"I've already told my wife that I would be late."

He had not consumed half his brandy when Mr Hudson-Smith came bustling in. He was a man built for anger, short, thick-set and red-faced. He acknowledged Greg with the briefest nod and turned to his wife. "Of all the witless things to do! And a fine night you chose! This whole area is crawling with police. They'll charge for towing away and probably fine you for obstruction. Damn it all, why didn't you run onto the verge?"

"It stopped so suddenly," she said meekly, and with a placating smile.

"How the hell did you expect it to stop?" And think how it would have been on a lonely road. Retford Heath . . . I'll buy you a Mini for Christmas!" With that his anger evaporated. He turned his attention to Greg and thanked him for looking after his half-wit of a wife. "Let me sweeten your drink."

"Thank-you no, I'm driving."

"And darling, I was just going to tell him about the back road. You do it, you're so much better at that sort of thing."

"It was the old farm road," Mr Hudson-Smith said. "I had it cleared up a bit. You're on our property for the best part of a mile, then there's a little lane – Pigeon Lane they call it and that takes you into Malwood. By that time a couple of drinks should be absorbed. And this man-hunt called off."

"Darling, why do you say man-hunt when they were looking for *me*?"

"May God give me patience," Mr Hudson-Smith said, but genially.

As he drove home by the deserted road, the Thing which had taken possession of Greg Anderson's mind, suddenly and yet so subtly that it seemed always to have been there, enjoyed a gloating session. He had now got even with three women against whom he bore grudges.

Old Miss Lowe had refused to accept Anna as a day, kindergarten pupil, saying that the kindergarten was phasing out; but she'd taken another little girl!

Becky Dalton had also rebuffed him, underlining their relative positions, by refusing to stay after hours and do a very small typing job for him. "No, Mr Anderson, I'm sorry, but I have a date." But Greg would bet his bottom dollar that had Mr Noble asked her to do two hours overtime, she'd have done it.

Lilah Noble had offended more often and for a longer period of time – giving Mary, and later on the children, things that he couldn't possibly afford; books for Mary, toys and treats for the children, always lessening him in his own eyes.

All these grudges Greg Anderson, poor simple soul, had forgotten or repressed and learned to live with. Then they had been resurrected and fully avenged.

What next?

The Thing laughed to itself. Chance could be relied upon to provide other victims. More exciting, really, because even to him, they would come as a surprise.

(ii)

Lilah rang Mary quite early on the Saturday morning. "Honey," she said, "I'm afraid I must call today's visit off. Believe it or not, I was burgled last night." She briefly described the incident and said, "So now there are police everywhere. I took a hell of a blow. My eye is bunged up and my face black and blue. No sight for the young."

Mary said sympathetic words, made sympathetic noises.

"The thing is," Lilah said, "I had a book for you, and such masses of stuff for the Young. Such a waste. Do you think Greg could run out and collect?"

"I'll just ask what his plans are. Hold on . . ." The consultation was brief and satisfactory.

"Lilah dear, he says of course he will. Fairly early, if that suits you. He has this session in the Long Bar at the White Horse. Lilah, is there anything you need? Anything we could do?" She was obliged to use the plural because she could not drive. She'd made several attempts and had mastered the mere mechanics pretty well, she could start and stop, she could steer a car; it was the other traffic that confused her and reduced her to gibbering idiocy.

"Nothing," Lilah said, "but bless you for asking. Mary there's a man here, puffing some sort of dust that shows up finger prints – they're all mine! And he fiddled about with a kind of miniature Hoover and little plastic bags. And he's getting nowhere, poor man. The hairs he collects are all Boru's. You see – don't be shocked – my burglar, except for a stocking mask and gloves, was completely starkers."

"How awful!"

"I must admit that I was a bit taken aback," Lilah said. "So Greg'll come. Tell him not to gloat."

"Why should he do that?"

"Don't you remember? The year we had the Staff Party here, Greg noticed the silver and said it ought to be put in the bank, or on show at some museum."

"I remember. Chris was *not* amused."

"He'll be less so when he hears about this. Mary, do you think I should tell him? Or wait until tomorrow? I don't want to spoil his lovely day."

"Leave it," Mary said. "It's not as though he could *do* anything."

To those who did not connect the two phone calls it seemed that Hardy was being unduly concerned about a simple break in. Nothing was missing, and Mrs Noble's black eye hardly ranked as grievous bodily harm. So why all the fuss?

There was some confusion over the method of entry. Mrs Noble said that she was absolutely certain that before going to bed she had checked that both the front and rear doors were locked; and in this old house there was no Yale lock which could be manipulated by any ingenious schoolboy. Both doors had solid, old-fashioned mortice-locks. Hardy and WPC Drabble had heard the lock in the front door turn before they were admitted; and WPC Drabble, asked to inspect the other, even before Hardy asked a question, was sure that the rear door was secure at that time. But there were other possible entries; windows, and two sets of French windows, opening on to a kind of terrace, and so warped that even when locked, a good shove could make them yield.

Detective Constable Madison, in a sulky mood, was investigating possibilities when Greg Anderson arrived, in exactly the kind of car as that being looked for last night! Old model, Ford Pilot, and black. Madison had attended a number of lectures and courses – he was ambitious – and great stress had been laid on *initiative*. Abandoning his inspection of a half-open larder window, Madison displayed initiative, wiliness and tact.

"Is this your car, sir? Then it would be a great help if you'd answer a question or two. I need hardly tell *you*, sir, that you're not obliged to answer." But he managed the inflection that said: It'll look very fishy if you don't!

"Ask away."

"Were you out in this car last night?"

"Yes."

"In which direction, sir?"

"This direction. On my way home from Thorington."

"And were you stopped by any of us?"

"No. Should I have been?"

"We were on the look-out for a car much like yours. And it is a fact that people notice cars similar to their own. Did you?"

"Did I what?"

"See a car, similar to this?"

"No. What is the object of this catechism?"

"A dark car, of respectable age, was involved in a crime, sir."

"Not this one. And the only car I took any notice of was a big Mercedes, run out of petrol and awkwardly parked. I stopped to see if I could be of any assistance, and I drove the lady who was stranded to her home."

"At about what time?"

Careful now! Careful!

"I couldn't honestly say very accurately. Soon after eleven."

If an imagination capable of making leaps in the dark guaranteed success, Detective Constable Madison would achieve his ambitions.

"Did you at any time last evening, leave your car unattended?"

"Of course. I attended a dinner at Thorington. My car stood, with a number of others in the yard at The Unicorn. But it was locked and the keys were in my pocket. Then, later on . . ." Greg hesitated; was this altogether wise? But Mrs Hudson-Smith was his self-supplied alibi. "Yes, I left it unattended and unlocked, but in a private driveway. The lady to whom I gave a lift is Mrs Hudson-Smith and she lives at Mason Croft. She asked me in for a drink."

"How long was the car left unattended?"

"Oh Lord! Who knows? Once I'd telephoned my wife to say I'd be a bit late, I took no note of the time. I had a drink. Mrs Hudson-Smith received a call from New York. Her husband came in and we talked for a bit . . ."

"And you noticed nothing unusual about the car when you did go out to it?"

"Only the usual reluctance to start."

Madison knew from experience that people who, talking to the police, admitted to having had one drink usually meant that they had two or three; talking for a bit could mean anything. There formed and hardened in Madison's mind the idea that this car had been borrowed and used and returned. He could hardly wait to lay his suppositions before Hardy.

Greg did not see Lilah that morning. Mrs Foreman, the daily woman explained. Yesterday that dog – she hated Boru and always referred to him in that way, had gone and run into

78

some barbed wire and cut his snout. "Mrs Noble didn't think it was more than a scratch at first. 'S'morning she thought different so she took him to the vet. But she showed me what the dear little children should have had and I've got it all ready. I must say there ain't many ladies being robbed – or nearly – and with such a black eye, would have thought of that dog and the dear little children.''

"Mrs Noble," Greg said, "is a very exceptional woman."

He drove home, delivered the provender, went into Hillchester, did a little office work and then, in good time, strolled across to the White Horse and into the Long Bar which was as much an institution as a drinking place. It was open to anybody with the price of a drink in his pocket, yet it practised its own form of apartheid. The shining mahogany counter, the crimson carpeted floor bore no dividing marks, yet everybody knew that the far end was the fiercely protected province of those who practised some profession or were self-employed.

There was a glimmer of sense in the arrangement. Nobody would have felt at ease, grumbling about how wages were going up in the presence of a wage-earner.

Wage-earners had a place at the end nearer the door and could, if they wished, enjoy a snack there: sandwiches, sausage rolls and wedges of pork pie, were always on offer. At the far end there were little bowls of salted nuts, potato crisps and – more and more rarely – olives. In the space between these two groups, at the foot of the stairs which led to the restaurant, lay a neutral zone reserved for women, alone or accompanied, and for strangers.

Now and again a stranger would try to join the group at the upper end; then some mysterious social litmus paper went into action. If he passed the test, he would be granted temporary membership; if not, everybody went deaf even to remarks about the weather.

Greg, when he was an employed person, drank with the younger and less exclusive group near the door, and shared its irreverent attitude towards the old fogies, yet he was flattered and gratified when invited to join them. It was Sims the auctioneer who promoted him, walking past, putting a light touch on his arm and saying, "Come and have a drink with me, Anderson."

The king-pin of the select group was undoubtedly Colonel Soames who lived at the White Horse and who when cold sober observed all the chill conventions of an earlier day: but a couple of drinks loosened his inhibitions and the talk in this rarefied atmosphere could become every bit as ribald as that at the lower end of the bar. Quite naturally the rape at the Old Vic had been thoroughly and salaciously discussed. Mr Rand who owned the Old Vic was no more informed than the others, but he was concerned. It was not the rent which bothered him; his tenants always paid in advance and he also demanded a deposit, in theory returnable if a tenant left a flat in good decorative repair. No out-going tenant had ever seen a penny back.

The point was, as Mr Rand pointed out, things like this gave a place a bad name; in fact, in future he would let only to men or married couples.

When Greg joined the group on this Saturday morning, Crawford the vet was holding forth about the fatuity of road-blocks.

"There I was, minding my own business, actually coming in from Ragmere – one of Dick Welland's prize cows had a difficult calving – and I was stopped and put through the mill. Naturally they didn't condescend to say *why*."

"I think I can tell you," Greg said, sliding into place and hoping that what he had to tell was news. "Chris Noble's place was broken into last night and the intruder hit Mrs Noble. I happen to know because my family was to spend the day at the Grange and Li – Mrs Noble rang my wife and told her."

"Was much taken?" somebody asked, speaking for all. Without exception, they hoped for a positive answer, for Chris Noble was most unpopular. A roaring snob. He would have been only too welcome as a member of this undefined club, yet he'd never shown the slightest inclination to join. Every weekday morning he passed, going upstairs to eat his lunch. As he went, he'd acknowledge anybody who caught his eye, but so curtly! Morning, Crawford, or Sims, or Argent. Well, everybody could not be an Old Lansfordian!

"Nothing was taken. The burglar was disturbed."

"By the dog?" Mr Crawford asked, hopefully. He'd often suggested to lonely people that a good sharp dog was better than any burglar alarm." He was ignorant of what had happened to Boru, for now that he had two assistants, each happy with every other weekend free, he did not go to the surgery on Saturday.

Greg thought: Better not to know too much; and said, "That I wouldn't know," and Crawford, resuming his tale, said, "I was stopped. Asked to identify myself. And asked my height and my age. And what that had to do with a bit of house-breaking, I entirely fail to see. I'm sixty-four and bald as an egg. Family characteristic; my father was bald at forty. As for height, well, in my prime I was about five-foot-six. Shorter now. Soft tissue, noticeably the so-called discs in the spine contract as the years pile up. So I didn't fit whatever they were looking for. But they took what I can only call a *morbid* curiosity in my overalls which I had stowed in the boot. They were quite heavily blood-stained. Any sort of birth is a bloody business."

At this point two young women, one in nurse's uniform, one in the ubiquitous sweater and jeans, entered the bar and perched on stools in the middle, central zone. One of them said, rather uncertainly, "Oh, shandy perhaps." The other said, "Oh, let's have a *real* drink for once!"

"Grace, you're driving!"

"I know that. But alcohol hasn't the slightest effect on me. *Not* an enviable condition! Two double dry Martinis," the brash girl in uniform said to Maudie, the barmaid, who always gave the impression of sauntering about, and yet seemed able to satisfy the most demanding customer in any section of the Long Bar.

"And we could do with a few olives . . ."

Colonel Soames glared his disapproval and muttered something about times changing – and for the worse, and Mr Kenyon, the retired bank manager, began to air his favourite grievance. "Just the type I complain about!" He shot an acidulous look at Mr Sims. "When I bought my house, two years ago, I understood that the Nurses' Hostel as well as the old hospital was closing down . . ."

"So it was." Mr Sims had put this defence forward many times before. "It was just that the planning fools had underestimated the accommodation needed by the staff. They made about every possible mistake – and won a prize, God help us!"

"God help *me*! A mob of girls, all with boyfriends, most of them with motor-bikes. Parties going on to all hours. Drunken orgies! I know, not only by the senseless noise, but by the number of empty bottles."

"Well," said Mr Argent who owned the Wine and Spirit Stores and had supplied most of the bottles. "You're only young once. And the youngest naturally get all the nastiest jobs. Mustn't grudge them a little relaxation."

"I know all about being young once. Gather thee rosebuds and so on. If they'd only be quiet about it. I have complained repeatedly. Not only about the noise. About the morals! The place is little more than an amateur brothel."

"Now that is libellous, Kenyon," Crawford said, and was promptly corrected by Sims.

"To be libellous a thing must be written. Spoken it is slander." And having made his point, he said, "my round, I think. Maudie!"

They drank in amity; but a seed had been sown.

Case Four: Grace Robbins

Grace Robbins parked her Mini in its usual place, to the left of the wide asphalted space in front of the Nurses' Hostel, and more passengers than anyone would have judged it capable of carrying, extricated themselves. They were all young and supple.

Grace said, to nobody in particular, "I've got one of my migraines coming on. I shall go straight to bed."

Madge Barker – Grace's best friend at the moment, and only a student nurse, had already learned that when people said *my* as a preface to any ailment or indisposition, they had not only accepted it but were hanging on to it, being possessive about it, so she did not argue. She said, "You do that, Grace. And by the time you're undressed, I'll bring you a cup of tea."

"That would be very kind."

Madge thought – almost *knew*, that Grace was dodging the party because she had been chucked once again. It really was extraordinary, the way Grace was chucked. For Grace had everything; she was pretty, she had more money than any other girl – and was generous with it. She had her Mini and was generous with that, too, so she acquired friends, both male and female, very easily and as easily lost them. Madge herself was wondering just how much more of Grace she could possibly stand. It was the gloom. And the discontent. Nothing done with Grace was ever fun. She'd treat you to a slap-up

83

dinner at the White Horse and decry everything that was served, so that you felt a fool for liking it all so much. It was far more fun to go with any other girl and eat egg and chips in Peg's Pantry.

With patients Grace was popular; they mistook her melancholy expression for sympathy and found her manner soothing. Most nurses spoke and walked in a hurried manner, Grace seemed to drift, yet she never got behind with anything.

Madge went into the kitchen to prepare the promised cup of tea. Signs that a party was pending were everywhere: plates of sandwiches and sausage rolls, jam tarts and slices of marzipan. Really Sister Fawcett was a good sort, lenient and eager to see that the girls enjoyed themselves. And eager also to enjoy herself? She did not know, Madge thought as she waited for the kettle to boil, that this was *her* birthday party. She'd said that, after the fiftieth, one should stop having birthdays – or, better still, stop adding and start subtracting. But somebody had discovered that this was her birthday and all preparations had gone ahead under the pretence that it was Rose Archer's. The cake was still a secret, hidden under Rose's bed. At the right moment it would be produced and everybody would chant; Happy Birthday to you. There was to be a bouquet, too, further proof of their appreciation of the fact that, appointed as Warden, Sister Fawcett could have been distant and strict, and was the very reverse. In fact, when that beast, Mr Kenyon had complained and threatened to carry his complaint further, Sister Fawcett had nipped in first and told everybody in authority that an old man, suffering from hallucinations, made a very bad neighbour.

Madge carried up the tray of tea. Grace, despite her migraine had not toppled straight into bed. Wearing a nightdress, extremely pretty and obviously expensive, she was putting her day clothes away. Her room was almost painfully tidy. Most of the girls lived in shocking muddles, maybe through a subconscious rebellion against the orderliness in the wards.

Grace looked at the tray and said, "Oh, no cup for *you*! I was hoping you'd stay a bit."

As usual, complaint where praise was deserved! Madge said apologetically, "Well, I rather want to snatch a bath. Shall I close the window and draw the curtains?"

"No, thank-you. I need air. And I like to see the moon behind the cedar tree."

Feeling snubbed and yet not knowing why she should, Madge said, "What about pills?"

"Worse than useless. The last lot that Doctor Lawson tried out on me made me hideously sick. Well, run away, have a bath and enjoy yourself. Good night." She had somehow contrived to dim Madge's happy anticipation of the party, but then, Madge reflected, that was Grace's way; gloom was contagious. Her own slight attack of it did not survive a hot, powerfully-scented bath and dressing for the party. It was nine o'clock before she thought of Grace again. By that time the cake had been presented and cut, the flowers displayed and Sister Fawcett had shed a few happy tears.

Madge collected a slice of cake, two sandwiches and a glass of the sparkling wine which Mr Argent always recommended to those who could not afford champagne, and carried another tray up to Grace's room. The sound of music and happy voices faded out as she mounted the stairs and went along the corridors. Grace's room was as far from the old lecture room in which the party was being held as a room in the same house could be. The house, a rambling old building, had been donated as a Nurses' Home by the last of the Copplestone family in 1904.

Grace's room was in darkness; Madge thought, hoped that she was asleep. Sleep cured all ills! And having done what she conceived to be her duty Madge was prepared to steal away, but was arrested by a querulous, "Who is it?" and the flashing on of the bedside lamp.

"Only me, Grace. I've brought you a little snack, dear."

"I couldn't eat anything. Thanks all the same."

"Could you manage a drink?" It was only fair to ask that,

for the party was the result of communal effort and whereas most of them had contributed one pound fifty, Grace had forked out ten pounds.

"I might. Presently. Just leave it there."

Some incipient professionalism awoke in Madge. Speech slightly slurred and now that she was near enough to see, the pupils of the eyes dilated.

"Grace, have you taken any dope?"

"Only a couple of those useless pills."

"Then do you think you should . . . drink? As well?"

"Save that kind of talk for your patients, God help them."

"Grace, I was only trying . . ."

"And trying you are! Get back to your party!"

Snubbed again, Madge hurried away. Her best party dress was no protection from the chill night air which poured in from the open window and she had the distinct feeling that Grace had not appreciated her kindness.

The pills, useless against migraine, were inducive to sleep; and half a tumbler full of sparkling wine – ugh! horrible stuff! – completed the job. Grace dozed off, leaving her light on and when, presently, through the haze, she saw a grinning skeleton, she took it for part of a familiar nightmare. Anything to do with blood or bones absolutely revolted her. Nursing was about the last profession she should have embarked upon, but the challenge had been issued and she'd taken it up and she'd qualify if it killed her. Sometimes she hoped that it would.

Then she was wide awake and realised that the skeleton was not a dream figure. She said, blightingly, "I didn't know it was fancy dress! Go away!"

The next minute she was fighting for her life. A hard heavy hand clamped down over her nose and mouth. "Make a sound," the skeleton said, "and you're dead." She could feel her eyes popping; inside her head lights flashed and there was a crackling noise like sticks breaking. She relaxed, flaccid, willing anything but death. Then she was raped. No hurt with that; she'd lost her virginity two years earlier. And then everything hurt, long searing pains ran the length of her body. The urge to scream was almost irresistible, but she dreaded the renewal of the stranglehold.

Her assailant laughed, nastily, jeeringly, went towards the window and so far as she could see, seemed to jump out.

She stood up; the pretty nightdress in shreds, the gashes bleeding, horrible, disgusting, obscene.

She had always been, always, so careful about appearances. Even after what passed in her generation as lovemaking, she had always smoothed her hair, used her lipstick, but now, heedless of everything except the need that the man should be caught, she ran, clutching her bloodied rags about her, along the long corridors, down the stairs, across the hall and into the room where the party was in full swing. Nobody who shared it could ever forget the moment.

"Raped," Grace said, "and clawed. Garden. He went into the garden."

After that all was confusion. Sixteen young men went charging out. Sister Fawcett, now supporting Grace who had gone into a spasm of shaking, shouted, "And the old hospital!" To Grace she said, "There, there, everything is all right. You just come with me . . ." For her age Sister Fawcett was strong and she had all a nurse's skill in handling people, but the poor girl sagged, a limp, dead weight. "Angela, take her other arm. Veronica dial 999 and ask for the police. Susie, make a pot of really strong tea." She had singled out three of the most self-controlled of the girls, several of whom had screamed at the sight of Grace. One had fainted. At the back of her mind Sister Fawcett planned some admonitory words. How, she would ask, would they behave if posted to Casualty and asked to deal with victims of a bad car crash?

When Grace was deposited on the sofa in the little room off the hall, and Angela despatched for hot water, Dettol and Bandaids from the First Aid cupboard, Sister Fawcett pulled off the shreds of nightdress and assessed the damage. Long symmetrical furrows ran the length of the girl's body. Only in two places deep enough to need stitching.

The girl, after the limpness and the shaking, had rallied surprisingly well, and when Susie came in with the tea, was able to sit up, propped on a cushion and drink a cup of the scalding, heavily sugared beverage. Sister Fawcett had naturally been one of the first to hear full details of a former case – that poor girl who was still in the mental hospital at Pykenham. And for one dreadful moment Sister Fawcett feared for Grace's sanity. For when she said, taking the cup, "Good girl! Now I know this is asking rather a lot of you, Grace, but when the police come they'll want a description of the man. Can you give it?" Grace said, "A skeleton. With sharp claws."

"A skeleton, dear?"

"I mean got up to look like one. For a moment I thought the party had turned into a fancy dress affair ..." She even managed a smile as she said that. "So I can't really describe him. Except he was tall. He laughed. I'd recognise that laugh anywhere. Oh and he smelt – like the monkey house at the zoo." She thought for a moment and said, "Agile. He went through the window. I think he must have jumped from that silly little balcony into the cedar tree."

"Well, the boys are searching the garden. And the old hospital. This time he is sure to be caught. But now, with the police on the way, we must make you decent. Have you a warm dressing-gown?" So few of them had. They always bought flimsy, pretty things made of nylon.

Grace said, "Yes. A camel-hair. In my cupboard."

Sister Fawcett said, "Angela, dear, would you fetch it?"

"No. At least not alone. I mean, he might be anywhere."

"Grace just said he went out of the window."

"And he could have come in by another." Sister Fawcett foresaw an unhappy time, with the general mood that of panic.

She said, "That is highly unlikely. But perhaps you're brave enough to go into the hall and fetch a coat, or a mackintosh."

Grace said, "My fur coat, Angela, please."

She kept it there because someone had told her that constant movement was the best guard against moth. And also because the clothes cupboard in her bedroom was always crammed. She gave things away, to other girls, to jumble sales, but then she went and bought new ones, so that the congestion never eased.

Angela fetched the coat; it was not mink, but the next best thing, dyed ermine, very light and soft. Like her Mini and her very generous allowance, it was what she called a guilt offering from her father.

Sister Fawcett, tucking in the glossy folds said, ''There you are, dear, quite decent. And when the police have come and gone, I think you may have to go to hospital.''

''I shouldn't mind that – if I could have a room in the private wing.''

''Sixty pounds a night,'' Sister Fawcett reminded her.

''Daddy could manage that,'' Grace said.

Once again Sergeant Saunders was the first to arrive. Not by chance, but because Mr Kenyon had lodged another complaint and said; ''Will you send somebody – not totally deaf – to listen to the noise.'' Tom knew Mr Kenyon, fussy old biddy, and guessed that he was exaggerating, but he also knew that since his retirement he'd taken to writing letters to the *Hillchester and District*, and, surprising to anyone who knew the writer, the letters were witty, and all the more telling for being so. Unless at least some token response were made, Mr Kenyon would sit down and compose a letter which in a sly way made fun of the police. And that was one thing which the Hillchester Force did not want at present. Enough had been said and written about their failure to bring Becky Dalton's assailant to justice. So Tom was on his way to spread what oil he could when he was given not a different destination but a different purpose. He trod on the accelerator, and at the entrance to the Nurses' Hostel almost collided with two young men on motor-bikes. The same thought had occurred to both of them – the man might have run up Hospital Road and into

Petticoat Lane, or down to the junction with Albert Street. Since they had no clue to his appearance theirs was a fatuous errand, but they, like the others, had been shocked and to do anything was a relief.

They hooted madly as they rode and a tiny section of Tom's mind sided with Mr Kenyon. Hooting after eleven o'clock at night *was* an offence. Another, larger part of his mind hoped that this case would be the break-through. Of course nobody wanted another poor girl to be hurt, but Hardy had once said that it looked as though their only hope of catching the man would be another case, less bedevilled, and with a victim able and willing to offer some sort of clue. Tom had looked at Hardy rather sharply when he said *willing* and Hardy explained, just a little too quickly, that he was thinking about the anonymous letter.

Now, awaiting Hardy's arrival, Tom made himself useful. The young men red-faced and panting, came back saying that they had searched the garden and the old hospital just across the road most thoroughly. There were fourteen of them – and the two who had passed him in the entry. Some of them, but for Tom's presence, would have gone away. "No, no," he said. "The Chief Inspector will want to see you all."

None of the girls made any attempt to move. They stood huddled together looking very young, and frightened, pitiably vulnerable. Say what you like about sex equality, a thing like this showed what a farce it was.

One of the young men, handsome, well-spoken, asked, "Is there anything against us having a drink, Officer?"

"Nothing – except a law against drunken driving."

Some of them grinned. The handsome young man moved to the big buffet table and said, "Ladies first! Come along girls. Nothing like a little drink to tide you over."

And if Hardy wanted a rape victim able and willing to talk, he had it in Grace Robbins. She was astonishing – and few things astonished Sergeant Saunders. Although she had suffered in exactly the same way as Becky Dalton, who was a much more robust, open-air kind of girl, there she sat,

90

swathed in fur, calm as a statue and, in a curious way, in control of the situation.

Hardy arrived, so did the two motor-cyclists, still hooting. Hot on their heels came Mr Kenyon, too far enraged to reflect that the police would hardly send a Detective Chief Inspector, a uniformed Sergeant and a WPC – the new girl, WPC Girdlestone, a replacement for Collins who had inexplicably resigned – to investigate a complaint about noise. "Ha!" he said, "I'm glad you people have taken some notice at last! All quiet now of course. I came to protest . . ."

"Not now and not to me," Hardy said frigidly. He went into Sister Fawcett's little room and found what he needed, a rape victim ready and willing to talk. Grace had by this time asked for and been given a glass of wine and a cigarette. Hardy attributed her calm self-possession to the numbness following shock. He'd seen it before and expected her at any moment to break down and become violently hysterical. So he must find out as much as he could, while he could.

And it was nothing much and none of it new. A tall man, and agile, and with an animal smell.

When Grace repeated the phrase about the monkey house at the Zoo, inside Hardy a nerve winced. After the Becky Dalton rape certain specimens had been sent to the central Police laboratory and twenty-four hours later somebody there had made contact with Hardy and said "Was that a practical joke? Or did you confuse us with the Zoological Department?"

Hardy, with some indignation denied both charges and the voice said, "Well, in that case you've got something very odd on your hands."

"And what is that?"

"A man with a blood group so rare that it falls into no known category. I've certainly never encountered it before, nor has anyone I have consulted."

While Hardy talked to Grace, Tom Saunders had gone through the whole house and could say with certainty that the man had not gone out of one window and in at another.

Reporting to Hardy, he said, "Now this would have been a chance for Dick Pettit and his dog, but with all these boys charging about like buffaloes . . ."

"All the same, let him try," Hardy said. His own feeling was that dogs were over-rated, but he knew from O'Brien that PC Pettit was longing for a chance to show off what he and his Alsatian, called Searcher, could do. After all, Pettit had gone on a dog-handling course and hated to think that the time had been wasted.

Having finished with Grace who was about to be taken into hospital for treatment for possible shock, and stitches for the two deeper wounds and antibiotics as a precaution against any possible infection, Hardy turned his attention to the old lecture room and asked all the young ladies to withdraw. Still in a huddle they did so.

"Now, will those who have cars and locked them, give the keys to Sergeant Saunders? And then, if you don't mind, line up."

"But surely, Chief Inspector, you don't suspect one of us." That was the handsome young man with the superior voice.

"It's my sorry duty to suspect everybody," Hardy said.

They shuffled into line like raw recruits.

Above average height. And what exactly was average height? The norm into which the majority of these boys fitted. Three of them stood out, a good half head above the others and one of these was young Graham Harper who had also been – and it might be mere coincidence – at the Old Vic when Becky Dalton was raped. Another three were definitely undersized, but tough looking and perky – probably jockeys from Newmarket. And there was Maxie Fisher, small and so thin as to be emaciated. The rest of ordinary size, varying by half an inch or so. But the fact remained that the rapist had used disguises which might include towering head-dresses.

"Please think back," Hardy said "and tell me exactly what you were doing just before Miss Robbins came down?"

There was a little silence while they remembered. Then Graham Harper said, "I dashed out to my car to fetch the

92

flowers. I'd been commissioned to buy them because my hours are – well, flexible.''

The other tall young man, with the voice said, ''I went out at the same time. For a leak. There was a queue at the downstairs cloakroom.''

''You were within sight of each other? All the time?''

''Naturally, I turned my back for as long as it took. Then Graham asked me to lock his car door for him. He was lumbered with the flowers, you see.''

Patient, sometimes seemingly irrelevant questions elicited seemingly candid answers until Hardy was reasonably sure that nobody had been absent from the party during the crucial quarter of an hour. And they all, with the utmost willingness, agreed to do the lick which constituted the saliva test.

Saunders came back and reported that he had found nothing suspicious in any car or in the things like saddle-bags attached to the motor-bikes. Yet the man had been disguised, and Grace Robbins had given a surprisingly detailed description of the disguise: a skin-tight garment of some black material, painted with white for the bones, and the hideous skull face.

A man could not have run away in such a guise. And yet he had. Not for the first time Hardy had a little creepy feeling. Something uncanny! He suppressed it.

Pettit arrived with his dog. Pettit stolid and matter-of-fact, the dog over-bred, inbred, over-trained, all a-quiver.

''Where do we start, sir?''

''Where the man was last seen. The girl's bedroom.''

Pettit and the dog stood by the bed and Pettit spoke gibberish, but obviously he made the dog understand that of the two scents one was to be ignored, the other followed. Nose down, Searcher made for the window which had a low sill. Outside was what Grace had called a silly little balcony and there Dick Pettit had the worst moment of his life so far, for Searcher scrambled over the low balustrade and hung, suspended by his collar and leash, in space. At some peril to himself, for the balustrade was no more than knee-high, PC

Pettit leaned downwards and outwards and hauled the dog in.

"Up the tree," Pettit said. "Searcher could have jumped it if I hadn't got a good hold on him. And any man could've. Now we'll go start at the base of the tree."

But there too many scents crossed and Searcher, nosing his handler in an apologetic way, gave up. Pettit said, "Good boy!" and delved into his pocket, bringing out the kind of mint-flavoured sweet that Searcher preferred.

And this time Graham Harper was not dependent upon hearsay or upon what the Public Relations officer chose to release. He could write from first-hand experience. He could really let himself go. Keeping well on this side of libel, he wrote a stinging article. By consulting his pocket diary he counted exactly how many days had elapsed since the first aggravated rape and without actually saying so, implied that the Police had been ineffectual if not inefficient. He reminded his readers that as long ago as September he had foreseen a reign of terror. Now it was here.

He could write with all the more authority because he had had an interview with Grace. He had not really expected to achieve that but there was no harm in trying. He went armed with a bunch of golden chrysanthemums from a shop which stayed open on Sunday for the convenience of those visiting the cemetery which lay on the edge of the town, or the hospital which stood about two miles out.

He put on his most winning manner as he talked to the Staff Nurse at the desk. "Would you be so very kind, Sister as to see that Miss Robbins gets these? And tell her that Graham Harper called to enquire."

Softened by his manner, by his mistake in her rank and the hint of romance in the air, the Staff Nurse asked would he like to see Miss Robbins.

"I would indeed! Would you allow me to?"

"It might cheer her. Her father came this morning and she was rather low after he left. And she seemed not to want to see any of the girls. I'll just ask."

She came back beaming and positively ushered Graham

into a little room off the main ward. Grace was propped up in bed, wearing a bed jacket foaming with lace. She looked pale – but hardly more than was usual with her and everywhere in the small room were signs that her father had been. Dozens of dark red carnations, a huge bunch of black grapes, a large box of chocolates, neat half bottles of champagne. The faint but unmistakable smell of cigar smoke lingered on the air.

"How *very* kind of you to come, Graham. And what *lovely* flowers! Do sit down. Have a cigarette. Have some champagne. Let's have an orgy!"

What on earth had happened to the gloomy, fault-finding, almost lugubrious girl?

He could not know that *now* Grace was enjoying being the centre of attention, a position she had held until her father went silly and married the nurse who had looked after him when he was operated upon for gall-stones. Grace had been sixteen at the time and since her mother's death, when she was twelve, she had absolutely ruled the big new house in a Letchworth suburb. The usurper's name was Nancy and one day, during an acrimonious exchange of insults, Nancy had said, "And let me tell you. You'd never make a nurse." Straight away, Grace had decided to show her that anything Nancy could do she could do better. So she'd come to Hillchester and hated every minute of it. The squarest of pegs in the roundest of holes. But now she had every excuse for quitting. There was, however something. Dad had come hot-foot, laden with gifts but he had not said: Come home and I'll see that Nancy behaves herself. No, he had suggested a trip round the world as soon as Grace felt like it.

"Do you mind talking about last night?" Graham asked, his voice gentle and solicitous.

"Not in the least. Why should I? It could have happened to anyone."

"So true! I'm trying, in an article, to make that clear. Until this man is arrested all women are in danger. Of course I would not give your name. Just *latest victim*. I would like to say you were clawed. That fact was suppressed last time and I

95

think people should know. I mean it shows what a fiend we have in our midst.''

To his surprise, Grace looked amused.

''Graham,'' she said, ''sometimes you talk just as you write. Fiend in our midst! But it is true. I was clawed. Probably scarred for life.''

He said earnestly, ''Really Grace, I do think you're awfully brave.'' He meant it but even as he said it he was toying with phrases. Deeply shocked but anxious for others . . . From her hospital bed the latest victim told me . . . Facing facts bravely . . .

And how extremely odd it was that the only fellow he knew who'd run around with her for a week or two, had described her as a wet blanket.

The Terror

The Terror did not really clamp down on Hillchester until Monday, Sunday being a bad day for the dissemination of local news; no *Hillchester and District* published that day and Peg's Pantry closed. But there were a few leaks.

Mr Kenyon was a fairly regular attendant at St Luke's for morning service, but what with one thing and another he did not feel in a mood to worship. He wanted a drink and unlike Doctor Brunning, he recognised the danger of drinking alone. Once you start that and who knew where you'd stop? He walked down to the White Horse and found the select end of the Long Bar unoccupied except for Colonel Soames, nursing a large whisky and wearing a slipper on his left foot.

They'd never been friendly. The Colonel, in Mr Kenyon's hearing, had once spoken disparagingly of office-wallahs and when an opportunity offered, Mr Kenyon had slipped in a reference to Colonel Blimp. But on this dull morning they were pleased to see one another.

"Gout!" Colonel Soames said, grimacing at the slipper. "What'll you have? Maudie!"

"Cheers," Mr Kenyon said in a rather non-U way. "Well, what I have long foreseen happened last night. One of those flippertigibbet girls was raped." He gave a blow-by-blow account of the previous evening's events, seeming to see in the rape a punishment for annoying one's neighbour and saying harsh things of Hardy's curt dismissal of him.

At the end of the tirade Colonel Soames asked, "And was she *clawed*?"

Mr Kenyon blinked. "Yes, as a matter of fact, she was. How did *you* know?"

"I merely wondered. There was a previous case. Back in September."

"September? I was away then, on my Mediterranean cruise."

"So you were. Lucky dog! That poor girl was clawed but it was not made public. There were rumours, of course, but I had first-hand information from Doctor Brunning. He had an interesting theory . . ." Colonel Soames paused and looked fixedly at his empty glass.

"The other half, Colonel?"

"Thank-you, yes. A double." And there was no need for Mr Kenyon to shout "Maudie". She was there, listening.

Taking his fresh glass, Colonel Soames said, "Brunning, during his comparatively short time in India saw a woman who had been clawed by a leopard. He said the poor girl's injuries bore a distinct resemblance. I thought at the time . . . But I did nothing. Now, with another poor girl mauled, I blame myself." He drank deeply for comfort.

"I don't see what you could have done," Mr Kenyon said in his plodding, prosaic way.

"We shall see," the Colonel said and most ungratefully, since he was drinking Mr Kenyon's whisky, changed the subject.

But Maudie had heard enough and therefore Mr Griffin who owned the White Horse, was the first person to realise what The Terror could do to business.

"Sorry and all that," Maudie said, "but 'less you can promise me transport home, I shan't be coming back tonight. And I shall warn Evie." She told Mr Griffin the news.

Mr Griffin was just old enough to remember the time when chambermaids and even barmaids lived in. Now, in order to maintain any kind of service at all he was obliged to employ a positive chain-gang of women, all young, but married, and as independent as the Devil. The Evie mentioned by Maudie acted as waitress in the upstairs restaurant four evenings a week of which Sunday was one, and at lunch-time on market day. Various other women did similar stints. Mr Griffin had some difficulty in telling them apart. His wife, Yvonne, a barmaid before marriage – but not in Hillchester – kept a chart, in different coloured Biros and knew who should be on duty at any given time. She also had a list of people who could be fallen back upon in cases of emergency and they were all too frequent. The young women had babies, their husbands became ill, they became ill themselves, they went on day trips to Zeebrugge or on holidays to the Costa Brava; to keep the hotel going meant the constant application of cajolery and bribery.

"I'll send you both home in a taxi."

Unimpressed Maudie said, "Better book it now. There'll be a run on taxis if this news gets about."

She was right. The news was spreading slowly but surely, and neither Call-a-Cab nor Hillchester Taxis could offer transport this evening. It was, in any case, Sunday, and both firms were operating with skeleton staffs.

"Then I'll fetch you and see you safe home," Mr Griffin said. "Where do you live?"

Maudie looked as though she thought he should know. "I'm out at Castlegate, and Evie's out at Fallowfield."

Out was the apt word; the two housing estates, one old, one new, lay on the extreme edges of the town, south and north.

William Selsey heard the shocking truth when he was at the very end of his round, delivering one pint of the superior milk given by Jersey cows. He saw this customer very rarely, for Oakey as everyone called him was a night porter at the hospital and was usually asleep when William called. The single pint, paid for by himself, was one of Oakey's gestures of defiance against officialdom.

He had worked for many years at the old hospital which was small, and intimate, even cosy. The Matron there knew the sort of milk he liked and always provided it. Then came the move to the new place, six times the size and horrible. The new place did not even buy its milk from Farmhouse Dairies; the stuff came in a tanker. There was no Matron to consider anyone's individual tastes, let alone those of a night porter. True, there were now machines for dispensing drinks but to Oakey they all tasted the same and all horrible. So now he bought his own, with the gold cap that signified its superiority, and he took care to carry it ostentatiously, though he feared nobody noticed.

"Morning Oakey," William said as the old man came to the door of the isolated cottage where he lived his curious hermit's life. "You up early? Or staying up late?"

"Either or neither." A typical Oakey statement, discouraging further conversation. William was actually turning back to his van when Oakey actually volunteered a piece of information. "Another girl brought in last night; raped and clawed."

William's tongue said, "Oh, no!" while all his vitals, turning to icy water said; "Oh yes, no more than I expected!"

"Somebody I knew, too. And a real nice girl. One of the young nurses. Had a little Mini. Once or twice when our times were coincidental, she'd give me a lift, to or from. Hearing what happened to her of all people, upset me. And I don't mind admitting it."

"Enough to upset anybody," William agreed. "Still, Oakey, you need your rest."

"There's something I need more. There's that shop at the end of Southgate Street. Open on Sundays. Sells flowers. You give me a lift down. Get her a bunch. I'll walk back."

The van had no accommodation for passengers, the only seat was the driver's, but Oakey crouched down on a crate of empties and only once tried to make himself heard over the noise of the engine and the rattling, but what he said was slightly, *very* slightly comforting to the anxious father.

"Funny thing," he said. "Both times a lot of people about. Not lonely girls, if you get my meaning."

And Lorraine used the same argument. "Oh, Dad where's

the sense in trying to keep me from the only thing I enjoy? Both the girls this loon has gone for were indoors; near other people. Not at the Disco and not walking home alone.''

''I know that, honey, but until he's caught and put away, I feel, well, like this was a jungle and some fierce wild animal was loose in it.''

There was a whiff of the jungle in Hardy's morning post. Nothing anonymous about this letter. A white horse rampant against a background of black and the full, correct address; then.

Dear Sir; this thought occurred to me when Miss Becky Dalton was raped and mutilated. I put it aside then. But now I learn that another unfortunate young woman has suffered in a similar way. Far-fetched as it may seem to you I think the wounds could have been inflicted by a claw cut from a trophy or a rug. I think you should investigate this possibility. Wishing to be helpful, I append a list of skins I know about. There may well be others. Yours faithfully, James St Barbe Soames. (Colonel)

''And I was thinking along some similar line myself,'' Hardy said to O'Brien. ''Parsons persuaded me otherwise – he even found the knife, thoroughly scrubbed, still damp, in Miss Dalton's kitchen. But Miss Robbins's injuries were so identical . . . And there is the time element. Both these were hasty jobs in places where he was liable to be disturbed at any minute. No time for fancy work with a knife whereas a couple of quick slashes with a claw . . . Maybe we should give this,'' he touched the letter, ''a grain of attention.''

He was desperate enough to try anything, for once again there was no clue, or at least no clue that led anywhere. The Scene of the Crime officer had found smears of white paint on the rail around the small balcony and similar ones on the dark flat bough of the cedar tree. Had he stayed in the tree long enough to divest himself of his disguise? He could hardly have walked or driven away wearing it. Grace Robbins said she had run from her room to the lecture room and that was probably true; her injuries, ghastly as they looked, would not have prevented her from running. Doctor Stamper whose turn it was to act as police surgeon said that Grace was not a virgin.

Hardy had timed a girl covering the distance at a run, at a walk, and hurrying without actually running; the young men had run out immediately, and even if the girl had come at the slowest pace, it hardly left time for the man to take off his disguise, descend from the tree and get away. Hardy was of the opinion that the man had stayed in the tree until the boys abandoned the search. Then he'd slipped down and probably made his escape over the wall into an adjoining garden. But this was mere deduction, with not even the dog's behaviour to back it up! Searcher was plainly a dog with a one-track mind. Pettit could lead him around the perimeter of the garden as many times as he liked; Searcher always pulled towards the cedar tree and stood there, waiting for his peppermint.

There were relatively few houses in Hospital Road. The old, abandoned hospital with its excrescences and grounds took up most of one side of the short street and the eight houses that flanked the Nurses' Hostel all stood in spacious grounds. Gardens, side entries, even dustbins had been searched and not so little as a further smear of white paint found.

Hardy read the list which Colonel Soames had thoughtfully compiled. He was evidently well-acquainted with the contents of every large house within an area of forty miles and his memory was good. In brackets he had often added the name of the animal; lion; tiger; leopard. And at the very end of the list was written; *Any house in Quarry Lane*.

And that was going to be difficult. The coloured community had a deep distrust of the Police. A that's-right-pick-on-us-just-because-we're-black attitude. The accusation of prejudice might be justified in some places, but not in Hillchester so far as Hardy knew. The fact remained that although practically everybody else on the list would co-operate and show off a hide, with or without claws, it would take a search warrant to get a policeman over the doorstep of any house in Quarry Lane.

O'Brien said, "I can't exactly see Sir Joshua in the role and Admiral Filby is well over eighty. Still, if there *was* a claw it must have come from somewhere. It's worth a try. I think Parsons – he speaks their lingo."

Parsons, whose work as Scene of the Crime officer, was often dull and usually squalid, had a delightful day, and the prospect of another tomorrow. All the people whose rugs or hunting trophies he must ask to inspect were willing to help and even when living in reduced circumstances where a tiger-skin rug covered most of the living room floor, they were hospitable. He drank several cups of coffee and as the day moved on – and he with it – was offered sherry. He said, "Not while I am on duty, sir." He had the ex-public school-boy's ability to say *sir* without the slightest tinge of servility. Then they said, "Half a glass and some blotting paper to go with it," and produced biscuits. Sir Joshua Richardson gave him lunch and after that he was offered tea in several places, and then sherry again, or in one case whisky. Followed by dinner, very simple but very good. However, it had been an abortive day, for the only pelt with a paw missing was that of a bear, now serving as a bedside rug and Admiral Filby had an adequate explanation. "Poor thing," he said. "He'd got his left foreleg in a trap. I shot him – out of pity. And there's his hide."

Parsons tipped up the truncated leg and saw by the way it had been mounted that what the Admiral said was true.

WPC Girdlestone said to Hardy, "I understand, sir, that you anticipate some difficulty in getting the Quarry Lane people to co-operate. I have an idea. May I tell you about it?"

O'Brien – only he could have told her – really was a gossip!

"Go ahead."

"I haven't been here long enough for my face to be known. And down in Thorington there is a far larger coloured community. So I am experienced. I could get a look at every pelt in that area for very little outlay. Do you know where we could borrow one."

"Yes. There's a very good specimen over the fire-place in the Constitutional Club. A tiger, complete with snarl."

"Splendid," she said. "Aside from that I only need a van. Quite a small one would do."

Afterwards she told Hardy that she'd hated herself and felt dreadfully cruel.

Wearing civilian clothes and with her head tied up in a gaudy head-scarf, WPC Girdlestone drove into Quarry Lane, parked, lit a cigarette and waited. In the open body of the small van were several bundles and stretched over them was the magnificent tiger skin which Sir Everard Richie had given to the Constitutional Club when he was Hillchester's M.P. On both sides of the van was a placard, lettered in scarlet. "I Buy Furs at Top Prices."

From an upper window a dark face looked out, then disappeared and shortly afterwards a West Indian woman came out and, studiously ignoring the van, crossed the road and vanished into a house. Pat Girdlestone took another cigarette and waited patiently. She knew that somewhere to the rear of the houses the community spirit was at work.

"And I could have kicked myself," she told Hardy, "I should have stipulated *rugs*. What most of them had to offer was so *pitiable*. Old fur collars and gloves; two nylon fur coats – very good imitations, I must say. I kept pointing to the borrowed tiger and presently an Asian woman came out with this leopard – as you see, all claws intact. I gave her ten pounds – I hope that comes under legitimate expenses. Oh, and I remembered to ask if her husband would mind her selling it, and she said he was dead that was why she was so poor and needed to sell it. Then the keeping-up-with-the-Jones spirit set in and another woman said she'd had a finer skin, but she'd sold it. She couldn't remember to whom, or even how long ago. So it was a wasted afternoon and I'm sorry.''

"Don't be," Hardy said. "You did your best."

I have, thou hast, he has, we have, you have, they have, all done their best. He wanted to tell her that he had more than once thought that there was a jinx on this whole affair. Nothing led anywhere. He said, "I may have made a colossal mistake. No real publicity about the Becky Dalton case; keeping a low profile as they say. That served no good purpose. Now this with every possible publicity has ended in the same deadlock. Hell!''

Every possible publicity included an article, front page, in Monday's *Hillchester and District*. Graham Harper had not broken any known rules; he'd named nobody, used no hearsay. He'd simply recounted his personal experience and reiterated his warning. And that women were heeding it became evident towards the end of the afternoon when there were hardly any solitary women to be seen on the streets, though the pre-Christmas shopping period had begun and the shops were gaily lighted. There was evidence, too, in the knot of anxious-faced women waiting outside the big new comprehensive school. Mothers always waited outside the primary school but it was generally believed that a child old enough for the comprehensive was capable of getting itself to and from school.

Jim Palfrey, Sergeant Saunder's brother-in-law, saw grim evidence of the prevailing mood in the empty seats usually occupied by elderly women taking advantage of prices so reduced as to show hardly any profit. Elderly men – and a few young ones – were there in their usual number. Jim had started charging less than half price, in fact barely more than a third on Monday afternoons because Hillchester Town Council – surely the most backward in the country – would not allow him to open on Sundays. An audience, however small the profit, made it just possible to turn on the antique heating system and have the place comfortably warm by six o'clock. It also gave him a chance to test what effect his Sunday's tinkering had had upon the near obsolete projector.

These were the reasons he could offer himself, and accept. There was another which he shied away from. Starkly simple. While the cinema was open he couldn't be with Lily!

Four years earlier Lily had been in a car crash. Her femur had been dislocated and broken. It had been expertly set and surgeons, doctors, X-rays had all assured Lily that she was as good as new. She refused to believe. She would not make any effort; she was still using the walking frame which far older patients discarded for sticks after about a month. Their flat was upstairs and Lily refused, absolutely to try to master stairs. She was no trouble – she could get herself to the bathroom, she could even take a shower. Anything to do with the kitchen seemed to daunt her.

Relatives and friends had been kind and helpful at first, but even good will was expendable and the help had tapered off, except for Amy. Amy had her two girls, and Tom who worked very odd hours, but she'd never yet failed to come and do what she called a bake-up, enough prepared food to last for a week.

The ailing old projector worked on this Monday afternoon and the ailing old people, only two of them women, watched, or dozed. The heating system displayed a burst of energy and the place became pleasantly warm, and although the seats were worn and shabby, they were still comfortable.

Diagonally across the Market Square, Greg Anderson said to Shirley Morrison, "How exactly do you get home, Girl Friday?"

"On the Castlegate bus. Then I walk along the Avenue. Pa often meets me, giving Bobbee a run. Bobbee rather favours the pillar box on the corner." Shirley heard her own voice a little shrill from the effort to speak lightly. Whistling in the dark!

Greg said, "Take the four o'clock. Today and every day until this scare is over."

Shirley said, "Really, Mr Anderson, you are the kindest,

most considerate person! And I will make up the time, honestly. I'll bring a few sandwiches and make a cup of tea in the cubby hole.''

On Tuesday the correspondence column of the *Hillchester and District* reflected the general concern about this second rape and the fact that nobody had been arrested. The longest of the letters made direct reference to the Cambridge rapist, and to the fact that when at last a man was arrested, the police admitted that they had had suspicions, but not enough evidence to warrant making an arrest.

"How much danger and misery could have been averted," the letter demanded, "had the police been empowered to take action sooner. The innocent would have nothing to fear and if, by some rare chance a mistake was made, is there not a Court of Appeal? Yours faithfully, Justice Before Protocol."

The next letter was brief and to the point. "Everybody should keep a dog. Both rape victims lived in places where there was no dog. Yours faithfully, Dog-lover."

Another letter advised all women to carry a dog-whistle – more penetrating than a human scream.

Then three letters asked, in almost identical words, would not the police be better employed in concentrating on actual crime, instead of checking licence dates on cars.

Such a criticism of the police was mild compared with some which arrived on Hardy's desk. Some letters were definitely libellous. One said that no arrest had been made because the police had been bribed. Another said that no arrest would ever be made because one of the police was the rapist.

Hardy knew that he was being ridiculous to care about such accusations, but they showed something he didn't like the smell of. But he must seem not to care. Making an effort, he said, "Tom. Somebody must have noticed that you were first on the scene. Both times."

"With you, sir, a close second," Saunders said. He added, in a different voice, "And when you think of the service we give the bastards . . .''

107

"But we seem to have failed them now."

"Given time, he'll overreach himself."

"And in the meantime how many poor girls are to be raped – or badly scared?"

That was the question which he faced every hour of his working day, and whenever he woke, as he now frequently did, during the night. The simile of a blind man hunting for a black cat in a dark room, struck him as apt. The only comfort – and sometimes Hardy despised himself for regarding it as a comfort – was that nobody was breathing down his neck from Thorington. Detective Superintendent Harrison had enough on his plate. A Securicor man had been shot dead and £80,000 stolen; and a pound of pure heroin, worth some incalculable sum, had been found in a derelict coastguard's cottage. A mere rape, however savage, seemed relatively trivial.

But . . .

The writer of the anonymous montage letter had used the word *progressive* and Grace Robbins, so calm and so explicit had said; "At first I thought he was trying to kill me. He put his hand over my nose and mouth and I couldn't breathe. I thought I was going to die."

And next time – almost inevitably there must be a next time, a girl might die.

Trade did not suffer so badly as the shopkeepers had at first feared. Women changed their habits and shopped earlier, or in groups. Tony's café was hardly affected at all, it had never been much of a resort for unaccompanied females in the evening. It was a roughish, toughish place which sold good Expresso coffee and solid spaghetti-based dishes prepared by Tony's Italian wife. Fights sometimes broke out inside the café, but were invariably finished outside, Tony being a match for any two men and an expert chucker-out. In his heart he hankered for a better class establishment and was sure that he could attain it if he could only get a drinks licence. He regularly applied for one and was as regularly refused for a valid enough reason, enough licensed premises within the area; the White Horse within a few paces; the Dog and Partridge at the end of Market Arcade, and three clubs.

Mr Quantrill who owned and, with the help of Poor Old Arthur, ran the Disco which operated only on Wednesday, Thursday and Saturday evenings, did notice a slight fall in attendance. Girls always outnumbered boys, especially in the over-twenty age group. Girls once hooked on pop music seemed to stay hooked; boys drifted away and took up other interests, crazy old cars held together with hope and spit, or marriage. Mr Quantrill rated the two aberrations as much the same. On the Wednesday after the second rape there were noticeably fewer girls on their own and five of them had clubbed together for a taxi to take them home. The driver would not wait a minute. He could well afford to be haughty. Both taxi firms were enjoying an absolute gold rush.

Nice regular bookings such as that made by Mr Griffin at the White Horse.

Mr Griffin had soon seen that seeing Maudie and Evie and Elsie who did the washing up, and Ruthie who gave a sketchy kind of chambermaid service to their respective destinations, meant that he was absent just at the time when Colonel Soames and other less permanent residents were exercising their privilege of drinking after hours. Why the Hell they couldn't order beforehand and take the bloody booze to where they wanted it, Mr Griffin could only explain by the thought that all men were perverse. And although Yvonne had been gallant about standing in and taking over, he could not feel easy about that. Yvonne, to his infatuated eyes was still no end of a dish, and commercial travellers were notorious. So Mr Griffin had given a standing order to Call-a-Cab. It would cost, but the cost should be tax-deductible . . .

Case Five: Gloria Woodford

Though the top end of the Long Bar had been severely male territory, it had been affected by the Terror. Men who had wives who were nervous of being alone after dark no longer assembled there for the happy after-work drink. Mr Sims could attend if he had earlier taken his wife out to play Bridge, or if she had friends in to play at her house. Greg Anderson could attend because Mary, imagining him to be working, had bravely said that she did not mind being alone. She pointed out that both rapes had taken place in the centre of Hillchester and both the victims had been young, unmarried women. Also she had Fritz who, though small, could be very aggressive.

Greg had won the bedroom battle. He'd come in one night, deliberately late and moving with great stealth had bedded himself down, fully dressed except for his shoes, on the unmade bed, with just the eiderdown over him. In the morning he said, "I did look in on you but you were asleep. I simply couldn't bear to disturb you. I did it twice last week. And I look like being late every night from now to Christmas."

"In that case you might as well be comfortable," Mary said. "I'll make the bed up today."

In the Long Bar one evening, Colonel Soames said suddenly, "Say what you like about them. They *are* brave!" The attenuated company, Crawford and Crowther, both bachelors,

Sims who had left his wife safely installed, and Greg, turned as one man and saw that the Colonel had been speaking generally; for they were singular. Gloria Woodford, the town's bad woman!

She moved to a stool in the central part of the bar, but nearer the lower end where a group of men stood. She slipped off a worn old beaver lamb coat and dropped it to the floor. Then she sat down and crossed her legs.

Everything about her was just slightly out of date. The black satin frock was too short, the red shoes too pointed and high-heeled for present fashions. Even her hair, suspiciously golden, was too rigidly, too regularly waved. Her nails and lips matched the scarlet of shoes and handbag.

She went into action with the precision of a machine. She took from the handbag a packet containing two cigarettes and a lighter. She put one cigarette in her mouth and laid the packet on the bar. She clicked the lighter several times. A man who earlier had joined the group near the door, detached himself, carrying his drink – a most promising sign to Gloria's experienced eye.

"May I give you a light?"

"Thanks very much." His lighter was noiseless, and it worked.

"Have one yourself," she said, smiling and offering her packet.

"No, no. It's your last. Wouldn't dream of it. Now, what are you drinking?"

"Dry Martini, please." Maudie who had carefully avoided even glancing at Gloria – she also knew the drill – came along.

"Dry Martini, double. And for me the same again. Oh and," he eyed Gloria's packet, "twenty Players, please."

Gloria realised that she would not have to draw on her reserves – the new packet and the lighter which did work, lying at the bottom of her bag. For the trick did not always work. More than once one of the young louts at the lower end of the bar had tossed her a box of matches, or brought a lighter

111

leaving his drink behind, and briskly going back to it. Tonight she had been lucky.

"See what I mean about them?" Colonel Soames asked. "They don't know their clients – I believe they call them that – from Adam. That chap she's going to take home with her, might well be the rapist."

"I wonder," Crawford said flippantly, "whether it is technically possible to *rape* a prostitute. Rape implies a degree of unwillingness on the part of the female."

"In short, a bargain," Sims said.

"All the same, they take a terrible risk," Colonel Soames said, sticking to his point with admirable tenacity. "Good God! Look at that!"

Gloria and her pick-up were moving towards the stairs which led to the restaurant.

Four evenings later Gloria lay on her day-bed and thought herself lucky not to need to go out into the wintry weather. A howling wind with a driving rain intermingled with sleet. Her latest pick-up client had been either madly generous or in a state not capable of telling a five pound note from a one. He'd given her four fivers. And today she'd accommodated one of her regulars, Reg Palfrey, who always gave her two pounds and, as a kind of bonus, some of the produce of his market garden. Of absolutely no use to Gloria with whom inertia was a congenital disease.

She'd been born, the sixth and least wanted child of her mother, a debilitated woman who lived on stewed tea and bread and margarine. Her father was a drunken, violent man known throughout Hillchester as The Sweep. He did sweep chimneys and by the time he was fifty was the only one of his breed – a black sweep. Some Hillchester housewives still believed that a black sweep made a better job than a white one.

He was a fiercely independent man and he owned his own hovel; Number Four, the Sheepgate. Most of the

112

neighbouring houses had been modernised and had he chosen to follow his neighbours' example, he could have obtained a grant from the Borough Council; but he had said, "Where I piss is my business. Bugger off!"

In what at best could only be called insalubrious surroundings Gertie – the Gloria was still to come – grew somehow into a most entrancingly beautiful child, golden-haired, blue-eyed and with an apple-blossom complexion. And she learned early that she need *do* nothing; just to *be* was sufficient. She was tone deaf, yet she was in the school choir with the teachers clubbing together to see that she was properly clad. And when a minor royalty had come to open a home for old people – tactfully called Sunset House – on the edge of the Common, the then Mayor of Hillchester, having no children of his own, had appealed to the schools and Gertie Woodford had been chosen to present a huge sheaf of flowers and make a little bob. The minor royalty – an impulsive person – had actually kissed her.

When Gertie was sixteen she went to work at Miss Morland's, the general shop just across the road and one of the last small general shops to survive in the face of savage activity and effort and she always felt tired. However salvation came in the form of a young man, a big, cheerful young man who owned a car and a nice caravan, and who was a good bricklayer and who always kept one jump ahead of the tax men, by moving away.

Despite his nomadic way of life his standards of domesticity were high – his mother had been a Yorkshire woman. With Gertie he had tried and tried. She just couldn't or wouldn't learn. While he was still infatuated with her he was content to do the cleaning and some basic cooking and considered himself well rewarded by the envious glances of other men whenever he took her out for a drink or a meal. He earned good money and delighted in buying her things. She was astonishingly undemanding which at first he considered a virtue, but eventually saw that she was too bloody idle even to shop for herself. She could quite happily spend a day doing

113

nothing, just slopping around in a pretty, but soiled, dressing-gown.

After three years of it he simply quit. And although she had been calling herself Mrs Woodford, he'd never actually married her; so he was not deserting. And he left her with the caravan, worth, he reckoned, at least three hundred pounds.

On the caravan site which was just outside Bristol, Gertie had been popular with the other women. Still as pretty as an angel she'd never even looked at another woman's man and she was generous. She'd lend anything, even money and forget all about it. So now, when it became apparent that she had been ditched, she had the sympathy and goodwill of her neighbours. Unfortunately this, all too often, took the form of finding work for her. Most of them worked and were prepared to slip in a good word for her.

She was hopeless; she failed to turn up for, or was late for, any interview. Just occasionally she made an effort and because she was still so pretty, got a job which she seldom held down for more than a week. Then one day a good neighbour came along with a newspaper cutting. A business calling itself Pretty Kitchens was inviting entrants for what was intrinsically a beauty competition.

"You oughta go in for this, Gert. You'd win hands down."

"What would I have to do?"

"Fill in this form and send in a photograph of you doing something in the cookery line. And I don't think Gert or Gertie. you want something more glamorous. How about Gloria?"

She won, of course. Two thousand pounds for doing nothing. She gave the good neighbour five hundred. But Pretty Kitchens wanted her to give demonstrations using their wares: saucepans, grills, ovens, mixers, knives. For such demonstrations they paid by the day and paid very well; but it was all too much. Gloria's arithmetic was rudimentary but she could count well enough to reckon that she had fifteen hundred pounds of the prize money left and she could get three hundred or thereabouts for the caravan. She need do nothing for quite a long time – if she went home.

Even her father had been susceptible to her looks, he'd never knocked her about as he had done the others. So she thought of home quite fondly; and, his down-trodden wife being dead, The Sweep welcomed his daughter fairly amiably. He'd always paid his self-employed person's contribution towards his pension and was now in receipt of it; and he still swept a chimney from time to time. He apportioned the financial liabilities; he paid the rates, the gas and the electricity bills. Other food and drink expenses were fairly shared.

They lived in indescribable squalor for just on nine years. Miss Morland's, just across the road, had changed with the changing times and now offered a variety of foods taken from a huge deep-freeze. Miss Morland had also obtained a licence to sell intoxicants so Gloria need not even dress in order to go shopping. She just slouched across the road and though regarded with disapproval, was treated with the respect due to a good customer.

Then The Sweep died, and Gloria, her small fortune almost exhausted, had to decide what to do in order to maintain her standard of living without doing any actual work. She settled on the oldest profession as the easiest. She spent what remained of her money in quite an imaginative way, having the dismal scullery converted into a downstairs cloakroom and what had been the front room into something which some of her clients, even the most casual, remembered with a kind of sentiment. As indeed, they remembered her. She was not grasping, she'd give you a drink before or after. Her very inertia made her seem kind.

When making improvements to what she regarded as *her* house – The Sweep's other children having gone away as fast and as far as possible – Gloria had ignored the upper floor, into which the roof leaked and the back door which had never closed properly since a bomb fell on the cattle market. When the door made its familiar noise, a kind of grating sound, Gloria was not alarmed. Only regulars came along Maiden

Lane and in by the back door. She roused herself enough to call, "Who is it?"

A voice which she did not recognise said, "It's all right."

Then the door to the room opened and he stood there. Nobody she recognised, at least if she should have done, she didn't because the man wore, across his nose a wide strip of sticking plaster extending to both cheekbones.

"Do I know you?"

"No. But you will," the man said and laughed. Not a nice laugh, but Gloria could overlook that. Some men, embarking upon a first visit to such as her were nervous.

"Who sent you?"

"Nobody."

"Oh well," she said easily. "Like a drink?" She had time to think that so far as she had any preferences, this was the kind of man she liked. Young, clean-looking, well-dressed. A jarring laugh, but a gentlemanly voice.

He pounced upon her and proceeded to prove that even a prostitute could be raped. Gloria's standard of behaviour was not very high, but she had never before been treated in such a fashion. She resisted with surprising energy until he put a hand to her throat and almost choked her. Then she gave in and lay passive until it was over. Not over! Something that felt sharp and red-hot at the same time scraped down the side of her face. She put her hand to it and it came away all bloody. The man by that time had gone.

She would have screamed then, but she realised the uselessness of it. She knew how her neighbours felt about her. They were not all estimable people though the Sheepgate itself presented a far more respectable appearance than it had done in Gloria's youth. Most of the old houses had been taken over by the Council and modernised, but the people who lived there were much the same, a fair mixture of unemployed, unemployable and a few near-criminals. But like people everywhere they felt better if they could look down on somebody, and the Sheepgate people looked down on Gloria. Envy had something to do with it, too. It irked the other

116

women when in the shop she said at the tail end of her haphazard shopping, "And a whisky; And a gin."

So in this extremity she did not scream. Holding a heavily scented but grimy handkerchief to her face, she struggled into her fur coat and her slippers, and went across the road to the shop. With the wind in a certain direction St Luke's clock could be heard even at this distance and it struck eleven as she crossed the road. Miss Morland had long been abed. She retired early because she rose early for the benefit of improvident housewives who had to buy food ten minutes before breakfast was due.

Gloria's first ring on the bell woke Miss Morland from her well-earned rest. The second, prolonged because Gloria kept her finger on the bell push, took her, in a state of righteous indignation, to the window.

"What do you want? At this time of night?"

"Telephone! Police!" Gloria shouted back. "I've just been raped! Hurry!"

In Gloria's sluggish mind a thought moved. By admitting that she had been raped, and instantly reporting it, she was making a claim to respectability. She had never fully accepted that she was a professional whore; just a decent married woman who happened to have a lot of men friends.

"I'll do that," Miss Morland said. "You go home and wait." She was prepared to do her duty as a good citizen, but she intended to avoid any personal involvement. There had never been and there must never be the slightest question about her respectability.

Gloria went home. She pulled the handkerchief away from her face and it seemed a bit stuck, a sure sign that the bleeding was drying up, all but in one place, the corner of her mouth. She took a clean handkerchief from a drawer, put the disgusting one out of sight, but easily available, behind the bottles. Poured herself a good gin – for after all, had she not had a bad shock? She took a cigarette. Her torn lip reddened it so she squashed it out and took another, carefully keeping it to the left, uninjured side of her mouth.

Hardy had been feeling off colour for two days. Some kind of flu bug was going about and men with comfortable homes and attendant wives had either taken their temperatures, or had them taken and stayed in bed. Hardy had only once taken his temperature and it was a hundred and two. But the service flat which was his home now, did not cater for people even temporarily indisposed.

Also he had a superstitious sort of feeling that if he did as he felt inclined and stayed in bed untended, something would crop up while his back was turned. Not, he thought gloomily that staying on duty was of much use. The rapist was still at large and all the information – piles of paper – was what Hardy called negative evidence. None of the saliva tests taken by the young men at Sister Fawcett's birthday party had indicated a blood group out of the ordinary.

Hardy dosed himself with aspirin and whisky; the alcohol, if it served no therapeutic purpose, helped to stave off depression. Then Sergeant Saunders – on night duty once again – arrived carrying a thermos flask.

"I told Amy how you were feeling, sir, and she fixed you a brew."

"Gypsy stuff, Tom." Saunders had once said that, way back, a Palfrey had married a gypsy, whose herbal remedies, charms for banishing corns and warts and so on had been somewhat shakily, because verbally, preserved and handed down for at least three generations.

"Could be," Tom said. "All I know is if I, or the girls, show the slightest sign of a snivel, Amy'll fix a dose and we're right as ninepence by morning."

"All right. And most kind of Amy," Hardy said. "Please thank her. And pour it out for me, please." He shoved forward the glass from which he just drunk the whisky. The liquid from the flask poured out, very clear, faintly green and smelling of thyme. It tasted of honey with a slight undertow of bitterness.

Tom Saunders watched while Hardy drank, and rather smugly congratulated himself on being diplomatic. Had he simply handed Hardy the flask the odds were a hundred to one against his drinking its contents. Now, once sure that Hardy had taken his medicine, he said, "There's just one thing, sir. After that you shouldn't drive. But that's all right. WPC Girdlestone will take you safely home."

Something, the aspirin, the whisky, Amy's brew or merely the healing process of time, eased the grinding ache in his bones, the hammer-knock in his head and the red-hot stabs behind his eyes. Even the feeling of defeat which had haunted him ever since the first reported rape, seemed to recede. He folded his arms on his desk, cradled his head on them and slept. And was rudely awakened to be told of the latest rape, reported from the Sheepgate.

He felt all right; it was everything he had to do with that was wrong. His room was upstairs and the stairs and the banister rail seemed to be made of rubber, rather soft and flexible. But he got down safely and out, over a floor that felt spongy and there was WPC Girdlestone, very trim, waiting to take him, not home, but to the Sheepgate.

The car behaved oddly. As he got in the roof came down and hit him, then the seat rose up and bumped him.

He felt obliged to say that most damning thing; "I am not drunk."

"I never for a moment imagined that you were."

"Do you know how to get to Sheepgate?"

"Yes. I even know the shortest way. Cut across the Cattle Market."

"Who told you that?"

"Nobody. I can read a map."

She drove very fast but very competently. She was, in fact, he thought muzzily, of a type; she belonged with Julia and Lilah Noble . . .

At the edge of the Cattle Market nearest Sheepgate there was a huddle of sheds, pens, and small offices. As they neared it, WPC Girdlestone gave a little muttered sound and swerved sharply. The headlights beamed upon the figure of a man who for a few seconds stood still and then dodged behind an outjutting building. WPC Girdlestone braked as sharply as she had swerved.

"Loitering!" she snapped and before Hardy could speak, far less move, she was out of the car and would have gone round the corner of the building too, but the man came out of hiding to meet her. She'd left her door open so Hardy could see and hear everything.

"I am a police officer," she said – somewhat unnecessarily since she was in uniform, "May I ask your name."

"You can ask, missy. I ain't obliged to tell you. You find out."

"I most certainly shall. And I shall have you charged with obstructing the police in their duties."

Oh God, Hardy thought, how young and confident she was.

"Thass right," the man said, unbuttoning his flies. "Harass a man for taking a pee." Deliberately he aimed at her well-polished shoes.

Damn Women's Lib; damn Unisex! This is really too much.

He fumbled with the handle of the car door intending to interpose his male presence; but before he could do so, the girl said, "Look behind you!" And there on the wall were the painted words; Commit no nuisance. The notice was very old and its legal power had never yet been tested.

"*And* with indecent exposure. With Detective Chief Inspector Hardy as witness!" She turned and came swiftly back to the car.

"Didn't you have a police-baiter down at Thorington?" Hardy asked. "That fellow – or his identical twin, hovers about wherever a crime has been committed – or a fire. It's maddening but there's nothing much you can do about it. I do wonder, though. How did he know that a crime had been committed?"

There was no real mystery about that. Gloria's shouting to Miss Morland had alerted the short street. Had alerted most sharply a couple named Shepherd who lived at Number 10.

120

They were sitting in their front room with two old, innocent-looking suitcases between them. Mr Shepherd had a job on the Waddington Air Base; Mess Steward and quite well paid. But he wanted more, much more; so he'd taken to knocking things off, a bottle or two, here and there, and cigarettes, mainly; now and again other things. Some thieves had difficulty in turning their loot into cash, but Mr Shepherd had an arrangement with a Thorington telephone number. When he had a load worth collecting he dialled this number and somebody came in a decent-looking car and collected the loot. Paying cash on the nail.

The Shepherds heard St Luke's clock announce the hour, and almost immediately, Mrs Woodford shouting.

"Get on the blower," Mr Shepherd said. "Say not tonight. Say to wait for a call. The place'll be lousy with fuzz within five minutes. I'll put these away." He lifted the suitcases and carried them upstairs, and making a super-human effort, hoisted them on top of the wardrobe. Under the bed was too obvious a place. The suitcase full of bottles was heavy and he practically *heard* the shaky disc in his backbone give way. And the familiar pain struck. Bent double, he got himself to the bed and collapsed.

Mrs Woodford was a willing, almost a garrulous witness. "Friends of mine often do come in by the back door. And there was this great strip of plaster over his nose. I felt I should know him. I gotta lotta friends, drop in for a drink. I actually offered him one! Then he set about me and he didn't claw me like he did the others, where it wouldn't show. He went for my face. Look!"

Her description tallied with all the others, tall, slim-looking but very strong; and she had seen what no other victim had been able to do. "Fairish hair," Gloria said. "Short back and sides, and wavy." Eyes? No she hadn't had a chance to notice them because as soon as he was near enough he'd set about her. She volunteered the information that he was clean-shaven and wore what she called a smart suit. "A business

121

suit, sort of. And yet, and yet . . ." For a moment she seemed
at a loss for words. "For all that, I reckon he'd been in the
market. There was a kinda animal smell about him."

The mixture as before, Hardy thought wearily, with just
that little extra touch about the hair and the clean-shaven
face.

At the mention of animal smell WPC Girdlestone's rather
supercilious-looking nose twitched. How could one stray
odour be detected in a room that held so many?

It was, superficially, a pretty room — if you liked pink! And
the rose-shaded lamps shed a kindly light over everything.
But it was dirty. Pat Girdlestone recognised the smell of
ingrained dirt, of too much usage and insufficient cleaning, of
cigarettes smoked and stubbed out but the ashtrays seldom
emptied; of food, of drink, of cheap harsh scent and of sexual
intercourse.

Hardy said, as though coaxing a backward child, "Mrs
Woodford, you said you had many friends. Did this man bear
any resemblance to anyone you know?" He was thinking of
that last ditch device, an Identikit picture and an appeal to the
public. Have you seen this man?

Gloria pondered. She brought her handkerchief away from
her face and studied it. Just smears now, except for that one
place on her lip. All this talking wasn't doing that any good.

"Not to *look at* exactly," she said, putting the handkerchief
back into place. "But he sounded a bit like somebody I know.
Young Mr Hooper . . . Mind you, it wasn't him. Of *that* I am
sure. Simon's a real nice boy."

As Mr Shepherd had foreseen, the area was now full of
policemen, rousing people and asking impertinent questions.

The swirling black-green darkness which had been
threatening to engulf Hardy ever since he was roused from
sleep, came nearer.

Pat Girdlestone took charge. "You should be in bed, sir.
You've done all you can. The Scene of the Crime officer is
here, and PC Pettit with his dog. And I think Mrs Woodford
should go to the hospital. She may need a tetanus injection and

possibly a stitch.''

In Gloria, The Sweep's fiercely independent blood surged up.

''I ain't going to no hospital. I don't need no injections nor no stitches. *I* ain't done nothing wrong. Harm was done to me and I've told you all I can remember. So you just go away, see!''

''I think you are most unwise, Mrs Woodford, but of course the decision is yours. Come along, sir. I'll take you home.''

(Afterwards Gloria told everybody who would listen that Hardy was dead drunk. She said it without malice, just a statement of fact. ''He was so drunk that but for her – bossy bitch – he'd have fell down. I knew. I could smell the whisky on him from the first.'')

Graham Harper

"Getting quite communicative," Graham said, glancing at the morning's release and seeing that it was longer than usual.

"Desperate measures, laddie. *We* are being spat upon – and not only by the public! And all that that will result in," the Public Relations officer's voice was bitter as he nodded towards the paper, "will be a lot of bumph about somebody's old Uncle Harry who bumped his nose on a door."

Graham read hastily. There was for the first time a full description of the rapist. Tall, slim, young, well-spoken, fair-haired and clean shaven. Possibly with some injury on his nose, or with sticking plaster over it. Then the appeal for anybody who knew anything to please communicate.

"Did the latest victim bite back?" Graham asked. Not that it was a subject for flippancy but he was anxious to preserve his hard-boiled image.

"She'd be capable of it! And our code of secrecy, preserving a damsel's reputation is in this case absurd. The victim apparently roused the whole street, telling all and sundry."

"Unmindful of her reputation?"

"Having none. Now buzz off before I become indiscreet."

Gloria opened the door and looked at Graham with disfavour. "If you're another busy, you can busy off. I've had enough."

"I'm Press, Mrs Woodford."

"Oh. Come in. I once had a lot to do with gentlemen from papers. And when I say gentlemen I mean gentlemen. They always treated me all right."

She was at that stage of inebriation known only to the steady drinker. Parallel red furrows ran down her right cheek and a blood clot had formed at the corner of her mouth.

"He properly did for me, didn't he?"

"Oh, I wouldn't say that."

"No, because you're a nice boy. Have a drink. Give me one . . . What! Another dead man? I shouldn't have thought . . . Still here they were tramping about, all night. One of them paralytic, couldn't walk alone. And a bossy bitch wanting to shove me in the hospital. I had a lot to bear. I needed my little nips."

"I'm sure you did. You need one now. Where's the nearest place?"

"Straight across the road."

He went and came back, poured her a drink into a glass heavily marked by lipstick, and himself one much smaller in a glass that looked relatively clean.

"You wouldn't think, to look at me now, but I was a beauty queen once. I'll show you . . ."

She kept the right hand top drawer of her chest of drawers for papers of some importance, receipts for rates, electricity and gas. She now had so many that when she pulled out the drawer they jumped out at her. Those that did not jump out, she shovelled on to the floor, and diving deeper, produced some newspaper cuttings, slightly yellowing about the edges. The beauty that had once been hers, still came through and made its impact.

Reduced to this, Graham thought. His mind could not catch the exact quotation: but beauty vanishes, however rare, rare it be; and when I crumble who will remember the lady of the West Countree?

"It was over in Bristol," Gloria said. "They picked me out of dozens. But then they tried to work me to death."

His mind threw up a good headline. Rapist's Latest Victim

was Former Beauty Queen: or Former Beauty Queen Rapist's Latest Victim.

He said, gathering the clippings together, "Mrs Woodford, have I your consent to use all this? It is quite a story, you know. And I'd be prepared to share the proceeds. With any luck we might hit the *Sunday Recorder*."

"Just take what you want. It never did me any good," Gloria said.

"And it'd be helpful if you didn't talk about this to anybody else."

"Not even the police? You've no idea how nosy they are." She grew expansive from the last gin. "And the time they waste! I mean I'd told them everything about the man, except his name, which I didn't know. Then they go mucking about looking for footsteps. What use do that serve? And that great dog! Downright unfriendly. I offered it a choccy and it wouldn't take it."

The *Sunday Recorder* reported very little that had not some sexual flavour; it escaped being sheer pornography by a hair's-breadth. But the great British Public, of which its readers formed a sizable section, liked animals, too.

"What did the dog actually *do*, Mrs Woodford?"

"Sweet damn-all so far as I could see. Waste of public money! It come in here and sniffed about a bit, then it went out the back door – but then I'd said the man come in and went out that way. And it went along the lane and then come back. Did that twice it did. Mind you, nobody told me nothing. And they'd have liked me to be in hospital, outa the way. But I wouldn't go and so far as I know they couldn't make me. So here I was and I couldn't help hearing, could I? The one with the dog said he reckoned the man who did *this* to me," she touched her face, "had left his car just at the mouth of the lane."

She hadn't talked so much for ages and the effort was straining her. But this extremely pleasant young man seemed interested. She took another little drink, another cigarette and said:

"There's something I didn't tell the busies. I had enough to do answering questions. But you just look at this!" She was wearing a pretty, though grubby what? Dressing-gown, housecoat, négligée? It was pink and at the throat and wrist ended with ruffles. She pulled the frills away from her neck and exhibited her bruise.

"He damned near throttled me," she said.

"Awful," Graham said. "It must have been awful!" His imagination was lively enough to enable him for a moment to become a prostitute, expecting a customer and being suddenly confronted by a rapist and potential killer. But at the same time part of his mind slithered away and thought: Best told in the first person, like the so-called confession stories – I was Hillchester Rapist's third victim. And yet a third part of his mind said, gloatingly: I now know something that Detective Chief Inspector Hardy does not! And although the police had always been so mean and cautious about what they released to the public via the paper, Graham was a sufficiently good citizen to see his duty.

As he went up the stairs to Hardy's room, he met a man coming down; or rather the ghost of a man. His mind flipped up with the relevant quotation: "Yesterday upon the stair, I met a man who wasn't there." Alan Douglas was there, he was even recognisable though haggard, wild-eyed and unkempt. They had not been friends, just bar acquaintances in the past, and after the Becky Dalton disaster Graham had sometimes asked himself what it must feel like to have the girl to whom you had just got engaged, raped and driven out of her mind. That amount of empathy made him, against his will, stop on the turn of the stairs and say, "Hullo, Douglas. How are you?"

"Bloody awful." A nerve twitched violently under his left eye. He reeked of whisky. "You know what they're saying now, don't you?"

"No, you tell me."

"That there's been no arrest because they know who the man is. One of *them*! And they're protecting him for all they're

127

worth. You hadn't heard that?''

"As a matter of fact I had. But it's just talk."

"Oh no! It's bloody true. I know. I can prove it. Man, I prove it once a week."

"That's dangerous talk, Douglas. Slanderous."

"All right then. If it is why don't they arrest me? I've said it to their faces. I said it not five minutes ago. You see, I tried to do it on my own. I chucked my job. I worked at it day and night. And I got nowhere. I kept going to see Becky . . . I reckoned that between screaming and talking about the Devil, she *might* say a word of sense and give me a clue. Before she could, I was warned off. My visits upset her. See? *They* told the people at Pykenham to say that! So I thought; If you can't beat 'em, join 'em. And I tried. Now you know how they're always moaning about being short-handed and advertising. But would they take me? Not on your life! I'm the right age, the right size and I can see and I swear I was dead cold sober the first time. They said not in this area; try Norwich, try London. What the hell should I have done there? But I kept trying. And this morning I heard the latest – I can't be enlisted because I am emotionally involved. So I am. And if they were straight they'd see that I was the best bloody candidate . . . But they're all bent.''

"Shush," Graham said, as though speaking to a child. His kind, sympathetic streak came uppermost, with just below it the cold, professional one asking – How can this be worked in? "Look." he said, "go and sit on that bench and keep quiet. My business here won't take long. Then we'll go eat. Right?"

And after all, what he had come to tell Hardy in a gloating, I-know-something-you-don't kind of way, fell remarkably flat.

"Mrs Woodford," Hardy said, "and I warn you, if you mention a name, you'll be in trouble – she was wearing a fur coat. When she stopped clutching at it it fell open and there were marks – red then, not bruises, on her neck. And I was not surprised. Violence, like everything else, is progressive."

"Unless arrested."

"Exactly! And I wish to God I knew who to arrest. We know everything about the blasted man, except his name. We know what size he takes in shoes, and where he buys them. We know his blood group. We know the make and age of his car. But not his identity – so far."

Hardy spoke wearily. Graham thought he looked ill. Or the events of the last months had aged him by ten years.

"But you still hope to find him? No, sir, I'm not trying to pump you. Just interested."

"Hope? Of course. So far he's had the Devil's own luck. It may run out. What I am afraid of . . ." He halted, realising that he was talking to a layman, and a newspaper man at that. "Since this is strictly off the cuff, what I'm afraid of is that he may kill some unfortunate woman."

"All too likely."

Hardy had expressed this same fear to O'Brien who had said, meaning to hearten, "Well, we'll deal with that when it comes. We've got enough woes without imagining one."

Compared with that reaction this young man, by expression of face and tone of voice, sounded sympathetic and understanding.

"And what bothers me is the fact that the victims are not the *only* victims. You may have passed Alan Douglas as you came in?" Graham nodded. "He's half-demented and an alcoholic. The young nurse showed remarkable resilience, but apparently the top brass mildly criticised the old dear who ran the Hostel and she is having a nervous breakdown. Things like that." Hardy could have added that it was Miss Dalton's case which had led to the resignation of WPC Collins; one of the very best and now being rather wasted as secretary to the Head of St Ethelreda's – a job any reasonably competent woman could do.

"I see what you mean," Graham said. "And I did meet Alan Douglas. He looked to me as though he could do with a meal, so I asked him to wait."

Abruptly Hardy became a policeman again.

"Take no notice of the rubbish he talks. For the price of a beer he'd accuse *me*. I appreciate your coming to report the marks on Mrs Woodman's neck. Good morning."

The Police Station stairs had a turn in them; so many stairs, a little half-landing, and then so many more down to the entrance lobby. Graham had reached the half-landing, glanced down and seen that Alan Douglas was sitting where he had been told to sit, when the entry doors burst open and a small, very neat woman positively erupted into the reception space. She made straight for the desk behind which the Duty Constable sat and said in a surprisingly resonant voice, "I have something to report. Mrs Coat is my name. I live at Number One, Sheepgate and last night I saw a car where it had no right to be. In Maiden Lane, just at the mouth of it I mean. I'm lucky you see, I can put my dustbin out just there and get it emptied. Other people have to cart theirs through the house. So last night, say about ten to eleven is near enough, I went to put my dustbin out and there was this car. I only just managed to squeeze past. Then there was that Mrs Woodman, screeching her head off and I went to the front and didn't see the car move off. But I did *hear* it. It didn't start easy."

The whole statement poured out in a stream, leaving no room for a question or an interpolation. Looking a bit dazed the man on duty said, "I think, madam, you should talk to Detective Chief Inspector Hardy. I'll see if he's there."

Having heard so much, and unlikely to hear more, Graham descended the last eleven stairs and took Alan Douglas by the arm.

"Come along," he said. "I don't know about you but I'm starving."

He'd always rather prided himself on being unconventional and was ashamed to find himself unwilling to take Douglas into the Long Bar at the White Horse. It would have to be Tony's. Better really, he thought in self-exoneration, the poor wretch had had all the drink he could carry. But in St Luke's Lane, Douglas took matters into his

130

own hands and at the yard entrance to the hotel, swerved in and made for the Shades. ''I drink in low places these days,'' he said.

''I was thinking of something to eat.''

''You can eat here, if you feel like it. I don't.''

The husky-looking barman behind the plain, cleanly-scrubbed bar, seemed to spring to attention.

''Morning Mr Douglas,'' he said, with a slight emphasis on the *mister*. ''Your usual?'' Douglas made a grunting sound which obviously stood for assent and the barman turned to the inverted bottle on the wall and worked the mechanism twice.

''Half a pint for me,'' Graham said and glanced over the food. It was exactly the same as that on offer at the lower end of the Long Bar. The only difference – and that not immediately apparent – was that it was a day older.

Douglas was moving towards the far end of the room and Graham, all his senses alert, noticed that men, even those seated at the scrubbed tables, seemed to give way to him; even if the giving way was merely a gesture, shifting a chair half an inch. And some seemed to be avoiding his eye, or, having looked just that half second too long, averting their gaze.

Carrying his half pint and ham sandwiches for two on a kind of cardboard plate, Graham followed the man he had intended to treat and sat down by him at a table in the corner.

''I drink in places like this,'' Douglas said, almost confidentially, ''but only to serve my own purpose. I do not welcome familiarity. In fact I made a bit of a rumpus. And once was enough.'' He took two gulping swallows and ignored the sandwiches which Graham pushed forward. ''I listen. One day, sooner or later, I shall hear something useful. The man's a maniac and maniacs all crave admiration. One day he'll let something slip. Maybe only a tone of voice; he'll say 'At least you must admit the chap is bloody clever.' Something like that, and I shall *know*. You'd be surprised what you can learn in places like this. Fr'instance,'' he lowered his voice still more, ''I know all about this car stealing, who does it and why and how. And I'd have told bloody Chief Inspector

Hardy if he hadn't treated me like a delinquent kid. And ask yourself, ask yourself about this car. They've never come into the open about *that*. I only know from hearing owners of such old relics talk about being grilled.''

"Then surely that shows that the police are taking notice.''

"Some, but not enough. No real drive. Because they just don't want to know. Or at least, they *know* and are covering up.'' He rapped his glass sharply on the table and the barman came, not to ask what he wanted, but with another double whisky in a fresh glass. Graham's sympathetic streak was almost exhausted. If the man wanted to drink himself to death, it was his own business. But other people's finances had always been of interest to Graham since his own were so narrowly budgeted. He said, almost without thinking,

"That's an expensive way to live.'' It was a mistake. Alan Douglas answered with searing words.

"I've been saving. For a house and furniture. With Becky . . . And what bloody good did that do me?''

Happy Christmas

"A card from Great Aunt Harriet," Greg Anderson said, recognising the postmark and the handwriting, shaky now but unmistakable. "Did we remember her?"

"The Royal plural," Mary said. "Yes we did. We sent her that very pretty book, all flowers and birds which Lilah lent us and didn't want back."

"Good for us!" Greg opened the envelope very neatly, using the unused butter-knife. Not the ritual card, a letter. Feeding himself with his right hand, he held the letter in his left, read it and gave a little laugh.

"Distressed gentlewomen as a breed are at last extinct. Therefore Aunt Harriet is betaking herself to a Nursing Home."

"Where she will shortly be a distressed gentlewoman," Mary said unkindly.

In fact the ill-tempered, snobbish, dictatorial old woman was Greg's great-aunt, his only living relative. As a gesture Greg had taken Mary to visit her soon after they were married and fundamental disapproval had been evident in every word, every glance. A horrible visit.

As a gesture, they had invited her to visit them, and that had been worse; she had dismissed their darling little house, their newly acquired furniture, their neighbours, with the single damning word, *suburban*.

"She has a few things which she regards as heirlooms and wishes them to be kept in the family," Greg said. "And she wants me to collect them over New Year.''

"How very awkward! We'd asked the Sullivans and the Inskips to eat our second turkey.''

A second turkey sounded rather grand, but farmers who reared them were very generous and appreciative of Greg's efforts on their behalf. He was their St George, fighting the dragon tax-man on their behalf.

"I think I should go,'' Greg said. "She had some rather nice things. And you could ask Doctor Roper to act host and carve. They say he can make a pheasant serve six – and some over.''

"I could do that,'' Mary said. But she shrank from it. She had never felt at ease with Doctor Roper since . . . well, since what? Since he made his mistake. Anybody could make a mistake; and she had agreed with him. Let that not be forgotten.

But before New Year could be considered there was Christmas, and all the evidence of the new affluence. A fur coat for Mary; a new bicycle for Jimmy, expensive new toys for Anna and Emma. And Greg was to take possession of a new car towards the end of January.

Greg was what the Malwood rector regretfully referred to as a Christmas-and-Easter Christian. Almost all men, except some very elderly ones, fell into that category. They devoted their Sundays to their gardens, or to golf, or to family outings. Yet most of them were very good; they kept the churchyard grass cut, they'd made a paved path from the lychgate to the church door; they supported good causes. But the average congregation at Morning Service was nineteen, three old men, sixteen old women.

Greg was going to church on this Christmas morning and Jimmy was eager to accompany him. "If I can take my bike. I want Ricky Sullivan to see it.''

Mary said, "Be careful crossing the main road. And Greg, don't forget to collect Miss Southey.''

"I should have forgotten. A Freudian forget! But I'll bring her.''

At the rector's suggestion, several young or youngish couples in the suburb had "adopted" an old, lonely person and the Andersons had fared rather badly in the lottery and drawn Miss Southey, who was, for seventy, in pretty good physical shape, but a born moaner. The Sullivans had been allotted a cheerful little hunchback.

The short stretch of tree-lined, house-lined avenue between Forest Road and the main road to Salford was excellent cycling territory on Christmas morning. Jimmy had learned to ride on Ricky Sullivan's bicycle and now happily showed off, making figures of eight around Greg, braking suddenly and keeping his balance, riding one-handed. But at the main road he stopped and waited, and they crossed together into what had been the original village of Malwood and still retained a few old cottages, a rudimentary village green, and beyond the green the relatively new school and the church which dated back to Domesday.

"I think I'd better put it in the porch," Jimmy said. "It might rain and I shouldn't like it to get wet."

Greg said, "Do that!" and reflected that before the coming new year was very old, the bicycle would be left out in all weathers. Outside the church gate, Dick Sullivan's car stood and Greg thought: Yes, of course, *their* poor old protégée can't walk very far.

There was the church porch, very ancient, with stone benches on either side. And there was the door; actually a double door, its left-hand half opened only for funerals.

The women of Malwood – even those who attended church but seldom, had risen to the occasion and superseded anything they had formerly done in the way of decoration. On the closed half of the door there hung a large cross, holly, ivy and a few icily white Christmas roses from Miss Southey's little garden.

It was as though Greg had received a violent blow to his midriff. He had the sense to turn away and then he could draw in breath enough to speak. He saw Jimmy carefully propping the bicycle against one of the stone benches.

"You go in, Jimmy. Find the Sullivans and sit with them. I'll come in later. Here, take this. For the collection bag." He gave Jimmy a folded one pound note and went and sat down on a low headstone.

He felt very – not ill exactly but very queer, as though all his bones had turned into jelly. As though he had made some enormous physical effort which had left him breathless and tremulous. From inside the church came the sound of hearty singing; "Oh, come all ye faithful". A couple of slightly late-coming faithful came hurrying up the path and Greg assumed the look of a man waiting, looking beyond them into the road.

Jimmy slipped into place near the Sullivans. There was just room for him, so he imagined that Greg would find a place at the back. "I got the bike," he whispered.

"I got two more trucks and a whole signal set and . . ."

Peg Sullivan said, "Shush!"

Presently the spirit of Christmas prompted Jimmy to whisper again, "You can ride it back if you like." That was only fair, since Ricky had taught him to ride on his bike but the offer made him feel pleasantly magnanimous.

To Jimmy and to everyone else, Greg pretended to have slipped in the back. Jimmy reminded him of Miss Southey.

"Thanks for reminding me."

"Dad, what is a Freudian forget?"

"When you forget something because you don't want to remember it."

"Oh! Then you don't like her either."

"Shut up!" But who could like an old woman whose idea of Christmas conversation was to remark that it was a fine day and a green Christmas foretold a fat churchyard?

William Selsey's Christmas had got off to a bad start. He'd gone to the most expensive shop in the Market Arcade and bought for Lorraine what was called a twin-set; jumper and cardigan matching. Pure wool which, the owner of the shop assured him, was not easily come by these days, and as a consequence, very expensive. He paid ungrudgingly; it was

136

exactly the right blue.

He always tried to be just; and having spent twenty pounds on Lorraine, he took considerable trouble over cutting little slits into a Christmas card, fitting two ten pound notes into the slits and writing above them: Gift Token, and below them; Exchangeable Anywhere. He was very punctilious and gave Liz hers first and she said, "Oh Bill! How lovely! I shall get a pair of fur-lined boots. And what a nice idea! Gift Token, exchangeable anywhere! Really, you are a one!" She gave one of the kisses, which, to be truthful, had never meant much to him and now meant nothing, just a gesture of goodwill.

Then Lorraine opened her parcel and stared at it with − no other word for it − dismay. She said, "A twin-set!" with marked lack of enthusiasm; as though he had presented her with a horse collar; or a crinoline. "Thanks Dad," she said and folded the pretty paper together again.

"I reckoned it was just your colour, honey. And pure wool. What don't you like about it?"

"Dad, nobody under fifty wears a twin-set."

"Well, it came from Annette's. She'll change it."

"I should hope so."

Liz Selsey gave her daughter an absolutely venomous look. She thought: bitchy, ungrateful little bitch! She could at least have *pretended*!

Liz was not unaware of the situation, nobody but a woman who was blind and deaf could be. It was a known fact that men getting on went silly over girls and Liz thought that perhaps she should be grateful that the girl Bill was silly about was his daughter. Not far down the road, a man had gone silly about, and finally run off with, a girl who'd been bridesmaid at his own daughter's wedding.

Lorraine carried away her unwanted present and soon came down carrying a gift-wrapped parcel. "I'm going along to Queenie's."

"All right," Liz said. She had long ceased to expect any help with the household chores. "Don't be late." Such warning was necessary because Queenie's family seemed to observe no regular meal-times, eating haphazardly out of tins and packets.

Bill went into the garden and gathered Brussels sprouts and a head of celery. The older houses on the Fallowfield Estate had been built when land was plentiful and relatively cheap, so they all had long narrow gardens. William Selsey had divided his with posts and trellis work covered with climbing roses and honeysuckle. The part nearest the house – roughly one third of the whole had a miniature lawn and two flower borders; on the other side he grew enough vegetables to serve the family for a year.

Had Lorraine showed the slightest pleasure in his present he would have been a happy man, for a free morning was still a joy. Until recently milk had been delivered every day, including Sundays and public holidays. He'd only had free mornings during his annual fortnight. But lately Farmhouse Dairies had fallen into line with bigger firms and he had Sundays off. The other holidays, like Christmas, the rounds-men arranged between themselves, taking on each other's rounds. This year he'd drawn Christmas, which was a Sunday anyway.

Back in the kitchen after using the scraper and the door mat, he proceeded to help Liz. He cleaned the sprouts and the celery and peeled the potatoes. The kitchen, indeed the whole house, was redolent with the odour of roast turkey and that in itself was a treat. He could remember the time, just after Nigel, the second boy, had married and gone to live in Birmingham, when all turkeys were monsters, far bigger than the depleted family could eat without becoming cloyed; but the supermarket had changed all that, and you could buy a turkey not much bigger than a large chicken.

As he worked, now and again exchanging almost routine remarks with Liz, his mind was busy, thinking about the twin-set. As was usual where Lorraine was concerned, he blamed himself. He should have asked somebody who knew what was being worn. Perhaps even the hated Queenie. He blamed her for all the change which had taken place in

Lorraine lately, most of all for introducing her to the Disco, but at least she would have prevented him from buying something which nobody under fifty wore any more.

Presently Liz said, "All under control," and produced a bottle of Cyprian sherry – and *two* glasses. "We'll have a Happy Christmas drink."

"Shouldn't we wait for Lorraine?"

"She's up at that Queenie's. Getting her hair done. And wait for her I will *not*. Happy Christmas, dear."

"Happy Christmas, Liz."

He was unused to anything stronger than beer, and that in small quantities. An occasional half pint in the Copplestone Arms at the end of the road, an occasional pint at the British Legion Club. Now the sweet, rich-tasting wine, tasted and slowly swallowed, ran about inside him, heartening him, dulling his sense of failure; even producing a half resentful thought: She could at least have *pretended*!

Blasphemy!

Then Lorraine came in and he was dumbstruck. Her hair, her beautiful hair, growing so prettily away from her forehead and then rippling down to shoulder length, an inturned bell which swayed when she turned her head and danced when she walked. All gone. What remained looked as though rats had been at it. No two hairs the same length, and a kind of lop-sided fringe.

"My *God*," William said. "What the blue blazes have you let that jealous bitch do to you now?"

"It's the very latest. Straight from Paris. Mrs Copeland went over there to a sort of exhibition and had hers done; then she did Queenie's and Queenie did me – as a Christmas present."

"I could have made a better job with the garden shears! Christmas present be damned! I've known all along but you were so simple . . . That Queenie is so blamed ugly herself she's set on making you worse. And my God, she's done it this time!" William remembered other times. He hadn't minded when Lorraine took to using a pretty rose-coloured lipstick and matching nail varnish: but he had hated the change which Queenie had brought about then, a whitish-mauve, a sort of dead colour, like frostbite. Nor had he approved of the heavy eye make-up. But such things were minor, just fads. This was real, permanent damage.

Liz said – after all it *was* Christmas, "Maybe it won't take so much washing and setting."

She spoke not only with tact but with feeling, for when, just after the war, the Hillchester Town Council had built these houses – every street named for some Mayor – they had cut costs by putting the lavatory and the bath and the wash basin together in one small compartment. This could be awkward at times, especially with somebody so utterly selfish as Lorraine who had her hair washed and set about once a month by Queenie, but washed it and set it herself at least once, sometimes twice a week.

"I don't reckon that fashion'll last long. Too goddamned ugly," William said.

Liz said, "I'm ready to dish up now."

It was a good meal, a proper Christmas dinner, well-cooked. But nobody enjoyed it much. Every time William looked at Lorraine his eye was affronted. She'd had such pretty hair!

Hardy's Christmas was bound to be gloomy from the haunting sense of failure, and his mood was not improved by Terry O'Brien's rather heavy-handed humour. "How about Alcoholics Anonymous, George?"

Hardy stared blankly. He had very little memory of the night of Gloria Woodford's rape, once her statement had been taken. He had no clear recollection of how he had got to bed. The combination of whisky, aspirin and Amy Saunders' brew had induced sound, dreamless sleep and he had wakened in the morning, feeling as Uncle Tom had promised, as right as a trivet but with a gap in his memory.

"I observe," Terry said, "that the latest gossip has not reached you. Well, as they say, the husband is always the last to know!''

Was Terry, with excessive bad taste, referring to the marriage, broken twelve years ago? (Julia had been characteristically gallant about it. She said, ''Even if you wanted to play the little gentleman and take the blame, I shouldn't let you. It would do you no good in your profession and an extra black mark against my name can't hurt me.'')

''What the hell are you talking about?''

''The tale started by that old bitch, Gloria Woodford. She told everybody you were too drunk to stand and the woman policeman had to carry you out.'' Just for a second the lurking malice in Terry's grin stood forward, naked and unashamed. ''Naturally, I forbade anybody to repeat the slander.''

''The best way of spreading it,'' Hardy said harshly. He thought glumly, *s'excuser est s'accuser*, but, dismissing this grain of wisdom, he said, ''I was *not* drunk. I'd had a little whisky, a lot of aspirin, and one of Amy Saunders' curious brews. It knocked me out cold. That I will admit. But I was *not* intoxicated.''

A constable came in and gave Hardy a letter. ''For you, sir. Delivered by hand.''

''I'll leave you to your fan-mail,'' O'Brien said. ''I'm off for the rest of the day. Have a nice Christmas – and take a little more water with it.''

Hardy thought bitterly of the eagerness with which the anti-Hardy section of the public would pounce upon the rumour, saying no wonder the mass rapist has got away with it since the officer investigating the case is a drunk! He opened the letter rather gingerly, expecting to find another anonymous, abusive letter, perhaps even mentioning this latest canard. The letter, however, was written on good headed paper; The Old Manor, Hickford. He turned the sheet over and saw that it was signed; Blanch Newton. He turned it again and read.

I am not a professional medium, but occasionally I fall into the state known as a trance. And lately, like most people in

141

the area, I have been thinking about the man responsible for these terrible crimes. Twice I have seen him very clearly. He is tall, slim but muscular and young-looking for his actual age. All this – as you are probably thinking now – I could have learned from the papers. But be patient with me. I know more about him than the papers have told. He has children, I think three. I see trees in his background; he lives in a very suburban house and when there is a model father and husband. Outside the ambience of his home he exudes evil, for which he is not entirely responsible. In bright sunlight he received an injury to his head. I have tried, so far in vain, to ascertain his name. If I ever do so, I will inform you immediately.

As usual at any awkward times, Sergeant Saunders was standing in, and as usual, he knew all the answers.

"Mad as a hatter," he said. "Lives on brown rice and raw cabbage. Still, there's no denying – long before your time, sir – Lady Hammersmith, not the present one, the old one, lost a very valuable ring. There was no end of a commotion, but Miss Newton said she'd *seen* it in the yard behind Hammersmith House. And believe me, we'd gone over it with a toothcomb. But found there it was. Socking great emerald, big as a postage stamp!"

"Well, all very interesting, but not any real help Tom. A suburban background and a happy family. It could apply to scores of men."

"Injury to the head," Saunders said meditatively. "In bright sunshine. That could mean summer. The hospital might know. They keep records."

"It's not much of a lead, but I'll try."

"There's just another little thing," Tom Saunders said, looking for once not in complete control of the situation. "That dose of Amy's . . . Meant for people taking to bed. You didn't. You went to see that old hag and she's been saying some very nasty things."

"I know. I was so soddenly drunk that WPC Girdlestone

142

had to carry me out . . .''

"Well, I've got an answer to that, inside the Force of course. I got Amy to make up a gallon of the same brew. And anybody says you were drunk, sir, I say, take a glass of this, and see how *you* feel. So far no takers."

Hardy found himself disproportionately, even absurdly touched by this concern for his well-being: but all he managed was a gruff, "Thanks Tom". Then he steered his mind in the direction Tom had indicated, and recoiled from the immensity of the work involved. In bright sunshine did not necessarily mean a day in summer; there were occasional bright sunny days in mid-winter. Nor did it necessarily mean in England – the man could have been holidaying somewhere abroad. And certainly hospitals kept records, but how many hospitals were there in England? And how far back must all their records be searched? It was an impossible task, and all to be undertaken on a suggestion made by somebody whom Saunders called mad as a hatter! And if the head injury, sustained somewhere, at some time, in some sunny place, were responsible for the man's atrocious acts, why had it not equally affected his family life in his suburban home?

What kind of head injury could result in a man being a model husband and father in one place and in another behaving rather worse than a wild beast?

Within himself, Hardy rejected the letter as a possible lead, but in deference to Saunders' suggestion, made what was merely a token move; a contact with the big new hospital, deliberately narrowing the ground to the summer months immediately preceding the first recorded rape . . .

With rather terrifying efficiency the hospital supplied him with information; all useless. A boy of six had fallen off a hay wagon and been mildly concussed: two women had suffered head injuries in a car crash; an old man at Sunset House had fallen downstairs and suffered a scalp wound; a boy of eleven had been hit on the head by a cricket ball; a toddler had fallen from the swing in the Castle Gardens; a young man of twenty-four – something in Hardy sprang to attention – had had an accident with his motor-cycle and had died without regaining consciousness.

And really, Hardy demanded of himself, what more could be expected of such a lead? He admitted to himself, though with the utmost reluctance, that the one hope was that the man would attack again, somewhere a woman, frightened, but not hurt, would scream and help be instantly forthcoming. So far the man had been singularly lucky, or cunning. At the Old Vic there'd been a party and Commander Lucas's T.V. in action. At the Nurses' Hostel there'd been a party in progress, with Grace Robbins' room at the extreme opposite end of the house. And down in the Sheepgate, congested as the houses were, nobody would be likely to investigate any noise coming from the house of the local whore. And if Mrs Noble – and despite everything Hardy held to his suspicion that she had been raped, not burgled – if she had been a victim, she could have screamed her head off and alerted nobody, the house was so isolated. Careful planning or sheer good luck? The luck of the Devil, Hardy thought, not for the first time and a phrase from the self-appointed medium's letter rang like a bell in his mind. *He exudes evil.*

A cold finger traced its way from the nape of Hardy's neck to between his shoulder-blades.

Six o'clock on Christmas evening, and for some reason a sad time Mary Anderson thought, as she began to clear up. In the corner of the living room the Christmas tree, of necessity small, still blazed bravely with the lights which Greg had rigged up but it was now denuded of presents, the little so-called "tree presents," and some of its silver foil glitter had been shed. Anyway, nobody brought up on Hans Andersen could avoid a slight melancholy in the presence of a Christmas tree. She could comfort herself with the thought that old Miss Southey, though grumpy as usual, had eaten well, that the turkey and the pudding had both been as good as they could be. The old gloom-monger had gone now, driven home by

Greg, taking with her a portion of scarcely cold turkey and a great wedge of Christmas cake. Jimmy was at the Sullivans' working the new additions to the train set; Anna and Emma were ready for bed. They were actually on the stairs when the telephone rang and Mary turned back to answer it.

"Mary, *dear*. Happy Christmas! I wanted to come round yesterday *and* this morning, but I've been *incredibly* clobbered. People in and out ... But I'm free now, for about an hour. Could I possibly *dash* over and wish you what are called the compliments of the season?"

"Of course, if ... Lilah, if you are fit to drive." Mary recognised, in the over-emphasis, a sign that Lilah was not drunk exactly, but slightly inebriated.

"I'm drunk," Lilah said, "but on a headier wine than comes in bottles. Wait till you hear."

Greg had said that if Mary didn't mind, he'd look in on the Sullivans and see the railway: and Mary had said, "It's true. All men are little boys at heart. I bet Ricky and Jimmy have hardly touched the thing all day." Now she was glad of Greg's absence for although he was always scrupulously polite, even amiable, towards Lilah, he didn't like her and it showed, and possibly the feeling was mutual for Lilah was never quite herself in his presence.

Mary finished tidying the living room and set a tray with the bottles, which reflected the new affluence. In the past they'd managed a bottle of sherry and hoarded it thriftily; now there was gin, and whisky, and vermouth.

Lilah arrived, very slim and elegant in a long, severely expensive dinner dress of black lace and a mink coat. They had not met for some time but their friendship was of the kind that could be resumed with ease however long the interval since their last meeting, so Mary was surprised to see that for once Lilah was not at ease; she kept moving about, examining the little Christmas tree, and then the cards on the mantelpiece. Her speech was still over-emphatic and a trifle jerky, but she was not drunk, she seemed rather to be labouring under some kind of excitement. Finally she turned from the cards and said, "I wanted you to be the first to know. Mary, I'm pregnant!"

"Are you sure?"

"*Positive*. There's some sort of test they can do. And yesterday, dear old Doctor Brunning said it was certain."

"Darling, how wonderful! I couldn't be happier for you. When?"

"Some time in August. I was due about two days after I was – burgled. I missed out, but I thought probably shock . . . Then again this month. So then . . ."

She sat down suddenly and lit a cigarette with an unsteady hand. Actually she had been pretty sure after the first miss and had lived with her dilemma for more than a month. Her first impulse had been to get rid of it. There were still places where money spoke – and loudly; you went in for a check up. Ten days and there you were as good as new.

Two things had deterred her; she could be ninety-nine per cent certain that Chris was not the father, but not a hundred per cent, for although they no longer shared a bed or a room, they had not ceased to have intercourse, less and less frequently, but often enough to account for her condition. And all the people consulted during the early years of their marriage had said that they were both normal. The other thing to be considered was that although this child might be the child of a rapist, a violent, cruel, possibly demented man, it would be her child too, and no young thing inherited all the characteristics of one parent. And surely environment and upbringing counted for something.

"How delighted Chris will be," Mary said.

"He most certainly will. Actually I feel a bit ridiculous. I'm thirty-seven. A bit elderly, don't you think?"

"No, I do not. You're in splendid physical shape."

And so was the man, Lilah thought; tall, muscular, agile.

"Well, Mary darling, telling you has really been like trying it out on the dog. And at least you didn't think I was raving . . . I'll tell Chris tonight. We're dining with the Hudson-Smiths. Hence all this splendour." She stood up and shrugged her way into the mink coat. "I find this keeping-up-with-the Jones a bit of a strain." She indicated the three parcels, wrapped in hollied paper that she had dropped on a chair near the door. "Just some bits of nonsense for The Young."

"And just think, this time next year . . ."

"I think of it constantly."

That night when she and Greg were alone by the dying fire, Mary said, "Lilah just looked in this evening. She had some wonderful news. After all this time she is going to have a baby!"

He seemed to be slow to comprehend and when he did his face darkened.

"Old Chris will be beside himself with joy! Well, as it says in the Bible; To him who hath shall be given." There was a jeering, unpleasant note in his voice and Mary thought she understood. In one department of life Greg had hitherto been able to feel superior to Chris Noble; now his one advantage – happy fatherhood – was to be wiped out.

Case Six: Lorraine Selsey

Much as she resented what she called Dad's old-fashioned fussiness, Lorraine had not objected to catching the four o'clock bus. It shortened the working day *and* it annoyed Mrs Fullerton for whom she entertained a feeling as near hatred as her torpid nature would allow. She was quite prepared to catch the four o'clock bus for ever; but William, over the years, had built up great reservoirs of good will, and naturally when the rape and the terror were being discussed, he had explained his own particular problem. On the Tuesday after Christmas, with the world creaking back to work, one of his customers had a solution to suggest.

"I gotta niece live up your way," an old woman said. "And she do cleaning, offices and such, from five to seven. I talked to her over Christmas and she said she could give your girl a lift home any time. She got a little car and it needn't take her an inch out of her way."

"That would be wonderful," William said. "Starting when?"

"Today, if you like. I'll give Lil a tinkle."

William stopped at the next call box and rang the Music Centre. Had Lorraine been an ordinary, lively kind of girl she would have reached the phone first, she was actually nearest to it. Then she would have suppressed this unwelcome piece of information. As it was, Mrs Fullerton took the call and her impatient expression changed to pleasure.

"Oh," she said. "That is excellent! We are rather busy just now. Thanks for letting me know."

Replacing the receiver and turning to Lorraine, she said, "That was your father. He's found somebody who will drive you home. She'll pick you up here at seven." She saw, not without a certain malice Lorraine's always rather sulky expression deepen.

The Music Centre was very busy, partly because so many people had received Gift Tokens for Christmas and were busy choosing records; and also because an incredible number of people wanted to familiarise themselves with the rhythmless, tuneless yet hypnotic noise produced by a group known as The Rogues.

For this Mr Quantrill, who ran the Disco, was responsible. Mr Quantrill knew his business. He made nothing of Christmas, a family festival, but concentrated upon New Year's Eve. So he'd hired The Rogues to make a personal appearance at the Disco and he had advertised them well. For a group not yet at the top, but up and coming, their charge was exorbitant – more than the Roaring Twenties could recoup in a single evening, however packed the long sub-basement room might be – but he counted upon gaining new customers, or as he put it, hooking more suckers.

During her lunch-hour that Tuesday, Lorraine carried back to Annette's the pure wool, mistily blue twin-set and received in exchange the garment of her choice. It was a kind of rug with a hole and a six inch zip in the centre. It was violently coloured, red, purple, grass green, pink and bright tan, woven in zig-zag stripes. It was heavily fringed all round. Absolutely right.

That transaction successfully concluded, she began seriously to consider Saturday; how could she make certain of attending the Disco without upsetting Dad. It was still only Tuesday, but when – without asking permission, Mrs Fullerton observed resentfully – she rang up the two taxi firms it was only to be told that they were booked solid. New Year's Eve was always a busy time, but this year, with

Hillchester still in the grip of the terror, each of the firms could have used half a dozen more men, half a dozen more vehicles.

Half-way through that afternoon a most remarkable change came over Lorraine. Mrs Fullerton noticed it with surprise. Ready and willing, lively, anxious to please. And the end of it something so sad, so absolutely immature that it left Mrs Fullerton with the curious feeling that her skin didn't fit. The wretched girl said, "I wonder, Mrs Fullerton, would you let me sleep here on Saturday night? You see, I absolutely must go to the Disco and Dad'd be quite happy about it if I slept here."

Months, Mrs Fullerton thought, of doing the least possible. Day after day coming from the bus stop straight past the shops, and never once an offer to bring in so much as a loaf of bread! Now the chance to be avenged. Unworthy, Oh God, how despicable of me, but I'm only human!

And apart from any personal feeling, the girl would have to have a key, and let herself in at midnight, so the door couldn't be bolted.

"No," Mrs Fullerton said. "It is quite impossible."

Lorraine who for so long, all through her formative years, had been given her own way – there was a little family legend that once, seeing a new moon in the sky she had said, "Baby wants 'nana," and had been given a banana – said, "But why? You've got two rooms, never used."

"So it may seem to you. But as it happens both my husband and I are expecting guests. Relatives."

And God forgive me, Mrs Fullerton thought; please God count it a white lie! Both Eric and I have relatives – but since his health failed and I took to shopkeeping, they just don't want to know.

After that Lorraine tried Queenie. "Queenie you know so many people. Wouldn't anybody let me doss down on the floor? I've got a sleeping-bag."

"I'll ask around. Not much hope though." She hadn't much patience with Lorraine who always wanted everything *done* for her, dim, wet thing without guts enough to stand up to

150

her father, even though she was earning her own living. Queenie's enquiries were casual in the extreme and produced only negative results. Forced into taking vigorous action on her own behalf, Lorraine tried the two bed-and-breakfast places and finally both the hotels. Not a bed to spare anywhere, for Mr Quantrill was not the only one preparing to usher in the New Year in style. There was a dinner-dance at the White Horse; a Meet-Your-Member-over-sausages-and-beer at the Constitutional Club and various minor events.

William Selsey had seen the posters advertising the visit of The Rogues; some bore blown up photographs of the four boys, looking, in his opinion, perfectly horrible; two had so much hair that they seemed to be peeping out from a tumble-down bird's nest and two looked to have no hair at all. Their clothes looked as though they had been stolen from scarecrows and all four wore deliberately ferocious expressions. William was glad that his honey had never once mentioned the Disco and the only interest she had shown in The Rogues was to play, over and over again, one of their records.

The fond father thought that Lorraine had simply been going through a phase and thought that on the whole he had managed things rather well. Twice, since the terror started, he had managed to book a taxi to bring her home, and then during the Christmas lull, he'd taken trouble to provide alternative entertainment for her. He'd taken her – and Liz, of course – to the British Legion Club, which being a club could discreetly ignore the not-under-eighteen rule, and Lorraine had drunk a glass of sweet brown sherry which she seemed to enjoy, though she said of the club that it was a bit like a museum, stuffed with mummies. Defending it, William said, "Well, honey, we can't all be young forever. And the Hitler War as we call it, is as far away from the young today as the Boer War was when we was young."

The club having been thus scornfully dismissed, William suggested a drink at the Copplestone Arms, just at the end of the road. Liz excused herself; she hated to see Bill try, and be defeated. "I'll just nip next door," she said, "and give the poor old dear a bit of help with her knitting." The poor old dear was a neighbour, and she had a name; Mrs Brooks, and she was not one of those pitiable old women who had outlived everybody; she had a son and a grandson who lived with her and maintained a roughish kind of comfort. Mrs Brooks was only partially sighted, but she could knit, and knit she did, squares of varying colour and varying substance which, when joined together, would make a blanket which some well-meaning organisation would send overseas, to warm the bones of some old person, living where the temperature at night dropped to about eighty degrees Fahrenheit, the heat of a hot summer day in Hillchester.

Cast on twenty-four stitches, knit twenty-four lines and you should have a square, but if the yarn supplied happened to be thin, Liz would say, "No dear. This ain't square. I'll pull it out for you and maybe you could make a baby's vest . . . Or something."

With Liz so happily and usefully engaged, William – limping slightly – took Lorraine to the pub, ordered one Coke, one brown sherry and then adroitly switched glasses. One or two old customers greeted him and he said, "Hullo," and introduced his daughter, feeling, rather sadly, that with the chewed-off hair-do and what she called a poncho – hideous thing! – she was less of a credit to him than she would have been a few weeks earlier. Even in the past when wages were lower and the boys both at home, Lorraine had been a conspicuously well-dressed child. William had always been willing to do a bit of overtime in order to provide pretty things for her, now she seemed to be deliberately making herself unpretty; or perhaps that was only his fancy, for the men appeared to see nothing wrong with her, addressed her civilly, if a trifle shyly and for their pains got treated to a fine display of indifference. No smiles; just bored, monosyllabic answers to direct questions. William's mind threw up a disloyal thought; If she's like this to people her own age . . . But his heart sprang to the defence. Poor child, of course she *is* bored, surrounded by us old fogies. "Shall we be moving, honey?"

She got up with unflattering alacrity. That little outing had been a failure, too.

Outside the night was cold, with a brisk wind which fluttered the fringes and lifted the edges of the ugly garment. William said, "You'll never convince me that that thing is as warm as your quilted coat."

"Oh Dad! That's the third time you've said that!"

Her voice was sharp with exasperation. Patience tried to the limit!

"That don't make it any the less true," he said and after that they walked home in silence. He really must remember, he thought, to refrain from criticism. It did no good, it altered nothing and simply poisoned the one relationship which he valued.

On Saturday, New Year's Eve, the Music Centre was extremely busy. A fair proportion of the customers hoped to take The Rogues' latest recording and have the sleeve of it autographed. Punctually at seven o'clock, Lil, that Good Samaritan, stopped outside the shop and hooted imperatively, and moving more briskly than she had done all day, Lorraine took her departure. Her going made no *real* difference, Mrs Fullerton assured herself, but it left her feeling abandoned, and if Eric – suffering another fibrillation attack – should ring his bell...Rather furtively, and ashamed of seeming so – for after all was this not her own place, a business built up from nothing? – Mrs Fullerton locked the door of the back room where organs and radiograms and guitars were stored. In the shop itself she began snapping off lights, indicating that she was about to close down. Slowly the shop emptied; and there was the usual chaos left behind. Let it wait till morning, Mrs Fullerton said to herself as she went upstairs to make one of the tasty little meals which Eric, even when feeling poorly, never failed to enjoy. And wasn't luck an odd thing? Up at St Ethelreda's the Headmistress, whom Mrs Fullerton knew slightly, had advertised just once for a secretary and chosen the first applicant, a young ex-policewoman who was good at all secretarial work, able to drive and to service a car, keen on all games, and happy in her spare time to act as second gym mistress. Mrs Fullerton's own repeated advertisements had brought her Lorraine Selsey! Life was bloody unfair. And that, she said to herself, is far from being an original observation!

Lil drew up outside Lorraine's home. This was the fifth evening they had ridden together and so far they had established no kind of relationship whatsoever. Lil was a garrulous woman, full of tales about those who employed her before and after office hours and the highly interesting things they occasionally flung into the waste-paper baskets. But even the most ardent gossip needed some response from her audience and Lorraine had made it plain from the word go that nothing Lil said, or could ever say was worth a second's attention. She did not show even basic gratitude. Lorraine was in fact not grateful. She'd preferred catching the four o'clock bus.

This evening, however, instead of getting out and saying, "Thanks. Good night" before slamming the car door with unnecessary force, she sat still, opened her handbag and brought out a pound note. "I want you to have this. For the extra petrol." (Actually that had been William's idea and he had provided the money.)

Lil did not pounce upon it; she said, "Really, there's no need. I hardly use a drop more."

"But you *do*," Lorraine said earnestly. She repeated what Dad had said. "You have to come right round the Market Square, and in at the top of this road instead of the bottom."

"That's so," Lil agreed, "But a pound's too much. Say 50p."

"Call it two weeks then."

"All right. Thanks." But even when the money had changed hands, the girl did not move. After a perceptible pause she said, "I've been wondering. If I paid, *properly*, would you drive in and fetch me from the Disco tonight?"

"No way! I'm off to a party myself. My sister up at

154

Retford. Family do. Fifteen of us . . ."

Lorraine wasn't listening. She jumped out of the car and slammed the door even more violently than usual.

She made a great effort to appear normal at supper. Normal, but terribly tired.

"Eat up," Liz said. "I thought you liked macaroni cheese. I made it specially for you."

"Actually, Mum, I'm too tired to be hungry. We've had a most hectic day."

"How about a drink, then? That'll revive you. I got it to see the New Year in with." William went and fetched the new bottle of Cyprian sherry and Liz produced three glasses.

Lorraine revived sufficiently to say quite amiably, "Well, Happy New Year, Mum, Dad. I can't wait up. I shall just wash my hair and have an early night. Anybody want the bathroom?" Both took advantage of this offer for even with so little hair to be washed, the ceremony took a good hour.

Back by the fire, William said, for quite the twentieth time – but then Liz, unlike Lorraine, did not chide him for repetition – "If only she'd got the job I earmarked for her, down at the office. Nine to five and sitting down all the time."

It was indeed an unexacting job, book-keeping mostly but it demanded an ability to add, and it had gone to a clever Asian girl, always known as Miss Lali because her surname was completely unpronounceable. She lived in Quarry Lane and even before the terror struck Hillchester, had always been escorted to and from work. Her escorts varied and included a boy of about twelve, very skinny and armed with an old cricket bat.

The office in the yard of Farmhouse Dairies was glassed in, rather overheated, and now and then, seeing the sari-clad figure, the sleek black head bent over the books, William Selsey had thought – a thought instantly banished, but nevertheless *thought* – *Is this what I fought for?*

Lorraine ran enough water to prove that she was washing her hair, then she pulled the lavatory chain and while the rush and roar of it filled the little house, stole out, very quietly and ran to the corner where Fallowfield Road joined the Common; she might, if lucky, catch the last bus there. But if she were too late, she wouldn't worry, for street-lighting had recently been installed so that the road across the Common was now as well-lit perhaps even better lit than the Market Square.

And in any case the rapist had never yet attacked in the open. Lorraine felt no fear.

This proclivity of the Hillchester Terror for attacking women indoors, in their own habitat, had been noticed by other people. At the upper end of the Long Bar, Mr Sims, tired of ferrying his wife, her friends and his relatives back and forth, had said irritably, "I keep telling Ada – and everybody else – that mad as he undoubtedly is, the fellow works to a kind of *pattern*."

"Modus operandi," the schoolmaster said.

"Exactly," said Mr Sims without quite knowing what he was agreeing to. "It's almost as though he *courts* danger. Twice in places simply crawling with young men, and even Old Glory could have had a man with her, or one due any minute."

"Unless he'd made a date with her," Colonel Soames said.

"Possible, of course. The point is, as I tell Ada – and she's too scared to let the dog out after dark – the blasted man has never yet done the obvious thing which is pick up some stray female and rape her on Goose Green or some other isolated spot."

The talk then drifted away; to Old Glory's accusing Hardy of being too drunk to stand. The Colonel pooh-poohed that, seeing in a Detective Chief Inspector something akin to, if not of, the officer class.

Then there was the amusing fact – and it amused young Simon Hooper as much as anyone else – that Mrs Woodford had said that her assailant had sounded like him.

Hardy had taken note of that fact and of the coincidence of young Hooper having been one of the party in the penthouse at the Old Vic and also one of the party at the Nurses' Hostel. But that horse wouldn't trot! The blood groups did not conform and young Hooper, when Gloria was raped, had been in London, eating one of those ritual dinners necessary to an aspiring lawyer.

Bright New Year

Matt Waterson placed the early-morning tea tray on the bedside table and poured two cups. He did not say good morning, or wakey-wakey, or even Bright New Year, because he was sulking and he had learned over the years that a stern, sulky silence, combined with meticulous service was the best way of bringing Georgie to heel.

Georgie stretched and yawned, and said, "Thanks, darling. What sort of morning?" He had learned over the years that a breezy insouciance was the best way of bringing Matt to heel.

"I don't know. I haven't looked." The penthouse had its own independent method of central heating and all its curtains were lined and interlined. Whatever the outside temperature, inside it was warm.

They drank two cups of tea and smoked a cigarette apiece, then Georgie, just to show that he could be independent of Matt, got out of bed and jerked the thick silken rope which controlled the curtains.

All the main windows of the penthouse overlooked St Luke's graveyard and when Georgie contemplated taking the place and fashioning it to his own comfort, somebody had asked wouldn't he find the view depressing? He said, "No. The graves are so *old*. Nobody has been buried there since 1896. Besides, in the eighteenth century, men who knew how to savour life to the full kept skulls on their library tables. I shall need no skull.''

This morning, narrowing his eyes against the glare of the sun rising over a world all heavily and whitely frosted, like an iced cake, Georgie saw something wrong with the Copplestone tomb, a massive stone edifice surrounded by iron railings. He had no objection to gravestones as a reminder that life was fleeting and should be enjoyed to the full, but if people were going to deposit rubbish . . . It looked like rubbish; a heap.

He said, ''Matt!'' but Matt was already back in the kitchen, making the breakfast which Georgie preferred above all others, the bacon grilled to a crisp and the eggs poached. So Georgie padded, barefoot, to one of his cupboards and took down his binoculars – last used at the Hickford point-to-point. He was a little older than he cared to admit and his sight was shortening, but after a few seconds he had the glasses focused and then he called, in a voice which Matt, even in his sulkiest mood, dared not ignore.

''Look at that!''

Matt looked, fiddled with the glasses and looked again.

''I think it's a girl . . . And dead. She must be. Frozen stiff . . . Ought we . . .?''

Georgie assumed the control which he had always exercised over his minions, not merely because he was rich and senior. He was quicker-witted. He now pulled the cord which jerked the heavy curtains together. He said, ''There was all that hoo-ha about Becky Dalton. This will be worse. Such a *bloody* bore! Let's know nothing; gobble our breakfast and get out to Leo's.''

It was over this invitation to lunch at Leo Attleborough's which had evoked the overnight quarrel. But that was forgotten now. Georgie might keep his head and plan a sensible, callous course of action; Matt simply felt sick.

One other window at the Old Vic overlooked the graveyard and the Copplestone tomb, and that was the window of the bathroom which was shared. The new tenant was singularly easy to share with for he was a nephew of Mrs Peacock and used her far more luxurious and warmer bathroom. Mrs Peacock's housekeeper took care of his laundry, so Lorna had the linen line suspended over the bath all to herself. Mrs Peacock's nephew used the communal bathroom for one necessary visit each morning; and that visit had already been made – Commander Lucas had heard the chain pulled.

The curtains in this bathroom were flimsy and even when drawn admitted enough light on such a bright morning as to shame a low-wattage bulb, so the Commander walked across and drew them back. A beautiful morning, he thought and then stared. His sight was still keen so that he could take in at one glance the full horror of the scene. ''Good God!'' he exclaimed aloud, and drew the curtains close. Within him the good citizen fought a brief, fierce and losing battle with the good husband. Poor Lorna had behaved so well on the night of the Dalton disaster but she'd suffered a sharp reaction, gone off her food, slept badly and jumped at the least sound. He'd spare her as much as he could of this new tragedy. The girl, whoever she was, was dead, nothing could help her now, poor thing.

He looked about for some kind of fastening and saw the clip-on clothes pegs on the line over the bath. He took two and pinned the curtains firmly. Then he hobbled into his flat and forcing himself to sound casual, said, ''Oh, by the way, dear, the bathroom is bitterly cold. The curtains aren't very substantial, but they provide a degree of shelter. Leave them closed.'' The thought of questioning an order or even seeking a reason for it would never occur to a well-trained naval wife.

It was, as Commander Lucas had remarked bitterly cold, and St Luke's Church at the nine o'clock early service was frigid. The heating system was obsolete and utterly undependable. There was a coke-fired boiler in the crypt and warmed air from hot pipes was supposed to rise through iron gratings in the floor. After the service, Mr Lummis went and stood on one grating and it was as cold as the surrounding stone. He

160

looked around for Pawsey, the old man who in these days of labour shortage combined the office of verger with that of handyman. He was nowhere to be seen – but then he never was when he was wanted! Mr Lummis must go round to the side of the church and down the steps and deal with the boiler himself. He proceeded, rather angrily, to do so.

St Luke's had been affected by the terror. Evensong at six o'clock in ordinary times had been attended mainly by elderly women and a not inconsiderable sprinkling of girls, going through the adolescent religious phase or imagining themselves in love with the organist, a handsome young man who gave private music lessons. This congregation had suddenly disappeared. So Mr Lummis had moved Evensong forward to three o'clock, with satisfactory results.

Descending the steps – and going carefully, for they were frosted, he had his back to the Copplestone tomb. He found the boiler just alight, but clogged with clinker. He raked and was rewarded by a soft roar. By eleven o'clock the church would be tolerably warm and by mid-afternoon quite hot. And really, he must have a word with Pawsey!

Mounting the stairs and thinking about his belated breakfast, he faced the Copplestone tombstone and noticed something odd. His first thought matched Georgie Turner's; somebody had deposited a bundle of rubbish! For really what people thought could be dumped these days in a disused, but still hallowed burying place was quite unbelievable: skeleton bicycles, one-wheeled push-chairs, once, even, an antiquated gas cooker!

Then he saw, and was appalled. He tore off his surplice and tossed it – for the out-curved rails prevented a close, or more decorous approach – over the body. It fell as directed, hiding the worst and holding his black shirt knee-high, he ran to his home and the telephone. He had lost all appetite for his breakfast.

This was what Hardy had dreaded, half expected, and felt himself responsible for, in that he had failed to find and arrest

161

the dangerous man. My fault, my most grievous fault! But what more could I have done? What did I miss, that could have prevented this?

The dead girl seemed to have no identity. Under her head, with a kind of dreadful mockery of consideration, was a folded kind of cloak such as ten girls out of twelve wore nowadays. Across her feet lay the ripped remnants of a pair of jeans, the pockets intact; one contained a pound note and a little loose change, the other a handkerchief and what looked like half a ticket, roughly torn. It could have been a raffle ticket; it was numbered 104.

She had been raped and she had been ripped – but differently from the others, from just below the ear to the collar bone, her jugular vein severed. Yet on and around the Copplestone tomb there was hardly any blood.

They could time, with some exactitude, if not the murder, the placing of the body in position, for the folds of cloth on either side of her head, and the torn jeans over her feet were frosted with white, and the weather station at Waddington had supplied the information that hard frost had set in at one o'clock in the morning.

Hard frost checked bleeding. Hard frost hastened, or blurred, the effect of *rigor mortis*.

Not that it really mattered when or where the poor girl had been killed; nor would her name, when they knew it, make much difference; the fiend had struck again, leaving his mark all too plainly – and they were as far from knowing his identity as they had been back in September.

The habit of early rising was not easily shaken off, so although William Selsey no longer set his alarm-clock on Saturday nights, he woke at five, turned over, dozed, woke, grew restless, wanted to be up and doing, wanted a cup of tea. He dressed himself quietly and stole down and made what he called a brew up, two tea-bags and the pot left to stand for exactly five minutes to extract the maximum flavour. On his round he was offered innumerable cups of tea but seldom a satisfactory one, either too wishy-washy or stewed. He drank with relish, and thus fortified, set about the job he had assigned himself for Sunday; New Year's Day.

This was to paint the little hall. Helped by Liz he had cleared it overnight, moving the hall-stand and the painted pedestal which upheld a flourishing aspidistra, into the front room.

Liz had scored over the aspidistra; for some unknown reason the innocent plant had become a joke and most people had tipped theirs out, but Liz had stuck to hers because her Gran had given it to her, and now people were cadging cuttings because the plant was fashionable again and to buy one cost one pound a leaf.

He painted diligently, applying the colour which Liz had chosen after much deliberation and vacillation; it was called Marshmallow and was a kind of pink. He'd almost finished one wall when Liz came down, studied his work critically and said, ''It's paler than I expected. Maybe we should have gone for Blush Rose. Never mind; it'll look nice and fresh.'' She went into the kitchen and presently called him to enjoy the one proper hot breakfast of the week.

After that he worked on and by about mid-day had finished the walls, but not quite all the paint. So he called her. ''Liz, how about my giving that stand the brush-over? It'll look pretty grubby against this fresh wall.''

''Lovely idea,'' she said. And just for a second it occurred to him to wonder why Liz, so easily pleased, so appreciative, should rank lower in his esteem than Lorraine whom nothing pleased. That was the kind of thing about which there was no understanding, so it was silly to fret over.

Presently, his work done, he went up to wash and shave, no longer bothering to move silently. He actually wanted Lorraine to wake up, and come out and show herself, rested and restored by the long night's sleep.

From the foot of the stairs Liz called, ''Bill, give her a rap! I shall be dishing up in five minutes.''

He rapped, he called, and receiving no answer, opened the

door. The room was small, but pretty. At some time Lorraine
had expressed a desire for a dressing-table with skirts, he had
bought it and Liz had made the drapery, with frills, blue spots
on white, and presently Liz, not yet too critical of Lorraine,
had made a bedspread and window curtains of the same
material. Now the empty room was tidy; the bed neatly made.

"Liz! She ain't there!"

"Then we know where she is. Up at that Queenie
Palmer's, getting her hair set. You heard her yourself saying
last night she was going to wash it. And now she's up there,
getting it set."

"But when did she *go*? I been in the hall. You been here!"

"Oh don't be so daft! Didn't you come in here and drink a
cup of coffee? She slipped out then. Come on, Bill . . . I'll keep
hers warm in the oven."

"No!" he said. "I gotta *know*!" He repudiated Liz and her
well-cooked dinner and went charging up the road to the
Palmers' house which had both a bell and a knocker. He plied
both with vigour and after a long interval Queenie, puffy-
eyed, in a sleazy dressing-gown opened the door. And even as
William asked the question, he knew the answer.

"Why no, Mr Selsey, what made you think . . .? Last I saw
of Lorraine was at the Disco. Last night."

"The Disco? You sure?"

"Of *course* I'm sure."

"Then where is she now? Where did she *sleep*?"

"How would I know?" Queenie was prepared to shrug a
bored shoulder, but Mr Selsey looked so stricken and she had
a flash of thought; fancy having a father who cared where you
slept, or with whom! She had enjoyed no such paternal care
since she was about ten! She said, rather hesitantly, "I
wouldn't worry, Mr Selsey. Maybe Lorraine talked Mrs
Fullerton into letting her sleep there."

"Mind if I use your phone?"

"Help yourself." Queenie shuddered. "It's cold down
here. I'll leave you."

Even as he dialled, William knew what the answer would

be. To some extent he understood his daughter; *if* she'd managed to cadge a bed from Mrs Fullerton, she'd have said so, bragged about it a bit. One up to her, as it were!

Mrs Fullerton used Queenie's very words. "Why no, Mr Selsey, what made you think . . .?"

"Just a chance thought. Sorry," he said.

He was now thoroughly alarmed. Lorraine had been at the Disco, and she had not come home. So something had happened. Something he'd dreaded. Something awful. He knew it in his bones. It seemed to him, as he hurried back to his own house, that he always *had* known, deep down in his mind. In this tricky world, it just didn't do to set too much value on any one person or thing.

He went in at the side entrance to his house, to the shed where he kept his garden tools and his bike. He rather hoped that Liz would not see him and come out and say he was making a fuss about nothing and suggest that he should eat his dinner. If she did, then he would know what he had really known for years – that he hated his good, amiable, faithful wife.

Liz came out and he snapped at her. "She's missing. Job for the police." Clumsily, as usual, because his lame leg had so little bounce in it, he mounted and pedalled away.

He did not take his usual route. Like Tom Saunders, he knew all the short cuts, and one short cut that he could take to the Police Station, was through St Luke's old churchyard. Not in ordinary times much of a short cut because at the gate in the back wall there was a notice, "No cycling". In his present mood William Selsey was prepared to ignore it and ride straight through. But a uniformed policeman stood there. William recognised him. He wobbled to a stop but did not dismount.

"Don't you go stopping me, Charlie Alston. I'm on my way to the Station. My girl's missing . . ."

"My God, Bill! I do hope . . . I hope with all my heart . . . Not the one up there." He indicated the upper end of the churchyard, where canvas screens had been erected. William rode straight towards it, threw down his bicycle with a clatter and pushed his way in. A uniformed arm tried to bar his entry and William Selsey, that law-abiding citizen, pushed it savagely aside and went up to the slab where the dreadful thing lay.

For half a split second hope danced in his heart. *Not* Lorraine's face. Her sweet, pretty face. Then he saw the ring on the limp, slightly bloodied hand, his present on her last birthday; a black stone with her astrological sign on it in gold. "My girl!" he cried in a terrible voice and dropped as though he'd been felled.

Dr Stamper, acting police surgeon again, said "Lying prone will bring him round." Then he added an unprofessional, "Poor chap!"

Well, now they knew the name of the latest victim. Even Sergeant Saunders who knew everything and everybody, had failed to identify her, though he had recognised the bit of torn green paper with the number on it as half an admission ticket to the Disco. "Mostly they just walk in, if they can get past Old Arthur, but on special occasions – and last night was one – there're tickets."

Hardy was being bombarded with information which he must arrange and correlate. Doctor Stamper said that the girl had been strangled before she was clawed – that word was freely used now. There was some cyanosis about the victim's face, and death before ripping would account for the absence of any great show of blood. "Once the heart ceases to function," he said. But he was also of the opinion that the girl had been violated – his carefully chosen word – before she was strangled. Raped – perhaps screaming, and therefore silenced by the suffocating pressure; then clawed, and brought here and laid out. Exhibition of finished work!

And how that was done was a mystery.

The first Copplestone to go to his final rest here had done so when grave-robbing was rife and all the medical schools avid for corpses, however ill-come by. Around 1829. Thomas Everard Copplestone – "twice Mayor of this Borough" –

buried in that year had been protected from post-mortem disturbance by heavy stone slabs and the out-curving iron rails which now added their little mystification to the general bafflement. The girl's body had not been simply tossed over the rails, that would have been understandable; she had been carefully laid out, the folded garment under her head, the tattered jeans over her feet.

Hardy, no dwarf, and Scene-of-the-Crime officer Parsons, a six-footer, had tried to reach over the railings and succeeded only in touching, with the tips of their fingers the edge of the table tomb. Someone with very long arms . . . Ape-like! For a moment the vision of something not quite human flashed across Hardy's mind. The pathologist's joke about zoological specimens. The recurrent mention of an animal smell . . .

That way madness lies! Get to work!

William Selsey regained consciousness and came back to a world bereft of all colour and light and purpose. He began to heave himself up and somebody lent him a hand. He blundered out and picked up his bike, tried to mount it and for some reason failed. Try again. No good. All right, push the bloody thing – it gave him a kind of support. News had spread and a crowd had gathered in the space between the Old Vic and the church. It was being held at bay by WPC Girdle-stone, very trim and authoritative; "Stand back, please! You there, I said, *back*!" A few venturesome boys had got into the backyard of the Old Vic and were standing on the dustbins in order to stare over the wall.

William pushed his way through. He was not making for home. Home was the last place and Liz the last person he wanted to see now. What he wanted was oblivion and he knew where to find it. In the river.

The river Starling curved around Hillchester like a half-embracing arm. It had played its part in the development of the town, having once been navigable, bringing coal in and taking corn out, but, moving slowly and shallowly and having lost its purpose since the railway came, it had silted up and during William Selsey's lifetime had offered only two places where a man might drown easily; one was called The Butts and one Holywell Pool. The Butts was the better known. There had been three suicides there within William's memory and generations of Hillchester children bent on bathing or swimming in the river were warned; Keep well away from the Butts!

William had never learned to swim and he thought; All I need is to fill my pickets with stones. He began to look about for them. Then he remembered, as clearly as though the voice spoke again, something someone had said as he got to his feet and stumbled out of that enclosure: I'm sorry, Bill. But this time we'll get him!

He stood transfixed, a stone in his hand. This time they'd get him. And then what? His thoughts were similar to those of Alan Douglas. There'd be no *punishment*. Somebody would be paid to stand up and say that the man was mad, that only a madman could have committed such a fearful crime, and they'd take him away to live in luxury for the rest of his days while Lorraine rotted in her cold grave.

"Oh no!" he said aloud. "Not this time!" He dropped the stone he was holding, and emptied his pockets of the three or four he had already gathered. He mounted his bicycle and rode home. To face Liz.

"To be quite honest, Chief Inspector, I don't notice individuals very much," Mr Quantrill said. "I have no time. People may think that a place like this runs itself, but that is far from true. During a session, I'm run off my feet. And the lights are, as you see, dimmed. They like it that way."

In the long, narrow, sub-basement room that was the Disco, all the lights, except those over and around the little platform at the far end, were on now and the light was dim because all the bulbs looked to be coated with thick red paint. What such muted light revealed was desolate indeed; empty cups and glasses, empty crisp bags, over-full ashtrays stood on black-topped tables in front of a black leather bench which

ran around three sides of the room's perimeter. By contrast
the dancing space was clean and shining. Mr Quantrill held
that people came to a Disco to hear music and dance, not for
the scenery or for comfort.

"Still," Mrs Quantrill said helpfully, "not so many girls
come on their own. Arthur may have noticed. *Arthur*!"

The door beside the little platform opened and Poor Old
Arthur shuffled in, betraying by his bleary eyes and shaking
hands that he had been drunk overnight. Hardy did not
regard him as a very likely source of information but he was
wrong.

"Bill Selsey's girl? Christ! Yes, of course I seen her. I was
there, at the door, getting a bit of a breather. The air in here
was thick. I said: Good night, miss. I always did if I noticed
her. I was a bit sorry for her. She always seemed a bit of a
loner. I mean she might come with Queenie Palmer and her
lot, and she did surely enjoy the dancing, sort of tranced if you
know what I mean. She'd dance by herself! She'd sit alone
most times. And go home alone . . ."

"She left alone last night?"

"She surely did. Thass why I said good night. It seemed
kinda sad with everybody else in here shaping up for Auld
Lang Syne."

"Was she followed?"

"Not so far as I could see her."

"And how far was that?"

"Clear up to the Market Arcade."

That would indicate that she had not taken the possible
short-cut, through the churchyard where she had been found.

"You're sure of that?"

"Of course I'm sure. I only drink *off* duty."

"That is correct," Mr Quantrill said as Arthur looked to
him for confirmation.

The whole business of who drank what, and when and
where was one which Mr Quantrill had tied up with his usual
ruthless efficiency. Unlike Tony with his café and his
ambition to turn it into a restaurant, Mr Quantrill had never

applied for a licence and in the Disco itself nothing but coffee and Coke were served, but as yet there was no law that he knew about that forbade him from asking a few friends in for a drink, and the room behind the Disco was well-stocked.

"I can even tell you the time," Poor Old Arthur said with the truculence of the drunk whose sobriety had been questioned. "Four minutes, afore midnight. St Luke's started to strike and I came back in."

(Mr Quantrill remembered, with some disgust, how deceptive in appearance The Rogues were, two of them total abstainers and one a fanatical Sabbath Observer or something. So Auld Lang Syne – that souped up version of it, had to be over before it was officially Sunday morning.)

Hardy visualised the doomed girl's progress.

"There were cars on the Square?"

"Dozens. And motor-bikes. And The Rogues' mini-van with all their gear. But I don't think . . . No, wait, I knew I was forgetting something. I *did* hear a car, just as I come down the steps. It started sorta jerky, and out of Charity Lane."

"An old car?"

"Or battery run down."

That final touch was not necessary to complete the picture. It was the rapist turned murderer – as Hardy had always feared he might.

Miss Marcia Lowe had been accustomed to attending Morning Service, but when the Terror thinned even the earlier-timed Evensong she had changed her habit, feeling that with so tiny a congregation every one counted.

By three o'clock in the afternoon there was nothing to show that anything untoward had occurred in the churchyard, except that the section of railing, removed from the Copplestone tomb in order to give access, had not been replaced, and WPC Girdlestone, seemingly still crisp and fresh, was controlling a small crowd of morbid, would-be sightseers. Curiosity was a vulgar trait, but Miss Lowe possessed her full share of it though she phrased her question discreetly, "Is something wrong, Constable?" Authority always recognised authority. "A girl who had been murdered was found here earlier today, madam."

"Another – victim?"

"We are afraid so. Stand back, there!"

Miss Lowe turned and walked, with speed but still with dignity, away from the church and along Castle Street, to the complex of buildings ranged about an open space which had retained its original name of Castle Meadow. The Public Library, the Borough offices, a health clinic and the Police Station.

"Good afternoon," she said to the Constable behind the counter. "I have something to report."

A lost dog, PC Pryke imagined, judging from her age, dress and bearing. Prepared to note down name, address, time of loss, breed of animal, he was startled when Miss Lowe said, "It may be concerned with the latest murder. I should like to see Detective Chief Inspector Hardy."

"I'm afraid that is impossible, madam. The Inspector is engaged."

Heavily engaged. Rape was rape, even when accompanied by such unusual features as clawing, but murder was murder, a thing of sufficient importance to bring Detective Superintendent Harrison and one of his minions up from Thorington on a Sunday afternoon. "If you would tell me what it is, madam, I'd see that the Chief Inspector . . ."

Miss Lowe gave him a look; he was exceedingly young.

"I think I will wait," she said and moved to the bench provided for people who waited. But almost before she had reached it, three men, all in ordinary clothes, appeared at the top of the stairs. No badges, no sign of rank, except the, not subservience exactly, the decent respect shown to the older, stouter man. The youngest of the trio – and the least worried looking, came last down the stairs, then, skirting the others ran forward and opened the door. "The car is here, sir," he said with as much satisfaction as though he had conjured it from the air.

In the doorway the obviously important man turned, gripped the other by the hand and said, "I wish you luck, George. You know – there is always an element of luck." Down at Thorington, lately, Harrison had had a one tiny stroke of good and then a clobbering of bad. The good was that an angry and rather drunken woman had denounced her husband and said that the police would be interested in a package in the garage. Interesting indeed! Another cache of heroin. Source still unknown and the man denied all knowledge of it; said it had been planted there. And nowadays interrogation was a farce, you practically had to have a medical team in attendance! And the bad, very bad part, was that the complete failure over the Securicor man's murder, had encouraged others to think they could get away with it too. Thorley's Bank had been held up, two cashiers, one man, one woman shot down where they stood, the Manager, emerging from his room, shot in the stomach and unlikely to live.

One had to keep a sense of proportion, Harrison had pointed out to Hardy; armed gunmen were a menace to the whole community; a rapist – even one who also killed – threatened only one section of it. He did not say so but the implication was there – silly little girls out alone at midnight in a town where a rapist was known to be at large, were asking for trouble.

All this, Hardy realised was the excuse – no! Be fair! – the reason why there could be little or no help from Thorington.

Hardy said, "Thank you, sir," and turned back. PC Pryke sprang up from his stool and said, "This lady, sir, has some information."

Nothing really new, but it helped to fill in the picture.

"It's just struck me as *peculiar*," Miss Lowe said. "A car after business hours or at the weekend in Charity Lane is a rarity. Parking, as you know is strictly forbidden there. But last night, just before midnight, I heard a car start – and very badly – in the lane to the south? Yes, south of my cottage. Then, four, perhaps five minutes later, just as St Luke's clock finished striking, I heard the same sound again, but this time to the north, just where Charity Lane runs into Market Square. It started in the same way, a kind of grating cough. I know this may sound very trivial, but I thought at the time, why here at all? And having started with such difficulty, why halt at the mouth of the lane and repeat the performance?''

''Miss Lowe, so far from being trivial, this information may be of the most crucial importance. I am much indebted to you.''

Hardy's imagination, at once such an asset and such a burden, saw it all with singular accuracy. A man looking out of the window of an office, bang opposite the Disco, seeing the girl come out, alone, seeing whether she turned left or right; and then, his old, coughing car in the mouth of Charity Lane, watching which way she went; catching up with her.

The Hunt

As though to compensate for the lack of help from Thorington, Terry O'Brien said, "Have 'em all, George. For the duration. There'll be no more traffic control. And if another poor bloody bullock runs out from the market, they can bloody well shoot it themselves." Shooting a runaway bullock was the latest service demanded of the uniformed branch.

"Thanks. One day, I'll do something for you, Terry. Catch me on an off day and I'll do a bit of traffic control for you."

"I'll take a rain-check on that," Terry said, speaking with a buoyancy that he did not, for once, feel, because George Hardy, for whom he had a genuine affection, looked so bloody awful, so grey all over, skin and hair and with a look in his eyes as though he had heard the banshee calling. And that, like all the other superstitions inherent in his blood and inculcated during his early childhood, Terry pushed aside with impatience.

He did it far more easily than Hardy could dismiss his private fantasy – a frail structure, based on what Poor Old Arthur had said, what Miss Lowe had heard. His tiresome imagination would persist in presenting him with a vision of the killer standing in a darkened office window, watching out for possible prey, spotting it, hurrying to the old, badly-starting car, parked on the hard-standing behind the offices, stopping at the mouth of Charity Lane in order to see which way the girl went . . . And then having the same difficulty in starting again.

"Tom, who has offices, opposite the Disco, with hard-standing for a car in Charity Lane?"

"Turner and Noble. Rogers and Ward . . . No, they've a car-park to the side. And Mr Anderson. *And* he's still driving his old Ford Pilot!"

"D'you know him by sight?"

Wasting no words, Saunders said, "He'd fit, sir."

The only trouble with that neat fit was that Mr Anderson and his aged car had not been in Hillchester at the time when Lorraine Selsey was done to death.

You had to move carefully these days when the overall breakdown of law and order was symbolised by the alienation of the middle-class, good citizens who had exceeded a speed limit, or parked where double yellow lines forbade all parking. There was really no good reason for Hardy to say: "Be a bit casual, Tom."

(And it was stupid, or worse, to think about what the self-styled medium had written about the guilty man being surrounded by trees – and a good family man.)

It was Anna's birthday and Mary had always taken great pains to see that this anniversary, important to a child, should not be overshadowed by Christmas. The tree had been refurbished and a special, be-candled cake produced. The party was in full swing – and very noisy, when the bell rang. Carefully closing the living room door behind her because of the noise, and opening the front door, seeing a policeman, put her hand to her throat and voiced her worst dread. "An accident?"

"Oh, no, no," Tom said using his most avuncular, soothing voice. "Merely a routine check on cars. Could I have a word with Mr Anderson?"

"He isn't here. He went to Broadstairs, yesterday. In the afternoon."

"Taking the car?"

175

"But of course. That is why I was so alarmed at the sight of you. The car is so old. I am always afraid that it might stall at the wrong moment."

Machiavelli, disguised as Tom Saunders, asked, "But he did arrive safely?"

"I can only assume . . . I have not heard."

Tom's gaze went to the telephone on the hall table.

"Would it be as well to make sure?"

The cold hand of fear clutched her heart again.

"Sergeant, are you trying to hide something from me?"

Wretchedly aware of what he was hiding – though only in the way of the vaguest suspicion as yet, Tom repeated his assurance that he was merely making a check on cars, but he was mentally willing her towards the telephone. And he invited himself in. "I'll just step inside and close the door. It's a freezing wind again." For a moment he found himself wishing with all his heart that the husband of this nice little woman – and his aged car – *were* in Broadstairs. But that was an unprofessional attitude.

Mary looked up and dialled the unfamiliar number. Great Aunt Harriet regarded the telephone as a thing for herself to use, not as a convenience for other people.

"Hullo darling. It's me."

"Hullo! Anything wrong?"

"I just wondered whether you got there all right."

"I did. But only just. Poor old Mr Ford is on his last leg but one. Children all right?"

"Unless they're murdering each other. Listen." She held the telephone away, towards the door.

"Very healthy by the sound of it."

"And how is *she*?"

"Mad as a dozen March hares. But I must say she has ear-marked some very nice things for us. Did Anna like her present?"

"Absolutely delighted."

"Good. Well . . . She's calling. See you tomorrow. I shall look in at the office first."

176

"We'll look forward."

Tom had the uncomfortable feeling that he was eaves-dropping on a perfectly normal, family conversation. He had heard the male voice at the other end of the line, even heard the light reference to the old car. For the nice little woman's sake he was glad. But sorry for George Hardy.

Hardy had had a frustrating yet not entirely useless after-noon. He now knew where the murder had been committed and that was largely due to a Thorington man, PC Armstrong, and his dog Oscar – all that Harrison could lend at the moment.

"Not much to look at, sir," PC Armstrong said. "And not college-trained. A bit like me. He's just, well, my hobby, so to speak. And there's a bit of bloodhound in him and they weren't named for nothing!"

Hardy who had no great faith in dogs, eyed the newcomer doubtfully. A bit of bloodhound, but far more bits of several other breeds.

Still it might help to know where the murder had been committed, and those who had faith in dogs always contended that one good dog could cover as much ground as four men.

"Better have a word with Sergeant Saunders," Hardy said.

Most places in Hillchester were pretty deserted by midnight, but some more so than others. The murderer had evidently taken his time, in a place where he felt safe from disturbance, in a place accessible to a car. Assuming – and of course at this point it was only an assumption – based on what Poor Old Arthur had said and Miss Lowe had heard, with a good dash of Hardy's imagination – the unfortunate girl had gone through the Market Arcade, which was the pedestrian precinct, emerged on to Forehill Street, a short, built-up area after that she would have been twice vulnerable. There was the vast, deserted Cattle Market and adjoining it the sinisterly named Shambles Meadow, where some doomed cattle, awaiting transport, spent the night. After that the

177

Sheepgate, densely occupied – but with Maiden Lane running behind it. And then the Common.

Not much remained now of the large open space where one of the great mediaeval fairs had been held. A stretch of new road, as brightly lit at night as any other section of the town, ran across it. On one side of the road was the big new primary school, the college of further education and the town's Leisure Centre, all three set in spacious grounds. On the opposite side was Sunset House and a bit of the original Common, now tamed, threaded by footpaths, dotted with seats upon which a few old men sat and smoked on sunny days. The rest of the space was devoted to allotments.

Behind Sunset House was space which everybody agreed was a disgrace to a self-respecting town, but about which nobody seemed able to do much. It was cleared at infrequent intervals and stern notices forbade dumping, but almost overnight old bedsteads, old cookers, old refrigerators littered the place again. It was a regular police job to see that refrigerator doors were unhinged, lest some child should shut himself in. The first matron of the old persons' home had called it an eyesore and had ordered fast-growing trees to be planted as a screen.

The space was known by its old name, Goose Green, but as though ashamed, the printers of the latest town map which PC Armstrong was studying, had omitted the name.

PC Armstrong was not troubled by the fact that his reception at Hillchester had been cool; he was that rarity in the police force, a born loner, and an eccentric and he fully understood that, with a serious case on their hands, the Hillchester people had hoped for more backing from headquarters, than one man and his dog – the dog not even trained!

Saunders, Armstrong admitted had been helpful, explaining the map to a stranger.

PC Armstrong, sufficiently briefed for the moment, turned away and experienced enough to conceal his most unpoliceman-like action, wetted a thumb and forefinger and from his pocket drew out a 10p piece; thumb was head, finger was tail, head, he said to himself was Cattle Market; tail was Goose Green. The covert lottery decided for Goose Green and PC Armstrong said, "Come along Oscar. Let's go!"

Although so prone to leave things to chance, Armstrong was observant. Off the brightly-lit and well-used main road was a service road, branching off towards the rear of the home for the old and where that ended, the track, indecisive, which led to the dumping ground. Once there, Armstrong removed the leash from Oscar's collar, sat down on the wreck of an armchair and lit a cigarette. "Trot along," he said, "call me if you want me."

It had worked before, and it worked now. Bloodhounds, as Armstrong had remarked to Hardy, were not named for nothing. Oscar ran about, quartering the desolate ground and presently stopped, nose down, then nose up, emitting a sound that was neither a bark nor a howl; something in between.

PC Armstrong rose and went towards the spot; he seemed not to hurry, but he had exceptionally long legs and covered the ground quickly. There was a considerable amount of blood, some actually frozen to the tussocky grass, a macabre kind of decoration.

"That's my boy!" Armstrong said approvingly. He snapped on the leash. "Where next?" Oscar circled the patch of bloodstained grass sniffing uncertainly; then his course fixed, he pulled urgently, but gently, nose down, towards the edge of Goose Green and on to the service road alongside Sunset House and there he stopped abruptly, sitting down on his haunches. Two feet away from what the dog had declared was the end of the trail was another dark patch, this time of oil, leaked from an old or faulty car.

"That's my boy," PC Armstrong said again. "Now let's go and see if you can pick it up at the other end."

Almost incredibly, Oscar did so. He ran distractedly and unhappily about the area between the church and the Old Vic where churchgoers and sightseers had blurred all scent. Then he checked and began to pull and led Armstrong straight to the Copplestone tomb where he again sat down. "Oh no, there's more to do. We aren't finished yet!" Armstrong said. Baffled again, the dog sniffed, hesitated and then led his master to the nearest spot a car could reach, coming down on the road between the church and the Old Vic.

It was, Hardy admitted, evidence of a sort, but it provided nothing new. It had been obvious from the start that a car was involved, in all likelihood an old car – for the car and its age kept cropping up – a recurrent theme. But not only old cars, all cars were under scrutiny since it was possible, if rather unlikely, that some blood smears might be found. The killer had obviously been very careful, had probably used a big plastic sheet . . .

On Monday afternoon the weather changed and down came the sleety rain, ready at any moment to turn into snow.

Greg Anderson said, "Oh God! Officer, must I? I don't know what you're looking for, but it can't concern *me*. I've been in Broadstairs – and some of this stuff is rather valuable. I don't want it out in this weather."

"Orders are orders, sir. I'll lend you a hand."

Out came all the pretty, rather fragile things which Aunt Harriet, in her bemused mind, did not want to take with her to the Nursing Home for which she was bound, or to send to the saleroom. The best of her Persian rugs, an elegant little Georgian work table, a pole fire-screen which held aloft a sampler worked by another, earlier, Mary Anderson, a bow-fronted corner cupboard with butterfly hinges. Nice as they all were they looked pathetic and shabby, standing out there on the grass verge of the road in the sleety rain while a police constable took his time over searching every inch of the inside of the car, and in the boot.

He found nothing, of course, because there was nothing to find. Once, glancing up, the policeman saw the car's owner regarding him with an expression half-way between a smile and a sneer: a look that said; "You're wasting your time!"

Not an unusual expression; in fact those whose cars were being examined, either looked like that, or angry: You're wasting *my* time! or anxious.

With Lorraine Selsey's murder the Hillchester Terror gained nationwide publicity and many papers sent down their own representatives. Graham Harper could have felt over-shadowed for, with one exception, the newcomers repre-sented papers far more important than the *Hillchester District*. But he was young and buoyant – and ambitious; he enjoyed rubbing shoulders with those who rated above him in the world of journalism and he had advantages; he was local, he knew the town and its people, and he had written that first, tentative, prophetic article – now often quoted. He found himself almost in the role of host, though they enjoyed generous expense accounts and always treated him both in the Long Bar at the White Horse, and in the upstairs restaurant.

Graham tried to prevent "Our Special Correspondent", who represented what was possibly the most influential paper, though not the one with the largest circulation, from inviting a snub in the Long Bar. "Jameson," Graham said, "that group of dummies is practically a club, and very exclusive." But Jameson had consorted with Presidents and Prime Ministers and would not be warned, he positively rushed upon his fate. He was a big, fleshy man, well-dressed for one of his calling and his fruity voice bore the stamp of a good accent but as he walked towards the group Mr Sims said, "Newshound!" and Colonel Soames said, "We called 'em tripe hounds in my day." The elite went into laager, backs turned.

"Good evening," Jameson said.

"Evening," said the only one who appeared not to be deaf. "Turning cold again . . ."

"Go on, Crawford," Colonel Soames said. "You were saying . . ." Crawford who had in fact been saying nothing, launched quickly into a tirade about the fatuity of road-blocks.

Jameson stared for a full half-minute; it was unbelievable. But it had happened. Jameson turned away.

The little group had abided by their own mysterious rules, but they had done Hillchester a bad service. Jameson could hardly be said to dip his pen in venom, for what he couldn't phone in, he typed; but the venom was there. And since there was now nothing new to report about the rapist, a little background piece was welcome and Jameson really let himself go about this backward town, still living in the Middle Ages and practising a form of segregation even in its drinking places. And, being clever, he managed without actually saying so, to imply that in a less mediaeval community the Hillchester Terror would not have had a long run.

Many people were offended by the article; perhaps only one deeply hurt – and that was Hardy. After one of the routine morning conferences, he said, "Terry, stand back; pretend you've just been called in to criticise. Tell me, what the hell more could we have done than we have done?"

"If I knew I'd have told you and helped you to do it. And, dear man, pay no heed to this kind of thing." He tapped the folded paper. "Tomorrow it'll be wrapped round the fish and chips."

In the Long Bar Colonel Soames said, "In a way, the most offensive article; but not actionable." And Mr Sims, absolutely fed up with taking his wife to where she felt safe, or bringing in people so that she felt safe, said sourly, "Mind you, it can do no harm. They need a prod. I often ask myself, what'd happen if one of their women was savaged? Would that spur them into action?"

One of *their* women. Not all that easy to find or track down. When, somewhere back in the thirties, the new Police Station was built on Castle Meadow, houses were built, too. Chief Inspector O'Brien occupied one, but, typically Irish, he was a good family man, and the house that was his sheltered not only his wife and two adolescent but very husky boys, but also his parents, a little old granny of a woman and a sturdy old father. There were other police houses, some with vulnerable women in them, but a couple of evenings' observation proved that precautions the police urged upon the public were not being neglected by themselves. Greg watched while two babies in carry-cots and a toddler, together with their mothers went into one house and were joined almost immediately by a police constable off-duty. Men were, indeed, always coming and going, and Greg Anderson, standing in the shadow of the Public Library, decided to abandon Castle Meadow Square as a hunting ground. But Chance favoured the prepared mind and one morning in the Long Bar Mr Sims was talking about the escalation of house prices in the last three decades. "Take Orchard cottage," he said. "In 1948 or maybe '49, no running water and a I-beg-your-pardon at the end of the garden. I thought myself lucky to get three thousand five hundred for it. Admittedly Sergeant Saunders *improved* it – but he did most of the work himself. And today it's a small Georgian house, in a unique setting, secluded yet within easy reach of the town centre and I could get fifty thousand for it. Probably more."

"Where exactly is this desirable residence?" The question was lightly asked.

"On the far side of the Castle grounds. It was the old Fallowfield place. Barlow's bought the big house and most of the grounds – and did they get a bargain, too? They did not want the gardener's cottage."

183

Case Seven: Amy Saunders

"I can't let Jim down," Amy Saunders said. "Poor old boy, he's been let down all round. Reg and Iris should be ashamed of themselves! *And* Cynthia and Muriel could have done more, if they'd put their backs into it."

"I'm not arguing that. But Amy love, facts must be faced. This man is a killer – and he's still at large."

"I'm not scared," Amy said and Tom thought; No, that's the trouble with Amy, she just didn't know what fear was. Out of his desultory reading, Tom's memory dredged up a scrap. It was Nelson who had said that he didn't know what fear was. And Amy was like that.

When she was nine, and a little shrimp of a thing, she'd been playing about, paddling and splashing in the river near The Butts. Every Hillchester child had been warned about The Butts, the point where the river had eaten away both its bank and its bed, making a dangerous pool. But it was without doubt the best place for swimming. Three boys, all teenagers were practising their strokes there, when one of them was taken with cramp. He let out a roar of agony and fear.

Afterwards the boys who were already in the pool, and others, who could swim, who were lolling on the bank said that *of course* they would have gone to his aid, but that kid Palfrey just didn't give anybody a chance. Amy gave nobody a chance. She jumped straight into the pool and by some super-human effort, dragged the boy, twice her size, to safety.

Asked about this gallant act she said simply, "I just didn't think!"

Her infuriated father said, "Thass your trouble, my girl! You ever do anything like that again and I'll belt you!" Her mother forbade her, absolutely, ever to go near the river again. But the *Hillchester District* made quite a thing of it and presently some society in London decided that she deserved a medal, which was presented to her by the Mayor, at a ceremony in the Corn Exchange. Tom Saunders, a stripling of sixteen, his career already chosen, and merely waiting for the moment to come when he could join the police force, had been present at this ceremony and had decided, then and there, that this was the girl he'd like to marry – one day.

He was impressed, not only by her act of heroism but by her demeanour; confident without being cocky; not in the least awed by the Mayor in full regalia and all the other paraphernalia.

There was, as the years mounted, a good deal of competition to face. Amy wasn't exactly pretty and she could, on occasion, be sharp-tongued, but she was very popular. However, Tom Saunders persisted and was rewarded and Amy had proved to be in every way an ideal wife.

But Amy's mother had said that people who didn't think would sooner or later run into trouble, and Amy's trouble began to overtake her as soon as she began to drive a car. The reckless, I-just-didn't-think technique had led, after many minor skirmishes, to total defeat, the smashing of her Mini – so carefully saved up for; and the cancellation of her licence for a year. Undismayed, Amy said, "OK; thank God I have the use of my legs still. And if that old booby thinks a year of being grounded will make me a better driver, he's daft!"

And it had not mattered much until now, with the Terror clamped down and her determination to help Jim with his cinema quite unshaken.

Tom said, "Amy, there're lonely stretches . . ."

"I know. But anybody sidling up to me with, 'Can I give

you a lift, miss?' I'll say; Yes! And I'll reach in and press his hooter till you all hear.''

Experience had taught Tom that arguing with Amy was useless, but he went about quietly putting pressure on relatives – or friends – who could go along and lend a hand in the cinema. It had been, before the Terror, the full-time job of Iris, Reg Palfrey's adopted daughter, who had ridden in from the market garden on a moped and, as Tom argued, if Reg didn't think she was safe, chugging along, well he could have lent her his Land-Rover, or, come to that, driven her in and then fetched her. Such exhortations, and even a little mild abuse, had been effective from time to time, but in the end Jim fell back upon Amy and Amy said she couldn't let Jim down.

Greg Anderson began an intense study of the habits and habitat of this policeman's woman. She was easily distinguishable by her flaming red hair. Her home, Orchard Cottage, though absolutely invisible from the road called Mount Road, was exposed at the rear to anyone who cared to climb the slight rise upon which stood all that remained of Hillchester Castle. And, Chance favouring him again, amongst the things he had brought back from Great Aunt Harriet's was a pair of binoculars which had belonged to her brother, a keen race-goer. Get them properly focused and the little house and those who lived in it could be brought within what seemed to be arm's length. There were two children, both girls and both quite small – he underestimated their age by some years – and from them he anticipated no trouble. If they saw him they would stand transfixed with horror.

Orchard Cottage had retained many of its old trees, so was well separated from its neighbours on either side, and between it and Mount Road ran a driveway, a slight curve, and so overhung by tree branches that it was like a tunnel. This tunnel ended in a space laid with concrete, upon which opened the front door of the house – actually in the side – flanked by neat tubs of crocuses. At right-angles to the house was a double garage. At night this space was well-lit by a pseudo-antique carriage lamp that projected over the doorway. When any member of the family was out this light was left burning.

He now knew all that he needed to know and it was merely a question of waiting for two things to coincide. They did so on the first Saturday of February.

A man standing, as Hardy had visualised him doing, at the window of a darkened office, looked out upon Market Square as upon a lit stage. A little less well-lit than it had formerly been on Saturday evenings, for the sign, Roaring Twenties, no longer scintillated over the Disco's entrance. Nemesis of a sort had overtaken Mr Quantrill; and all because PC Pettit's feelings had been injured by the Thorington dog's success. He had said to Chief Inspector O'Brien, ''I'd give a lot, sir, to get into that Disco – with Searcher. He's a lot better with drugs, sir. But I reckon we'd need a search warrant.''

''Not hard to come by! What are *you* hunting?''

''I depend upon Searcher to tell me that, sir. He's a lot better . . .''

Mr Quantrill was accustomed to policemen by this time, but at the sight of Searcher, his swarthy skin took on a greenish tinge. ''I'll just turn him loose,'' PC Pettit said. ''Don't worry. He's house-trained.'' Searcher scurried about, taking great interest in ash-trays and in certain places on the floor. His erratic progress brought him to the door alongside the little dais. He could manage push down handles, but knobs defeated him; he looked for assistance. Mr Quantrill made a last ditch stand:

''That door leads to my private apartments!''

''And a search warrant covers everything from attic to cellar – sir,'' said Pettit opening the door. After that the game was up. Mr Quantrill whose account at his Hillchester bank was quite modest – no more than a fairly successful Disco warranted – had other deposits, under other names, in various places and was planning an early retirement. To Acapulco? To Tunis? But the magistrates in this backward area took a very serious view of anything concerning drugs –

187

even cannabis – and remanded Mr Quantrill without bail.

The Comet Cinema, upon which the watcher's stare was fixed, was doing good business. *Inner Circle*, a controversial film, a hotch-potch of Satanism, sex at its rawest and a whiff of Dracula, would undoubtedly have been banned by the Borough Council had it not been for Jameson's article about backwardness. Also as one logical member remarked, nothing in *Inner Circle* could be much worse than what was going on here, under their very noses.

Amy Saunders appeared, wielding a broom in a furious manner. Iris had come in for the matinée that afternoon, but she hadn't done a thing about clearing up the place. Together with the litter, Amy broomed Iris out – Iris and *all* of them, lazy sluts! She pushed the rubbish out of the foyer, across the pavement, into the gutter.

So! She was there. And, almost immediately, so was Sergeant Saunders, in the police car, sliding smoothly to a halt. They exchanged a few words. Tom was still worried, but she soothed him. "The place is packed; somebody must be going my way. I'll get a lift." From Amy that was a concession and he greeted it as such. "Mind you do."

And he need not worry about Kate and Alice, for Miss Gilman, up at St Ethelreda's had been very sensible about the day girls who had to go back, in the winter after dark, for such things as special lectures, concerts or dress rehearsals for plays. She had bought a minibus, and this, driven expertly by ex-WPC Collins, collected and brought home the girls.

Amy raised the broom in a kind of salutation as Tom drove off and then whisked away inside to serve cigarettes, sweets, potato crisps and peanuts from a kind of pedlar's tray slung from her neck.

Two separate young men, two together and then a man and a girl came out of the Music Centre and made for Tony's café. Poor Old Arthur appeared in the doorway and took a few deep, appreciative gulps of the crisp, cold air. In rather less than three weeks he had changed so much as to be virtually unrecognisable; rejuvenated, rehabilitated, and clad in one of

Mr Fullerton's suits, now outgrown by its previous owner whom a sedentary life had rendered bulky. Since the moment when Mrs Fullerton had taken him in, much as she would have taken a homeless dog, Arthur had not taken a single drink – not even a beer. Mrs Fullerton cooked like an angel and he found in the food what he had formerly sought in the bottle. And Mrs Fullerton had found what she had craved, ever since Eric opted out – a man about the place. And not merely that. Arthur knew as much, or more, about the noises now regarded as music . . . Let's not think of Lorraine Selsey!

Arthur closed and bolted the door of the Music Centre. Presently, at the cinema, the red-head reappeared and in the same angry way began to wash the glass of the doors. The watcher gave way to a curious impulse, a desire to see her, close to, to indulge in a preparatory gloat. He strolled across. If she recognised him, if she addressed him by name, even, it would not matter. Next time she saw him he would be utterly changed – and she would not live to tell the tale.

"Good evening," he said.

"Good evening." She was brusque. The glasswork was a disgrace and the brass was worse; nobody had really done anything since her last clean-up here. She took the man for a stranger, probably staying at the White Horse, perhaps lonely . . . But she had no time to talk. She said, "The film's half-way through, but everybody says the second half is best. I could find you a seat – half price."

Close to she looked so much older! She had that pale, papery-thin skin which sometimes went with red hair; myriads of tiny creases. She'd fought this affliction indomitably, and Tom and the girls had aided her, giving her for birthdays and Christmas the most expensive, sweet-scented, preparations, some of them guaranteed not only to prevent wrinkles, but to remove those already there. Then Kate who had an enquiring mind and ambitions to be a scientist, had analysed, as she called it, one of the preparations and said it was good honest stuff, so far as it went, based on lanolin and that she could make something every bit as good at a tenth of the price.

The man said, "Thanks. I saw it in London . . . You look to be busy."

"Somebody must be," Amy said, as she wiped the last smear of Windolene from the now gleaming glass surface and prepared to tackle the brass. But she looked at him as she spoke and something which she did not recognise because she had never felt it before, struck at her.

She attributed it to the cold. She'd shed her good old sheepskin jacket and now found herself longing for it. But not until this job was jobbed. She said sharply, "If you wouldn't mind moving, I could get to the other door." The man said, "Oh, sorry!" and moved. He said, "Good night," and Amy responded and he went away.

Despite her vigorous exertions, she did not warm up and a little later, huddling into her old jacket, fleece inside, she found it less comforting than she had expected. The cold was too deep-rooted; she felt as though she had swallowed an icicle.

Tom had said that there were lonely stretches. So there were, but not like, *not like* the place where Lorraine Selsey had been done to death.

And must you think of that now? What the Hell, Amy Saunders: are you scared?

Because she was so small, Amy always wore very high-heeled shoes but never until this evening had she been aware of how they rattled on the pavements of almost deserted streets. Almost; not quite. Guildhall Street which took her away from the town centre was mainly offices now, but there were some houses, some lighted windows.

At the end of Guildhall Street, where it split and became Westgate Avenue in one direction and Curlew Lane in the other, there stood what remained of a venerable oak-tree, banded and strutted and propped up with iron. Everybody regarded it as a traffic hazard but it was protected by its age – said to be four hundred years. At this point she must make her choice.

It was not all that late and in the Avenue there were lights in windows, lights over porches, people still astir. But to take it was to go far, far out of her way for the Avenue debouched at the Triangle, on the very edge of the town. Curlew Lane led almost directly on to the place where Mount Road opened off Castle Road.

Approaching the moment and the place of decision, Amy experienced yet another new feeling – tiredness. Always her energy had seemed inexhaustible; and today had been no different from most days; a bit of washing and what she called a bake-up, for she never went to the Comet without some substantial offering, some kind of meat dish which poor old Jim could easily heat up, a cake or a tart which her sister-in-law would enjoy. This evening she'd been rather busier than usual at the cinema because the audiences were better. What of it? Getting old, my dear. Well, that happens to anybody who lives long enough!

A man came out of the nearest Avenue house. He stopped near his garden gate and lit his pipe, then he emerged, followed by a large, bouncing young dog. Amy, with self-disgust, found herself wishing that he would turn into Curlew Lane and give his dog a good run. But both man and dog were creatures of habit; they halted on the pavement while the man looked about for traffic, scanty at this place, at this hour. ''All clear, Jonah. Go ahead!'' The dog bounded towards the old tree and lifted his leg four times in rapid succession. Amy swerved into Curlew Lane.

On one side the playing fields of the old grammar school – that sanctuary of learning having been built, without grounds, long before games had any place in the curriculum. On the opposite side Norton's Garden Centre which had started in a small way, selling roses only and had expanded vastly, now selling anything remotely connected with gardens – greenhouses, summer-houses, lawn-mowers, dried pampas-grass . . .

Again she was aware of the clatter of her heels – almost like teeth chattering. Once she thought she heard something else

191

and stood still, listening and doing a thing she had never dreamed she would ever do – looking back over her shoulder. Nothing!

She'd never been much of a scholar but she had for about a year, been exposed to the influence of a teacher obsessed with the idea that young minds, while they were plastic, should memorise . . .

To Amy it had all seemed nonsense then and she had found little use for it since. Now it sprang up, unwelcome, hateful.

> Like one that on a lonesome road
> Doth walk in fear and dread.
> And having once turned round walks on,
> And turns no more his head;
> Because he knows, a frightful fiend
> Doth close behind him tread.

She did not look back again, but she had an impulse to run, difficult in such high-heeled shoes. Take them off and run in stockinged feet? What a confession of weakness!

She emerged into Castle Road, more brightly lit than the lane and with cars going both ways. Choosing her moment she crossed, tapped her way into Mount Road and to the opening of the dark tunnel that led to her own door.

On the softer, leaf-strewn ground her heels made little sound; the noise of traffic on Castle Road was here only a murmur. But so deranged were her nerves that she was capable of finding something sinister about the very quietude. It would have been nice to think that the girls were at home, but they were at a music recital at the school, and, the first to be collected by the minibus on its rounds, they were the last to be delivered.

Good girls! They had remembered to leave on the light. With a feeling of relief, as new to her as the feeling of fear, Amy stepped into the lighted area and put her hand into her pocket for the key.

The nightmare thing stepped from behind the open garage door. Immensely tall. An animal's head with snarling mouth showing white teeth and eyes like green glass. She just saw, and then he was upon her. Intent to kill.

Even the old Amy to whom fear was unknown could hardly have fought more bravely, squirming, kicking, trying to claw his face which seemed partially covered by some slippery stuff upon which her fingers made no impression. The upturned collar of her coat impeded him for a few seconds but he got his hand inside it, got an iron grip on her throat and squeezed. She made one last desperate effort, twisted her head and with her last breath let out an animal scream.

Answered, echoed, as she slid into unconsciousness, by others, louder and more frenzied.

Kate and Alice had not gone to the recital. Just before Betty Collins — so happy in her new job — was due to appear, Kate said, "I don't know about you; for myself I'm sick of Culture, capital C. I like drama. I like music — at least, I *did*. But they do make such an issue of it!"

Alice said, "I've suffered more. I never liked any of it. Let's have an evening on our own. I can tell a good lie if I have to. Leave it to me."

A very good lie. "I'm so sorry, Miss Collins. Kate isn't very well. Flu, I think. Her temperature is up, so I've put her to bed and I think — don't you? — that I ought to stay with her."

"But of course. Wish her well from me. And don't *you* catch it," ex-WPC Collins said, executing one of those neat three-point turns which she had learned in the police driving school.

Giggling, the girls had gone to the little amateur laboratory which their father had rigged up for them in a little summer-house. And they'd had a very happy evening until disturbed by that first, choked off scream. Then — they were Amy's daughters — they moved as one girl.

Afterwards Alice was asked, "Did you do it deliberately?"

"Of course. I thought he'd killed Mum. Whatever I'd had in my hand . . ."

What she happened to have in her hand was a beaker containing sulphuric acid.

193

The Cupboard

The bedevilment which Hardy had sensed in this case, continued. They now had their man but still no clue to his identity. He wore a dark off-the-peg suit of the kind sold by the thousand; his underwear and handkerchief bore no laundry marks. There was a black plastic bag of the most common variety behind the garage door. In it he had, presumably, carried his horrible head-dress and the claw which he wore on his left hand. The snarling head had been mounted upon a rubber mask which covered the upper part of his face and had protected it both from Amy's clawing nails and from the sulphuric acid. The claw had not been cut from an old hide; it was home-made and Hardy examined it with fascinated repulsion.

It was a stout glove of dark leather, lined with fleece. Some men still wore them in very cold weather. Into the inside of each finger and the thumb had been glued a small square of wood, and into each square, from the outside, had been screwed an ordinary kitchen cup hook, filed sharp. Staring at it, Hardy saw again the marks left on the bodies of Becky Dalton and Grace Robbins, on the face of Gloria Woodman. He also saw Lorraine Selsey's torn throat. He dropped it hurriedly.

How had the man come? How had he intended to get away? The most rigorous search of the neighbourhood showed no car to be unaccounted for and with the full backing of their union, the bus-drivers in Hillchester had ceased to work after eight o'clock soon after the Terror clamped down. After all, with the exception of one woman they were men and were needed at home. Neither taxi firm had any knowledge of a passenger being delivered to Mount Road or anywhere near it.

So, as usual, out of the night he had come; but this time he had not gone away into it; he had been taken to hospital in an ambulance.

It was Doctor Brunning's turn to act as police surgeon. Of the acid burns he took a light view. "Superficial. Painful of course . . . But here, I think, if you don't mind my saying so, we have to be a *little* bit careful. Technically, caught in the act as it were, he should go straight to the prison hospital at Thorington. Eh?" Hardy nodded. "*But*, do that and suppose some unexpected complication set in, all the do-gooders would be out for my blood. You and I know that he's guilty but the law holds that he's innocent until proved guilty and to subject him to a journey of forty miles would be, on my part, an act of barbarism. Better the local hospital?"

Hardy agreed and Doctor Brunning was able to give a little attention to Amy Saunders who was suffering, understandably, from shock, rather shaky; and from a bruised larynx – her voice was a feeble croak. Rather more in need of the comfort of sedation was poor old Tom Saunders, not first this time, but last on the scene because there had been boxing in the Corn Exchange that evening, and although WPC Girdlestone said of course she could manage, he'd doubted it. So he'd stayed around and he had been needed.

PC Pettit came along, with Searcher, in whom his faith had not merely been restored, but had became fanatical. At first Searcher had behaved queerly, dodging away, hackles up, tail down. Then he had sensed what Pettit wanted, lowered his nose and pulled. Along the short dark avenue and into Mount Road. There he checked suddenly near the verge of the road, just as his rival, Oscar, had done at the rear of Sunset House. And there, for all to see, a few feet away, was a little patch, no bigger than a saucer, of oil.

The same old car, Hardy realised when this was reported to him. But whose car? There was irony in the thought that a car could be identified – given its number – in less than five minutes; for a man it took longer.

For the first time Hardy considered the possibility of an active accomplice: someone who had taken fright at the first scream and driven the old car away. Well, it would be found, it *must* be found. Not, of course, that it mattered so much now; they had the man and it was interesting to note how accurate the descriptions of him had been; he was tall and slender, but well muscled and when the disgusting head-dress was lifted away it revealed fair hair, slightly darkened and dampened by sweat. He looked to be about thirty-five.

Student Nurse Barker, whey-faced but determined said, "I don't care what anybody says. I won't give him even a drink of water! Becky Dalton was a friend of mine."

Sister Grant, in charge of the Intensive Care Unit – six beds in an open ward and two small rooms for patients on their way to recovery – said, "That is most unprofessional conduct! A nurse is a nurse. In prison hospitals even *convicted* criminals who need nursing, are nursed." She chanced her arm slightly. "If that policeman by the bed there sounds the buzzer, you will go in there and behave quite normally."

"Must I?"

"You must. Now what are you doing?"

"Resigning." Madge began to divest herself of all her admittedly rather humble status symbols.

"But you can't. You can't resign in the middle of the night . . ."

"I've done it. On a matter of principle."

"Then be so kind as to lift that phone and report yourself sick and say that I need a replacement *immediately*."

Sunday again. Five weeks since . . . Bill Selsey pulled on his heavy boots and went out to dig in his garden. Only in violent

196

physical exercise could he find any relief these days. And he must get away from Liz.

Liz had been very good at first, crying all the tears which he himself could not shed. They ran down inside him, corrosive on his heart. He'd been grateful to Liz for weeping. Then there'd been the formality of an inquest, and then the funeral, with more flowers than had ever been seen at a funeral before. And from that moment Liz had begun to go wrong – gloating! Oh, what a wonderful wreath, and from absolute strangers, too! One hundred and thirty-seven wreaths conveyed by Interflora, from absolute strangers, from all over the country. The flowers had their own odours, but they all stank of death.

The boys, Nigel and Francis came home and in an unguarded moment Liz said, "You boys haven't been together here since I can't remember when." Gloating! Of course she had always preferred the boys, just as he had preferred Lorraine, and of course she enjoyed having them both home together. But she seemed to have lost sight of the reason for this reunion. And wasn't the church crowded? Hadn't the rector conducted the service beautifully?

Near neighbours and a few relatives must be offered refreshment; a kind of buffet with a whole ham and a turkey, left over from Christmas and kept in the butcher's cold-room. There was sherry. There was beer.

All, all completely disgusting; making a party out of the laying away of his darling. But what followed was worse.

Liz said, "There's ways of looking at things Bill. And you should think – she had a happy life. She'd always done exactly what she wanted and nothing she didn't."

He didn't accept this in quite what Liz thought was the right spirit; so she ventured out upon much more dangerous ground. She dared to say, "You know, Bill, Lorraine was spoilt! No use arguing about it. She was spoilt and *you* spoilt her. *You* gave her the idea she could get away with anything. So she did go slinking off . . ."

William said, "Shut your trap!"

Since then they had held no real communication.

Through it all, he had done his rounds, never missing a day. It had been rough at first, with people tending to avoid him, leaving milk-bottles, and requests for tomorrow's supply, out on front-door steps. Then gradually, they'd emerged, and faced him and said how sorry; how deeply they sympathised. And they were all aware of the change in him; for many – especially the old – he'd been the one bright thing in the day. Now no more, and to ask him to post a letter seemed an imposition.

He was digging without purpose, not preparing the ground for any crop, for who knew where he might be when the seeds sprouted. Presently Liz appeared at the back door and called his name. When he looked up, she said, "You're wanted." He drove in the spade, leaving it upright and went towards her.

"What is it?"

"Man to see you. At the front door."

"What man?"

"How should I know? He wouldn't come in."

William limped to the front door and saw with a jolt of surprise, the hosital porter called Oakey.

"Hullo," he said.

"I reckoned you ought to be the first to know. *They got him*!"

"You sure?"

"Sure. From what I could make out he set about Tom Saunders' missus and one of her girls chucked some acid in his face. They brought him in last night."

"Much hurt?" Not that any degree of hurt would be enough. Not all the fires of Hell could sufficiently punish the man who had killed Lorraine.

"Well, he looked a bit of a mess; but I heard somebody say the burns were superficial."

"Where'd they put him.?"

"Intensive Care Unit; but in a little side ward. Well, like I said, I reckoned you should be the first to know."

"And I do appreciate that. I . . . I'm grateful."

"No need. Be seeing you."

"Be seeing you."

William Selsey turned after closing the door and did a thing unheard of; he went upstairs in his filthy boots. In the conjugal bedroom there was chest of drawers and one of the top, half-size drawers had always been known as Dad's.

There wasn't much in it; his Life Insurance Policy, his Military Medal in its case, the only letter Lorraine had ever written to him – she'd been, very briefly, a Girl Guide and gone to camp at Frinton for a week – another envelope containing a curl of very fair, almost silver hair. Below these in a handkerchief was the Luger, taken from the dead hand of an officer in the Afrika Korps. Its magazine had been empty then, but sometime afterwards Corporal Selsey had found some bullets which fitted it.

It was forbidden to hoard such things; it was illegal to possess a fire-arm without a licence, but some kind of perverse sentiment had made him cling to it. And it had never, since it came into his possession, done anybody any harm.

His intention had been to take it to the trial, when the murderer was caught and to shoot him, straight through the head – a fate too good for him, of course, but it would ensure that he wouldn't live to be cosseted and then eventually set free to kill again. He had also intended to shoot the judge if he summed up too leniently, and the man the daft government paid to speak up for such fiends.

He had a good eye and swift hands; he reckoned that the first shot would paralyse everybody and he'd have time, after the second and third, to turn the Luger on himself.

Now everything had altered. Instant death by a shot through the head still seemed too easy and painless an end for the man who had killed Lorraine. And the Luger was too good an instrument. It had belonged to a very brave man who'd stood up and fired it to the last bullet when he knew he was facing certain death.

William Selsey looked down at his hands.

The war had ended a long time ago; the weight of years and his lame leg had slowed him down considerably; he was no longer the man who had taken a course on unarmed combat; but there was nothing wrong with his hands! He re-wrapped the Luger and returned it to the drawer.

Mary Anderson gave the children breakfast. They made no distinction between Sunday and weekday and were always on the move early. She said, "We must all be very quiet. Daddy's still asleep." But she knew that he had promised to play golf with Dick Sullivan down at Salford at eleven o'clock, so at half-past nine she made fresh tea and carried it up. There was the empty room, the un-slept-in bed.

Panic did not seize her as it had seized William Selsey in a similar situation. She could think of a number of explanations. The most disturbing – that Greg had met with an accident, she dismissed. She would have heard by now; the road between Hillchester and Pykenham was well-frequented, part of the road to Colchester. It was Pykenham, wasn't it? She looked at the combined calendar and diary that hung on the kitchen wall. Yes, Pykenham.

The more likely thing to think was that the old car had at last given up the ghost and left Greg stranded. But where? Where could a man be stranded out of reach of a telephone nowadays? Her mind, anxious for comfort, reminded her that the Manor House, Pykenham, stood a good mile and a half off the main road. She visualised Greg saying good night to Mrs Denning – and it would be late; he was always late when he went to help sort out the hopeless mess that Mr Denning had left when he died suddenly of a stroke. The old car had broken down; Greg had not liked to walk back to the house to request the use of the telephone, and it would be a long walk to the village. So he'd slept in the car. Overslept, for there was no doubt about it he was over-working to a fantastic extent. He could still be asleep.

Or he could have found somebody, up at Manor House Farm or down in the village of Pykenham who could do yet another running repair job. In which case, hoping soon to be home, he might not bother to telephone, though he was usually so considerate . . .

Ten o'clock. Half-past and Dick Sullivan sounding his horn.

Now what has come over me? Why can't I just tell him the truth? Simple enough. Greg went out last night and isn't back. Dick would be kind and helpful; he'd get busy, telephoning, driving hither and thither. But there was in the man a coarse streak; he'd inevitably think that Greg was up to a bit of no good.

She went out and said, "Sorry, Dick. Greg was terribly late last night and he's sleeping it off."

"But a good round of golf in this bracing air would do him the world of good. I'll wait ten minutes."

"I'm sorry, but he definitely said not." She turned and went back into the house to avoid further argument.

She went straight to the telephone table, looked up Denning and dialled the number. A pleasant young male voice said, "Pykenham 28204. Yes?"

"I'd like to speak to Mrs Denning."

"So sorry. She isn't here. In London for the weekend. Can I take a message? I'm Mike Denning."

"No. No message. But perhaps you could tell me something. I'm Mrs Anderson. My husband – he's your mother's accountant. Was he there – at your place – last evening?"

"No, Mrs Anderson."

"You are sure?"

"Of course I'm sure." A tinge of impatience in the pleasant voice. She faced another fear. She had not forgotten that June evening when Greg had seemed dead enough to deceive Doctor Roper. That blow on the head. She'd always had a submerged dread of recurrence. She now visualised Greg slumped unconscious in the old car somewhere along that mile and a half of drive.

"Tell me . . . I am sorry to bother you . . . Has anybody been along your drive yet?"

"Milk has to be collected," he said rather severely. "The stockman came up to feed the horses. I went down on my motor-bike to collect the papers."

"I see. Thank-you."

Back in the kitchen she tried to remember what Greg had ever said about Mrs Denning. It wasn't much. She was young-looking. "You'd never think to look at her that she had a son of seventeen." She was very business-like. "Quite amazing considering that the old man, even when his mind was tottering, wouldn't let her know anything. If only he had, my job would be a lot easier." And of course she was rich: acres and acres of rich arable land, a prize herd of Jersey cows, a lucrative horse-breeding business.

Suspicion, so vague as to hardly merit the name, drove her upstairs. The room which Greg now occupied was too small to contain a wardrobe; his clothes still hung in the bedroom that they no longer shared. She knew his clothes as well as she knew her own and could tell at a glance what was missing – his best dark suit. City suit. London suit?

And she had last seen him wearing the clothes that symbolised his emancipation: slacks, a sweater and tweed jacket. That was at lunch-time yesterday. She had not seen him leave the house because Polly Inskip was giving her belated Christmas party and, as usual, counted upon Mary's help.

What had he said? What exactly had he said?

"Enjoy yourselves. Think of me, grinding away all afternoon. And Mary don't wait up. I'm going to Pykenham to grapple with the affairs of the late Mr Denning, and that is an apt word. Late. He was late with everything, including his Income Tax. A privilege only accorded to the very rich."

Then he must have come up here and changed and gone – where? Ask yourself that question often enough and up came the answer; absurd, disloyal and monstrous. But it could be true.

The *why* of it was easily understood. Their sex life was a thing of the past. And Greg was still young-looking and attractive.

The *how* of it was more difficult to explain to herself; for if Greg wanted a weekend with Jennifer – yes, that's her name – with Jennifer Denning, why the hell hadn't he arranged it better? Made some kind of excuse for being in London? Anything would have served. Anything would have been better than his rack of suspense.

Am I that comic figure, the Deceived Wife?

It did not occur to her to make contact with the police, for a friend of Peg Sullivan's had done just that when deserted by her husband; and the police had said that unless the missing man had committed some crime, or unless foul play were suspected, they could do nothing. There was at this moment, nothing that anybody could do. Except wait. Wait through an endless day, an ear cocked for the telephone which remained obstinately dumb.

If Chief Inspector O'Brien could have spared the men, he would have stationed one at the point where the Intensive Care Unit branched off the main corridor; but, with this flap on he could spare only two, one to sit by Greg's bedside, and one to sit by the fire escape. Each couple worked a four-hour shift; it was a sitting-down job and indoors, but it was intensely unpopular work.

The cynic who had said that it might stir the police if one of their own women should be attacked was wrong, but not entirely so. They had all stirred themselves over the former atrocities; those who had seen the victims had been rightly shocked. But there was something a little extra provoked by the fact the man had come within an inch of killing Amy Saunders – Uncle Tom's missus. It made it feel personal, almost a family affair.

On top of this there was the physical discomfort entailed. No smoking anywhere; the light in the corridor too far away from the fire escape to make reading easy. And the chairs! The one by the bed was fairly comfortable, intended for patients when they could sit out, the one in the corridor, like hundreds more scattered about the building, was designed as an instrument of torture. Yet the post near the fire escape was preferred to the one in the room, for there was something uncanny about the man, even when he was under sedation the animal odour seemed to be mounting. An hour of it was about as much as one could stand; so they changed over after that period.

Whether on duty inside or outside the room the watchers seemed to be in that state of nervousness that made frequent trips to the lavatory necessary. Very odd! Subject to hours on point duty or in the control of crowds a policeman was supposed to have an elastic bladder and cast-iron kidneys. Between themselves they called it "going along". "Keep an eye open, I'm just going along." "Right. And when you come back, I'll go along myself."

PC Alston, an addicted smoker opened the fire escape door when it was his turn to guard it, and was enjoying a cigarette at the top of the iron stairs when Sister Grant positively attacked him.

"Surely you should know that that door and that stairway are only for use in emergencies."

She was in her element; in place of that silly Barker girl she now had a thoroughly reliable, almost middle-aged woman, fully qualified, who did three nights a week for the sake of the money needed to pay a daughter's fees up at St Ethelreda's. With such support and only three people in the Intensive Care Unit – and all doing well – Sister Grant could relax a bit and think. And remember. Somebody saying; "Well he should thank God he didn't need a blood-transfusion. We couldn't have matched it."

Then that was forgotten in the tussle over the chairs. The police watchers changed shifts at the dead hour of four in the morning and one of the newcomers came in pushing a wheel-chair.

She pounced upon him. "What is this? I've had no instructions. Are you proposing to move him?"

PC Pettit said, "No. This is for me. I know them cardboard chairs you have here and I can't sit on 'em in any comfort for ten minutes, let alone hours.''

"I don't think I can allow it. It makes my ward look untidy.''

"Not if you take this away,'' Stebbing said, giving what he called a cardboard chair an irreverent kick.

So presently it was Monday again, and as could happen overnight, a beautiful day. A touch of spring, everybody said. And the terror lifted. Nobody as yet knew any details, but the rumours had scuttled around and the whole town seemed to draw a great breath of relief. A man was helping the police – and most people knew what that meant.

But a mothy little woman – grey hair, grey face, grey clothes – who came into the Police Station soon after eight o'clock had nothing to do with the brightening morning. With a peculiar combination of diffidence and aggression she approached the reception desk and said, rather breathlessly, "I want to see somebody who can *do* something. About my boy, my Les. Les Avis. I'm Mrs Avis and he's got in with a bad lot. That Maxie Fisher . . . And I've put up with it and put up with it . . . But now . . . There's this car . . . And Les, well they only wanted him because he could drive. You can't call it stealing. At least, a kind of borrowing . . .''

The constable behind the desk pounced on the word car. The whole of Sunday had been spent in a fruitless search.

"What car, madam?''

"Not a very valuable one,'' she hastily. "Old. It broke down, you see. On the Heath. They had to walk home. I nearly went out of my mind with worry and I thought . . .''

"I think Chief Inspector Hardy would like a word with you, madam.'' She looked very dubious.

"I work at the laundry, you see. And they start at half-past eight.''

"We'll arrange a lift for you.''

There was really no reason for Hardy to be in his office so early. They had the man now, even if they did not yet know his name. But he'd been at the Station at such odd hours lately that he now felt uneasy anywhere else.

205

Mrs Avis repeated her story, emphasising that the boys did not *steal* cars. They just borrowed them. "Mainly to go to Retford. Not that I like that much, either. There's this club, you see, drinking after hours, and gambling. But they'd have put this car back if it hadn't broke down. And it ain't that I want any of them to get into trouble – except Maxie Fisher. I just want somebody to talk a bit of sense into Les, before it's too late. He won't listen to me – and his father died when he was four." That sentence summed up the not unusual situation. And putting a scare into Les Avis was just the job for Tom Saunders.

"I'll arrange that, Mrs Avis. And don't worry. If the car is the one I hope it is, your information will prove very useful and in view of that we may be lenient over a youthful prank."

But that was not exactly what she wanted. Or why she had come.

"Maxie Fisher ain't all that young," she said.

Hardy had no more time to give her. Even as he thanked her and dismissed her, he was reaching for the telephone.

Retford had its own little Police Station – and needed it. Once, before Hardy's time it had been a tiny village, isolated amongst acres of gorse and brambles and rabbit warrens and pine trees. But it did run alongside the main road and it had expanded. Two caravan sites – not that Hardy, or anybody else for that matter had anything against caravan dwellers, most of them quite ordinary decent people, using Retford as a commuter base and even making little flower gardens. But there were others. And there was the Club. And although the man in charge there – Sergeant Bates – was not directly Hardy's concern, being part of the uniformed branch and therefore Terry's pigeon, Hardy knew that he was dead lazy; and here the two forces overlapped. So he spoke sharply. "Sergeant, there is an abandoned car on the Heath. About six miles in the Hillchester direction. Will you go immediately, get its number and tell me."

Sergeant Bates who was fond of his food and whose breakfast was about to be served by his ever-loving wife, said,

"Keep it hot, Nell. Shan't be long."

And as Hardy had known, a car could be identified, through a computer in London, within five minutes. The aged Ford which had served its third owner so well, and finally died out there on the Heath, was the property of Gregory Anderson; of 12 Forest Road, Malwood, Hillchester, Suffolk. But that was not positive proof that the man in the hospital was Mr Anderson. Various other possibilities – some of them very remote – presented themselves to Hardy's mind as, with PC Stebbing he went to the office on Market Square.

"Mr Anderson hasn't come in yet," Shirley Morrison said. "It's rather late for him. But he's on his way."

"How do you know?" He willed her to say that Mr Anderson had rung her up himself. For however detached and dispassionate one could be in one's profession it was appalling to think that a respected citizen, a good family man had been responsible for such macabre crimes.

"I know because Mrs Anderson rang up a few minutes ago to ask had he arrived in the office yet. I imagine that she had forgotten to tell him something. She didn't leave any message."

"You have his home number?"

"Of course." She told him and he dialled and an eager, rather breathless voice said, "Yes. Yes, I am Mrs Anderson. What is it?"

Hardy said, "Mrs Anderson, when did you last see your husband?" And it sounded exactly like the caption of a very well-known picture; When did you last see your father?

"On Saturday. At lunch-time . . . Oh for God's sake, tell me the worst. Is he hurt? Is he dead?" And Hardy wished that he could say yes to the last question. But he reminded himself sternly that his first duty was to the public, that curious conglomeration of individuals who paid him his salary.

There was nothing in the least incriminating in Mr Anderson's office, or in Miss Morrison's smaller one. But there was the cubby hole and there beside the little wash-basin, the electric kettle, some crockery and a biscuit tin was the cupboard. It had always puzzled Shirley because it was always locked and even the most private and confidential files were neatly ranged in the fireproof filing cabinet in Mr Anderson's office.

"I don't know about *that*," she said. "And I don't have a key."

Stebbing tried with the thickest blade of the old-fashioned shut-knife which he always carried but the thick doors, solid mahogany, resisted him. The cupboard had once been part of a prosperous coal-merchant's dining room. "It'd take a stout chisel, sir."

"I can borrow one from the Do-It-Yourself shop." Shirley said. And she had gone, come back almost before you could blink.

The splintered wood around the lock seemed to scream at this outrage. But there it all was. Awful and yet satisfactory.

It was a very neat cupboard and nothing in it looked to be actually dirty, yet it stank. On the bottom shelf there was a folded square of plastic which explained why no blood had been found in any car. There was a garment of black cloth with the main bones of the body painted on it in white and a mask – a leering skeleton skull. On the shelf above was another mask – a goat's head complete with horns – which had made one woman think of Pan and another of Satan. There was a card which had contained six cup hooks and now held only one and there was the file with which the other five had been sharpened. There was an object which neither Miss Morrison nor Pettit recognised but Hardy did – a penis sheath of rough leather. It was this which had done Becky Dalton the internal damage.

Shirley Morrison said, "I don't believe it! I can't. Mr Anderson is the *kindest* man. When I had flu he sent me freesias and a message not to come back till I was *really* well. There's been some awful mistake. He ... he lent the cupboard to somebody. Or something like that."

Hardy said gently, "I'm afraid it is true, Miss Morrison. Mr Anderson was arrested on Saturday evening. Caught in the act . . ."

The little sink against which she had been leaning seemed to give way and she fell to the floor in a faint.

Mary Anderson

Turning smoothly off the main road and towards the suburb of Malwood, WPC Girdlestone said, "You really are a glutton for punishment, aren't you? Anybody else could have done this. I would have."

"I know. I was brainwashed too early and taught not to ask anybody to do a job you'd shirk yourself."

"How very archaic! I hadn't noticed that you were a centenarian."

He recognised, and was grateful for, the goodwill behind the jibing. "I wasn't, until recently. This thing has aged me rapidly."

"But it is over now."

"Over, bar this. And small thanks to me! I did all I could but nothing, absolutely nothing got us anywhere near the truth. It took a girl of sixteen . . . ."

"You take things too hard. He was a very cunning, lucky Devil."

"Every now and then I think he *was* the Devil."

"Possessed?"

"Something like that. I wouldn't say I'd led a sheltered life exactly, but that cupboard stank of evil of a kind I can't remember encountering before . . . And now there's this poor woman, in for a ghastly shock."

"She may know," WPC Girdlestone said in her level-headed way, bringing the car to a smooth halt.

"I could almost wish that were so." But by that time Mary had torn open the door and was out on the short path between the crocuses and snowdrops.

"An accident?" Her voice was high and unsteady. "Has Greg had an accident?"

"Not exactly . . ." Really, in what words could he tell the truth to this white-faced, wild-eyed woman?

WPC Girdlestone said out of the corner of her mouth, "She should sit down first."

"May we come in, Mrs Anderson?"

She led them towards the kitchen. The living room door was open and they could see a little girl busy with a doll's house and a resigned looking dachshund wearing a doll's bonnet. Oh God!

"Tell me the truth," Mary said. "Is he dead?"

"No. Mrs Anderson, I'm afraid this will come as a terrible shock to you. Your husband was arrested on Saturday night. He is the rapist."

Mary closed her eyes and seemed to sway. WPC Girdlestone moved, ready to catch her if she fainted. In the circumstances there were no words of comfort to be offered. There was a silence which Mary broke.

"You are quite sure?"

"Quite."

"I must have been very blind . . . You see, you grow used to trusting . . . I believed what he told me. I'll show you." She made a move to stand up, but quickly sat down again. "My legs have failed me. Would you mind? The right-hand top drawer of the dresser. My diary."

It was one of the five-year kind, now in its second year of use. The entries were very brief, almost staccato. A mention of the weather; something about the children, something of the day's activities. All the dates of the attacks were graved in acid on Hardy's memory. He turned quickly to the most important one, the last day of the previous year, the night of Lorraine Selsey's murder. He read; "Too cold to snow.

211

Children all v. good. Peg in for coffee. Greg at Broadstairs.''
For most of the other crucial dates the poor woman had
written, "Greg v late", and once an addendum; "He works
too hard!''

Obviously she had been totally deceived. But then, wasn't
the Devil known as the Father of All Lies?

The enormous pity of it all slammed Hardy at the base of
his throat and when Mary asked a very natural question,
"How did you know? What happened?'' he was obliged to
give two hard swallows before he could answer and tell her
about the happenings on Saturday night.

She said, "Poor Greg! Poor man! Where is he now?''

"In the local hospital. Temporarily. If you wish to see him I
could arrange . . .''

"Oh no!'' she said, quickly, violently. "What you have
there is not Greg.''

"I think she took it remarkably well,'' WPC Girdlestone said.

"Yes. She's a lady. Breed will out.''

"What an interesting theory, sir! I'm a Doctor Barnardo
girl myself. And I think that what you want now is˜a stiff
whisky.''

"Maybe, but as you remarked not long ago, I'm archaic.
No drinking while on duty.''

"In uniform,'' she amended. "And I know a place . . . I
have not been wasting my leisure hours.''

She turned towards Salford, then swung off into a long
drive and drew up before a most imposing residence. She
entered it, indicating to Hardy to follow her, as though it
belonged to her. Hardy wondered if this luxurious place had
been turned into a club. WPC Girdlestone called, not loudly
but in a carrying voice, "Molly!'' A door opened and a short,
plump woman came out, embraced WPC Girdlestone fondly
and kissed her upon both cheeks. "Pat, darling! How lovely.
And unexpected. I was just thinking I'd have to drink alone
and Vic says that is so bad.''

WPC Girdlestone introduced Hardy, adding, "And we

have just had a most distressing time. We need a drink very badly.''

Pouring the drinks, Mrs Hudson-Smith said in her pretty, confidential way, ''Pat is one of my very *oldest* friends. We were at school together. It *does* make a bond.''

William Selsey

Oakey made his daily report. "They're getting ready to move him. Prob'ly tomorrow. They've had him up and walking and he ain't hurt anything like he deserved."

"Thanks, Oakey." Bill drove back to the yard of Farmhouse Dairies and spent some time checking the mechanism of his van. Then he fuelled it at the petrol tank and drove it near to the yard's opening. He had mulled over his plan of campaign until was was perfect – so far as he could see.

A milk delivery van was self-explanatory; it could stand anywhere without attracting attention or arousing suspicion. He parked it near the foot of the one special fire escape, walked round and found the door he wanted.

The whole ground floor of this purpose-planned hospital, except for the department called Emergency and Accident and the adjoining Geriatric Ward, was exactly like a deserted village. By day so busy, overcrowded, now it lay silent, empty and extraordinarily silent. Rather eerie.

William first made his way to the laundry and out of the mass awaiting attention in the morning, chose a surgeon's gown and cap. Then he proceeded to the corridor flanked by small rooms in which various experts held clinics. They were all open for the convenience of the cleaners and William could help himself to a stethoscope left hanging over the back of a chair. He took one and hung it about his neck. Thus disguised, he took the lift up to the first floor where the wards were.

Earlier in the evening, during visiting hours he had done what he called a recce – prepared, if accosted, to say he was looking for a patient named Smithers. Nobody had even asked what he wanted and he had stood by the glass doors and registered everything in his mind.

In the afternoon there had been two nurses behind the desk near the entry and he was prepared for another two to be on duty tonight. In that case he knew exactly what to do. He had, after all, spent a lot of time in hospital when his knee was mending and he reckoned they were all much of a muchness. When surgeons visited patients a nurse was always in attendance. But he'd give an almost playful wave of the hand indicating that this was not a formal visit and there was no need for them to stir. Then he'd point to the room at the end of the corridor and put his finger to his lips, a gesture demanding silence. During his days in hospital what a surgeon asked for, he got.

But tonight there was no one behind the desk. Sister Grant's assistant was having her supper and Sister Grant herself was in the main ward, checking blood-pressures.

The far end of the corridor was, as those policemen who had tried to read had discovered, badly lit and Bill was quite near the old wheelchair before he recognised its occupant. Charlie Alston. It was nearing the end of the four-hour stint and weariness and boredom were taking their toll. Charlie just glanced, saw what he might expect to see and took no interest.

Bill stopped, facing him foursquare, so that his own bulk served as a screen. He said, "Sorry about this. It's for your own good . . ." and hit him. A knock-out blow on the point of the chin. Charlie Alston's head snapped back and his body sagged. Had he been sitting in one of the cardboard chairs the task of propping him up and making him look natural would have been far more difficult. As it was, it was dead easy. Bill simply pushed the chair far enough from the fire escape door to allow for free passage when he needed it. Then he went into the little room, where another constable, not known to him by sight or name, sat reading. To him Bill did not apologise; he simply hit him. And to the thing – it was an insult to humanity to call it a man – to the *thing* in the bed he said, "Come along and look sharp!"

All along Greg had known that he would be rescued. His luck had been so phenomenal, he'd got away with so much. Rape, mutilation, murder.

"Down there. Into that van," William Selsey said, opening the door upon the fire escape steps, a door geared to open easily if pressed from inside. Greg went swiftly down the iron steps and his rescuer followed, then ran ahead of him, jumped in and started up the engine. "Get a move on," William said.

There was no accommodation for passengers, but there was an empty crate. Even without the other crates and the milk bottles in them, the old van rattled. And the man who was driving it, pressed it hard. It made its clanging way past the Triangle, along the road towards Salford, but ignoring the turn off to the village of Malwood.

To Greg it all seemed unreal – except for the salient fact that he had been rescued. In the hospital everybody had been so anxious that he should not suffer, that he had been sedated most of the time; but during his conscious spells he'd lain and thought about rescue and the form it would take. The fantasy most often centred about a rescuer posing as a police constable and he'd turn his stare upon the watcher by his bed, hypnotic, compelling; but whenever he felt that some contact had been made, up the man would jump, go to the door and say to his fellow watchdog, "Keep an eye skinned. I must go along." And after the heaviest dressings had been discarded he'd tried the effect of words. "There's been a terrible mistake . . ." The PC had turned upon him with loathing and fury. "Shut up, or I'll make you! I have to sit here with you. I don't have to listen to you!" The threat had been effective for

Greg knew that the policeman had only to say that he had turned violent.

Still his faith in a rescue had never failed and it had come in the form of a surgeon in a milk van. How very clever!

Neither rescuer nor rescued spoke for some time. William was silent because he had only one thing to say to Lorraine's killer, and Greg because he was waiting for his friend to speak first; but just as the turning to Malwood suburb was passed, he ventured a question. ''Where are you taking me?''

''You'll see,'' William said, sounding – God forgive him! – mild and friendly.

Presently the van turned left, into Malwood, the forest from which the village had taken its name.

William knew it very well. A boyhood haunt. A little far out for walking, but easily accessible to boys on third or fourth hand ramshackle bikes. It was, in daylight, a happy hunting ground, for there were clearings where blackberries and hazelnuts were to be found in abundance. Once William and his friends had come across a great patch of mushrooms. But William's mother had distrusted them and put them in the dustbin.

Apart from such loot, going into Malwood provided just that pleasing little touch of adventure; for the wood had a bad name. Nobody knew exactly why; and none of the boys knew then that *mal* was French for *bad*. They were just the stories which none of them believed so long as daylight lasted. When the light began to fade credulity took over. Long ago a battle had been fought in Malwood and – it was said – the clash of steel on steel and the cries of wounded men, and horses, could still be heard. And more recently, no more than two hundred years ago a girl had drowned herself in one of the pools, and came up occasionally, white and yet transparent.

These outings to Malwood always ended rather abruptly. There'd be a subtle change in the quality of the light and a boy would say; ''I ain't got no lamp on my bike;'' or ''My mum'll be on the warpath if I'm late.'' Then they'd leave, helter-skelter, nobody wanting to be last. Though, of course nobody believed the old stories.

William remembered this path into the woods very well. It had not changed at all. He came to a clearing, a rough oval, with a pool to one side. He halted. He said, "You get out here. Stand in the light."

Greg obeyed and looked about eagerly. The space was fully adequate for a helicopter.

Then the man who had rescued him, stripped of his surgeon's disguise, came limping round into the light. He said, *"You killed my Lorraine! And now I'm going to take you to pieces!"* With no more warning than that, Bill struck; his clenched fist sinking deep into his enemy's belly, low down. Greg grunted and doubled over for just long enough for Bill to get behind him and administer a kidney punch.

After that the fight evened out, for Lorraine's killer was the younger by more than twenty years, and he had been very well looked after during his short stay in the hospital. Bill was handicapped by his lame leg and also by a silly little scruple – he fully intended to kill this vermin, and as painfully as possible, but if he could avoid it he wouldn't hit him on the lower part of his face where the new skin was forming. Anywhere else. Everywhere else. And Greg fought for his freedom. He had instantly seen that though this was not the rescue he had counted upon, it could, nonetheless, be his salvation. He had only to down this man, take his clothes and the van and make off. His luck; the luck of the Devil, was serving him still.

They fought; they grappled. Once Greg got a killer's hold on Bill's throat, but Bill knew the answer to that! He brought his good knee up sharply. Slam! Bang on what everybody acknowledged as the most sensitive part of a male animal's body. It worked. The strangling hands fell away and the man held off just long enough for Bill to regain his breath and his balance. Then he came in again and struck Bill such a thundering blow on the side of the head, that betrayed by his lame leg, Bill fell. And hundreds of stars fell out of the sky with him. Down and down and down.

His last thought was for her; honey, I failed!

The descent into the abyss had been slow. The recovery was a jolt. A sudden, Oh still here! flash of consciousness and an awareness of pains in various parts of his body. He'd administered some hurtful blows himself, but he was the one who had been floored, and probably would be again. Unless he could play foxy. With this in mind, he lay very still, his eyes closed, his breathing so controlled as to be imperceptible. He hoped that the brute would come near enough, perhaps even stoop to see what damage he had done. Then, in a flash, he'd reach up and twist his head off.

That did not happen. Greg cast one careless glance; knocked out or dead, what did it matter? He turned and made for the van. William Selsey, the trained man, got up without any of the floundering hard breathing that would have been justified, and from behind administered what was known as the rabbit chop; the side of a hard hand smack on the point where the skull joined the neck. And administered with all the force one could muster; so much force, in fact, that William overbalanced again and they fell together.

But one was alive and one was dead. Honey, I did it! I did what nobody else could, or was prepared to do. I did it!

He reached into the van and brought out the surgeon's robe and cap, and dressed the man in them, over the hospital pyjamas. Then he dropped him into the pool. And that should exonerate everybody.

In fact it was over. Driving the van back to the yard, he realised that the desire for vengeance which had kept him going since Lorraine's death was no longer an excuse for living.

Nothing now to live for.

He and Liz had really parted when she stopped crying and began gloating. And once paths diverged, they continued to do so; every step, every day widening the difference. And this very evening when he had said he'd be late she hadn't asked why, where he was going or with whom. She certainly wouldn't miss him. Only his pay packet! He thought; What a summing up of a marriage after all these years! But he felt no self-pity or resentment; he'd never loved her, either.

The face he shaved in the morning was a right old mess; a black eye and one side of his jaw all swollen from chin to ear. But he doubted whether any other van driver would notice because lately he'd been surly and was now avoided, misery being as contagious as smallpox.

He had a tidy mind and didn't like to think of the police wasting more of their time in a fruitless search. So at the call-box on the corner of Guildhall Street he dialled 999. A voice so impersonal that it must be taped asked what service he required and he said "Police".

A different voice then asked his number and he said, "Never mind about that. If you want the killer, go and look in Malwood, the second pool."

He was now a rather different man from the one who had, on New Year's Day, contemplated drowning himself in The Butts. Then, distraught, he had given Liz no consideration at all. Now he did. And he had read the small print on his policy. Liz would be all right; she could go and live with Nigel, and enjoy being a grandmother.

In his army days he had been a great one for courses; the driving one had made him expert; he knew how to handle a skid, how to avoid a crash, or, in an emergency, organise one.

Everybody had always said, hadn't they, that the ancient oak was a traffic hazard. And sleet was falling at the time.

Liz was wonderfully brave. She said; "Well, poor Bill! He buried his heart with Lorraine. And now he's gone to join her." The first few times she said it, she meant it, but it was a good remark, so she repeated it so often that it became meaningless.

NORAH LOFTS

GAD'S HALL

Gad's Hall was for sale – and at a price so ridiculously low that even Jill and Bob Spender, to whom life had recently been unkind, could afford it.

But when Jill and others sense something wrong emanating from the attic, it takes a switch backward to 1841 to explain fully how a happy, ordinary family is infiltrated by positive Evil. Evil so well-disguised that it is not fully understood until the dreadful climax . . .

'A cleverly-constructed spine-chiller . . . it's my pick of the season.'

Sunday Telegraph

CORONET BOOKS

NORAH LOFTS

THE HAUNTING OF GAD'S HALL

No one at Gad's Hall could admit what they knew about the room in the attic. The locked room that held the Thorley family's most shameful secret. The terrifying room that had once been the living tomb of a beautiful young woman possessed by the darkest evil. Years had passed but the relentless diabolic force abided — waiting until it could once again possess an innocent and inflict its horror upon the living. It was a force countless centuries old. It was simply a matter of time before it would strike again. And when the Spender family moved into Gad's Hall, that time had come...

'A compulsive and riveting read by a storyteller writing at the top of her form.'

Daily Telegraph

CORONET BOOKS

ROBERT MARASCO

PARLOUR GAMES

Peter Drexler, the charm and genius behind Playcraft Toys, was a rare find. Maggie Newman, the stunning and vivacious advertising executive, found him. They were a brilliant duo. Under the bright lights of New York's glamorous night spots or relaxing at the beach, they seemed born to happiness ... until the phone rang out in the hall ... until a madwoman accused Peter of murdering her beautiful daughter ... until Gail – Peter's exquisite, beloved sister – told Maggie to run ... run for her life!

CORONET BOOKS